Robin Hood
freedom's outlaw

AIRSHIP 27 PRODUCTIONS

Robin Hood: Freedom's Outlaw
© 2013 I.A. Watson

An Airship 27 Production
www.airship27.com
www.airship27hangar.com

Interior llustrations © 2013 Rob Davis
Cover Painting © 2013 Mike Manley

Editor: Ron Fortier
Associate Editor: Rachel Davis
Production and design by Rob Davis.

ISBN-13: 978-0615852942
ISBN-10: 0615852947

Printed in the United States of America

10 9 8 7 6 5 4 3 2 1

Robin Hood
Freedom's Outlaw
by I.a. watson

Contents

The Tale Told in the Taverns

Being a summary of relevant events in
Robin Hood: King of Sherwood & *Robin Hood: Arrow of Justice*

Matilda of Leaford was supposed to be a pawn in a Prince's plot. While Richard Lionheart crusaded in the Holy Land, his scheming brother Prince John "Lackland" sought to take power in England by cowing the Barons. What better way, to show the consequences of criticising the Prince or denying him his will than to make an example?

When Prince John came to Lady Matilda's bedchamber to take her maidenhead he expected one of two outcomes. Either the red-haired beauty would yield, shaming her crusader father Sir Richard at the Lee, or she would resist, giving the Prince the excuse to destroy the old knight who'd been too honest in his appraisal of John's deeds and character. John hadn't expected Matilda to stun him with a chamberpot.

Lackland's malice led to Matilda's brother being provoked into an unwise duel with the Prince's envoy then being charged with murder for his death. Lord William de Vendenal, the newly-appointed, ambitious, ruthless High Sheriff of Nottingham imprisoned young Adam Fitzwarren in durance vile in Nottingham Castle. Sharing Adam's cell was the minstrel Alan a Dale, whose only crime was to protest the arranged marriage of the innocent Lady Elaine of Loughborough to the cruel Sheriff.

Sir Richard sought to protect his daughter from Prince John by sending her to sanctuary at Kirklees Priory. On the way she was abducted by Sherwood outlaws. Yet somehow she ended up fleeing with the wildest of them, the young bandit Robin of Loxley, and joining with him to rob and con the rich – to feed the poor! Amongst the villages of Nottinghamshire and Yorkshire Lady Matilda became known by her childhood pet-name: the Maid Marion.

As Robin's fame grew, the Sheriff of Nottingham and Prince John were inconvenienced and embarrassed by his exploits. The Prince's envoy, Sir Guy of Gisbourne, was captured by the outlaws and only escaped by murdering an innocent girl. The Sheriff's tax incomes were stolen then given away by the popular rebels who hid in the greensward.

De Vendenal's response was to use Marion and her family as bait to trap Robin Hood. The Sheriff ordained an archery contest on the day of his wedding to Elaine of Loughborough, offering as prize a golden arrow – and the hand of Lady Matilda. He expected Robin Hood to fall into his snare and so destroy the borning legend of the outlaw king and his Queen of May.

Robin came; but with a quiver-full of tricks as well as arrows. During the archery contest Marion's family, friends, and retainers were lowered by rope from the castle wall to safety beyond. Robin aided Alan a Dale to snatch Elaine from the Sheriff at the very wedding. At last Robin and Marion escaped together while the Sheriff called for their destruction.

Robin's courage, trickery, compassion, and élan were seen by the whole of Nottingham. The legend the Sheriff sought to destroy instead grew. Robin Hood had become freedom's outlaw, the people's champion, and Marion was his lady.

At least so the tavern songs and the storytellers told. The lady and the rogue still had a few things to work out before their happy ending. A dozen weak and injured escapees from Nottingham castle had to be spirited to safety. Prince John still demanded Lady Matilda, still wanted Sir Richard at the Lee destroyed, still expected the Sheriff and Gisbourne to crush the Sherwood rebels. A nation failed by the law still cried out for justice.

And so our present tale begins…

Dramatis Personae:

Being a list of the principal characters and their status and situations

The Merry Men of Sherwood Forest:

Robin in the Hood, outlaw rogue, leader of the bandits of Sherwood, the people's hero

Lady Matilda Fitzwarren of Leaford, beloved by the common folk as Maid Marion, the Queen of May

John Little of Hathersage, Robin's right hand man, known for his giant stature as Little John

Brother Thomas, a fat monk nicknamed Friar Tuck; Robin's boyhood tutor

Will Scathlock, a professional soldier; his violent tendencies have earned him the nom-de-guerre *Scarlet*

Alan a Dale, a minstrel who understands the power of legends

Much, the Miller's Son, a handsome lad of limited intellect

Will Stutely, a wise old bandit

David of Doncaster, a fiery young wrestler

Arthur a Bland, a cunning poacher with woodcraft and tracking skills

Gilbert with the White Hand, the band's cook

Riccon Hazel of Flintshire, a handy lad in a fight

Ros of Waltham, a camp follower, mother of the infant Tad

Elaine of Loughborough, a noble damsel who eloped with Alan a Dale

The Authorities of Nottingham:

William de Vendenal, Lord High Sheriff of Nottingham

Mereward, Castellan of Nottingham Castle

Matthew Shankshard, Chief Constable of Nottingham

Aelstan, captain of the guard

Morgan of Shrewsbury, the Sheriff's personal bodyguard

Gill o' the Red Cap, the Sheriff's finest archer

Sir Gerold of Kilington, squired by **Turstin Guillaurme** and **Naisen Renouf**

Reynold Greenleaf, bigger than Little John

The Court of Prince John:

Prince John, Count of Mortain, Lord of Ireland, younger brother of King Richard I

Rothmere, the Prince's lackey

Marcel of Flanders, Prince John's finest archer, currently held by the bandits of Sherwood

Sir Guy of Gisbourne, Prince's emissary, a ruthless and sadistic opportunist

Quimper Kinstain, Gisbourne's right-hand man and toady

Rulf Blackhelloc, Gisbourne's war captain

The Tattooed Woman, a Moorish hag of unnatural perception

The House of Fitzwarren:

Sir Richard Fitzwarren, *Sir Richard at the Lee*, knight of Leaford & Verysdale; an old crusader out of favor with Prince John; Matilda's father

Lady Mary Fitzwarren, his wife

Sir Mark Fitzwarren, his eldest son, absent from England

Lady Anne Greystoke, his elder daughter, married to Lord Greystoke

Sir Lucas Fitzwarren, his second son, married and settled in Sussex

Adam Fitzwarren, his youngest son, recently imprisoned in Nottingham

Lady Matilda Fitzwarren, described above, object of Prince John's desires, beloved of Robin of Loxley

Constanza, Lady Matilda's formidable old nurse

Loren de Weynold, captain of Sir Richard's guard

Aliss, Lady Mary's handmaiden

Kent of Verysdale, Sir Richard's steward

The Nobility and Clergy:

William Longchamp, Lord Chancellor, Bishop of Ely, master of the Tower of London, Grand Justiciar in the South; his youngest sister is **Melisend**

Hugh de Puiset, Earl of Northumbria, Bishop of Durham, Grand Justiciar in the North; Longchamp's enemy

Geoffrey Plantagenet, the Archbishop of York, Henry II's bastard, half-brother to Richard the Lionheart and Prince John

Baron Robert de Lacy, previous Sheriff of Nottingham, lord of Pontefract Castle

David of Scotland, the Earl of Huntingdon, an heir to the throne of Scotland

Sir Edward Lambert of Loughborough, husband of **Lady Hilda**, father of **Artus** and the absconded **Elaine**

Canon Steven, Archbishop's envoy from York Minster, currently held by the bandits of Sherwood

Thieves and Murderers:

Dunstan of Hucknall, a pardoned child-murderer working secretly for the Sheriff

Pendelou and **Oggesfot**, Sheriff's spies and agents

Tod Gallows, a would-be bandit king

Black Dane, a former outlaw of Sherwood, sworn enemy of Robin Hood

Slafot and **Evalgast**, the scum of Gisbourne's army

And a full cast of knights, damsels, archers, footmen, cutthroats, villagers, tradesmen, townsfolk, revellers, heralds, raiders, mendicants and spectators appropriate to the narrative (with a dancing bear in the wings).

I

obin kissed Marion.

The world stopped.

The brooding bulk of Nottingham Castle loomed over the water, just beyond bowshot. On its battlements the furious Sheriff gestured down towards the men and women that had just escaped over the outer wall. The rope had been cut too late to stop the outlaw-king of Sherwood and his lady from sliding to freedom, too soon to allow any of Lord William de Vendenal's guards to follow.

Marion's lips were soft and sweet. She'd kissed Robin once before, late after the dancing on May Eve when the common people had crowned her Queen of May. That kiss had been everything Robin had dreamed it would be. This was better.

Nearby, Little John of Hathersage was organising the getaway. The family and retainers of Sir Richard at the Lee had all been extracted from the Red Tower. Gilbert Whitehand and Will Stutely brought forward horses to get the old knight and his lady mounted. Sir Richard's son Adam carefully lifted Marion's old nurse onto a placid pony; Dame Constanza's Sheriff-inflicted whipping wounds were still raw. Aliss, a much younger house servant, rode pillion behind Captain Loren de Weynold.

Robin embraced Marion in his arms. Their bodies pressed together in a perfect fit, as if God had matched them.

"Look at them," said Alan a Dale, eyes alight at the adventure he'd just survived. "Have you ever seen two people so much in love?"

Lady Elaine of Loughborough—Elaine of Nowhere now since she'd foresworn her family and fled the Sheriff she was to have wed—threw her arms around the young minstrel and kissed him too. "I have," she confessed. "I am!"

Alan laughed out loud, though once he'd thought never to laugh again. The bride in his arms wore wedding finery for her match to William de Vendenal. Instead she was eloping with the man the Sheriff had planned to torture to death. When Alan kissed his true love, his heart soared. His mind teemed with new ballads.

Much the Miller's Son and David of Doncaster made mock kissing-faces at each other in the background, then grinned.

Robin's lips tasted of passion, of desire. Marion surrendered her mouth to that lust, hardly realising that her own lips conveyed the same yearning to her man.

Brother Thomas, known to the common folk as Friar Tuck, brushed the debris of his unceremonious descent from Nottingham Castle from his habit and staggered over to Will Scathlock. "Everything ready?" he asked, checking the horses and the travel preparations made by Robin's men at the riverbank. "It would be very terribly embarrassing to get caught and hanged after all this."

"All's ready," Scathlock replied tersely. He was a dour professional soldier, sometimes called Scarlet for his killing ways. He still bled from a hastily-tourniqeted knife-stab to the calf. He'd found a heavy branch to use as a crutch and was pretending he wasn't hurt

"Almost ready," Little John corrected. He gestured to Robin and Marion. "We still need to find a bucket of water."

Friar Tuck grabbed the young couple by an ear each and pulled them apart. "That's quite enough of that for now," he announced to the surprised lovers. "I know there was a wager about archery contests and kissing and so on but all debts can be settled later. After we're not shot dead by the Sheriff's men."

Robin managed a rueful chuckle. Marion blushed right down to her neck.

"I suppose we'd better escape," Robin admitted. "Marion?"

"Escape's good," the lady admitted. "I presume you have a clever plan?"

Robin's smile broke into a big beam. "I'm me," he boasted.

Before Marion could find the right words to put him in his place he turned his attention to the mounted party at the treeline. Sir Richard had his company in good order. Alan was helping Elaine onto his horse. Scarlet stiffly climbed onto the last available mount. "You know where you're going?" Robin Hood demanded.

Sir Richard at the Lee nodded to Stutely beside him. "This man knows the forest tracks. But we cannot…"

"The Sheriff will be after us soon with all the men he can muster," Robin warned. "Gisbourne, Shankshard, Aelstan, Morgan of Shrewsbury, everybody who wants us dead. We'll need to discourage them."

"You won't be able to keep up with us," Sir Richard warned the men on foot. "De Vendenal will have fast horses."

"We won't be keeping up with you," agreed Little John. "That's not the plan."

Robin Hood nodded. "Sherwood's mine. The Sheriff has to learn not to chase us there."

Marion saw that every man with Robin carried a bow. She remembered the devastation those bowmen had caused at the battle in Minsthorpe woods.

Sir Richard had slowly drawn the same conclusions about Robin's intentions. The old knight knew well what damage concealed archers could do to a riding column. "Very well," he conceded. He beckoned towards his saddle. "Matilda."

Lady Matilda Fitzwarren, Marion of the Greenwood, shook her head. "I'll be staying with Robin," she announced. "For the battle, I mean."

Robin cast her a look which said I-never-expected-anything-else.

"Somebody has to do the thinking for him," Marion continued, crushingly.

Little John snickered audibly. "Best get started then, lads an' lasses. We'll have unwelcome company soon enough judging by all those horns. Time we were into the forest."

Adam Fitzwarren's injuries were hurting him. The hot-headed young squire didn't like feeling weak or dependent. "Father!" he protested as his sister clung to a wanted wolfshead–albeit one that had saved the young nobleman from slow tortured death. "He's an outlaw!"

Sir Richard at the Lee looked down at the laughing blonde rogue beside his red-maned daughter. He glanced over at his own lady wife, her faded beauty an echo of his daughter's radiance. Lady Mary returned his gaze, sharing silently in some ancient treasured memory. "No, Adam," the old knight replied carefully. "Not an outlaw. *The* outlaw. Matilda will be safe with him."

"She'll never be safe with him," Lady Mary corrected her husband, "but she'll be alive!"

John gave the signal. The horses moved off along the forest track, away down the road. The archers broke into two and threes and vanished into the thick greenery of Sherwood.

Robin's arm still clasped Marion's waist. He turned back with her to look over the water at the dark castle.

"The Sheriff's going to have to kill you now, Robin," Marion advised.

Robin stared at the fortress. His eyes narrowed. "He's going to have to try."

Sir Guy, the black knight of Gisbourne, damned his wounded leg and limped around the outer ward of Nottingham Castle in a blind fury. He grabbed one of the passing guards, cuffed the man so hard his helmet flew off, and shouted. "Find me Quimper Kinstain! Get me horse and armour! Do it now!"

Around Prince John's furious envoy the holiday crowds had turned to riot. The threat of bowmen on the curtain walls no longer held them back. There were far more men and women gathered at the free festival for the Sheriff's marriage and archery contest than there were defenders of Nottingham Castle. Castellan Mereward had sensed the people's mood and had prudently closed the gates to the middle ward.

"Kinstain!" roared Gisbourne, buffeting grubby peasants out of his way. "Where's my horse?"

Just minutes before, the Sheriff's carefully staged event had fallen apart. His new bride had run off with a minstrel; already the peasants and serfs were gossiping that the wedding had been a sham and the supposed priest had been Robin Hood in disguise. The archery contest to win the golden arrow and the Lady Matilda's hand had gone wrong when the winning archer was not Marcel of Flanders, the Prince's chosen man, but the same laughing outlaw that the crowds adored. Now word passed that Robin and his merry men had escaped clean away over the walls of Nottingham Castle safe into Sherwood. Gisbourne was livid.

His attendant Quimper shouldered his way through the throng, pulling a fully-decked warhorse. The stallion spooked as some of the festival trestles were overturned. "Sir!" Quimper called to the black knight. "My Lord?"

"Get here!" shouted Sir Guy. "While you're admiring the rabble there's a wolfshead getting away!" He still favoured the leg where Robin's arrow had caught him almost two months earlier, and he'd just sustained a kicking from the fat Friar Tuck, but he could ride. "Where's Shankshard? What's the point of having a Constable of the Watch if he goes into hiding as soon as the rabble shout 'Boo'?"

The experienced Constable Shankshard was at the stables, trying to organise confused and party-drunk grooms to saddle horses for a forest pursuit.

"And those men on the battlements?" went on Gisbourne. "Why aren't they firing into the crowd?"

"They wait for word from the Sheriff, sire," Quimper called back, still struggling with agitated warhorse and pressing crowds. "And William de

Vendenal is in the Red Tower."

That was where Hood had retreated with his outlaws, the family of Sir Richard at the Lee, and the Sheriff's bride. It was from the battlements there that the fugitives had made their rope-drop over the moat into the greenwood beyond.

"Tell the fools to shoot!" demanded Gisbourne. "Tell them to *kill* someone!"

"But who?"

Sir Guy viciously punched the nearest serf, crumpling the man's nose with a steel-shod fist. "Anyone!"

But the guards on the battlements were uncommanded. Below them the feasting tents collapsed as peasants raided the banquet. The riot continued.

The villeins[1] called out the name of Robin Hood.

Canon Steven waited until the women watching him moved off to domestic tasks then began to work at his cords again.

The captive tied beside him in the shade of the Major Oak, deep in Sherwood, shook his head ruefully. "You are wasting your time," he told the clergyman. "These 'ellions understand 'ow to tie a good knot, and they use stout rope."

Canon Steven scowled at his fellow prisoner. The captive had the close-cropped hair of a professional soldier but he spoke with a courtly French accent. As with the clergyman, the bandits had taken his rich outer garments but he was clad in a good linen undershirt.

The Canon decided it would be acceptable to speak to him. "It is blasphemy to bind a cleric of God in this fashion."

---

1 Villeins and serfs are interchangeable terms for the most common class in England at the time of this story. A villein had the lowest status above slave, a man or woman who "belonged" to a particular estate or village, and therefore to the owner of that land. A villein was compelled to labour for his lord for a certain number of days a week and to render other duties. On strict estates he could not move away, own property, nor marry without his lord's consent. He had certain rights of protection and maintenance by his lord which were more observed in the breech than in the observance.

Peasants were a class above serf, usually free men that farmed land they leased on better terms or who carried out skilled labour. However, the term "peasant" was also casually and confusingly used to denote anyone of less than noble status.

The other prisoner seemed more sanguine about his captivity. "What is the appropriate manner for a cleric of God to be bound?" he enquired.

"You know what I mean! They have profaned a holy man on God's business. I was travelling to Nottingham to celebrate the wedding of Lord William de Vendenal, the Sheriff himself, to the Knight of Loughborough's daughter. Those…those outlaws waylaid me, despoiled me, and left me here with these hags!"

The Frenchman looked appreciatively over the clearing to where Ros of Waltham was bending down to gather washing from a wicker basket. "I have seen worse hags, in truth."

Canon Steven was outraged. "You have no idea what these brigands have done! Somehow they stole gold from the Archbishop in his own counting house. A full chest of money, four hundred pounds! Now they have robbed me of my goods and have interfered with my sacred duties. They will be damned to hell for it!"

The other captive snorted. "And my master will see them sent there. But until that I'll not waste my breath on choler."

The clergyman cut short his tirade and stared again at the Frenchman. "Who are you?" he demanded. "How came you to be a hostage of these vile wolfsheads?"

"Now you ask? Well then, I am Marcel of Flanders. I am a soldier in the service of Prince John of Angleterre. I am an archer of repute. I too was for the Sheriff's fair at Nottingham when I fell foul of Robin in the 'ood."

"The Prince's man?"

"His finest shot. I was sent to win the archery contest for his 'ighness. There was a golden arrow offered as a prize, and a fair maiden that John desired more."

"And these outlaws have prevented you from winning?"

Marcel shook his head. "I 'ad my contest with Robin Hood. When they took me, they promised to free me if I could beat their leader in a fair test of archery. I could not."

Canon Steven frowned. "He is that good?"

"He is that good. The best I have ever seen. He 'as other archers not far from his equal," the Frenchman confessed. "When Prince John comes to hang these men he will take some casualties beating the woods."

Ros of Waltham was back within earshot. "Then tell 'im to stay away," she advised the Prince's man. "Remind 'im what happened when Black Guy of Gisbourne brought an army into the forest. How many of them went home happily, eh?"

Marcel remembered the Prince's reaction to news of the massacre and of Gisbourne's capture and ransom. "That was a small force. Less than a hundred men, and poorly organised from what I have heard. What though when the Prince sends a thousand men, with dogs and foresters, who can come on day and night beating the woods as if for game? What when he places watchmen at every village, closes off every retreat? Your Robin 'ood has played a dangerous game. It is not one he can win forever."

"You will all pay for your lawlessness," promised Canon Steven, "in this world and the next."

Ros spat. "If I'm to fry in hell then I reckon as you'll be roasting next to me, holy man. You was the one what tried to break that Sir Richard Fitzwarren, Richard at the Lee, wasn't you? Made a loan you thought he'd never be able to pay then let the Sheriff steal what you'd given the old knight so's he had no chance at all. I don't call that very Christian."

The Canon blanched in the face of such furious accusation. "I know nothing about any theft. Except for the loss of four hundred pounds from the Minster counting house when a chest was found empty and bottomless."

"And you know nothing of them vile thugs what murdered the old knight's men on the road and took all the money for the Sheriff? And nothing of the Sheriff's plans to wed that poor Loughborough girl for her father's estates then do mischief to her brother to inherit all?" Ros moved in close. "You and me, when we get to the pearly gates and St Peter asks us about our sins, we'll both have a lot of explaining to do, won't we?"

Marcel of Flanders had regained his humour. "It seems Robin 'ood has the best theologians as well as the best archers, Canon."

The clergyman gave his bonds another useless tug. "The words of a nobody mean nothing. This bandit whore will doubtless be dead before winter comes."

Ros had no answer for that. She turned away.

"You realise now that she will spit in our food?" Marcel chided his fellow captive.

William de Vendenal stalked out of the Red Tower and looked down at the chaos that had overtaken his celebration day. The Midsummer crowd had broken into the beer and wine kegs and the fighting had now become factional. The inhabitants of the old Saxon settlement had reopened ancient quarrels with the incomers of French Town[2] and a general brawl had begun.

Aelstan, Captain of the Sheriff's Guard, hovered nervously at the Sheriff's shoulder. "What are your orders, sire?"

De Vendenal's eyes narrowed as he looked at the scene. "One volley of arrows at the men looting the drink tents. Soldiers to chase the rest out of the gate. Let the revellers burn their own houses and good riddance to them. I want twenty outlaws arrested for hanging tomorrow. I don't care who they are. I want order restored in the outer ward in a quarter of an hour."

"Sir!" saluted Aelstan. He hurried off shouting orders.

The Sheriff's gaze turned upon his bodyguard. Morgan of Shrewsbury limped up, his face a mass of contusions where he'd been slammed down by the minstrel Alan a Dale. He was more afraid of the Sheriff than of his own injuries.

"We were all caught off guard!" Morgan blurted before his master could speak. "Everyone. Even you. It was a trick. Who'd have thought the priests would turn on us?"

The priests had been Friar Tuck and Alan a Dale, seeking to liberate Elaine of Loughborough from a loveless marriage.

"Thought?" snapped the Sheriff. "There was thought today? Any thought? From anyone?"

"Sir…"

"Shut up. Shut up and stand there. Give me your crop."

Morgan handed over the stiff hide-wrapped rod he used to clear a way through serfs.

De Vendenal slashed him across the face with it three times then threw it back at him. "Learn," De Vendenal instructed.

"Yes…" gasped Morgan of Shrewsbury, not daring to flinch or turn aside even though his cheeks now welled blood. The marks would stay with him for life.

Castellan Mereward hovered nervously, worried that he was next in line.

"I see that Shankshard has mustered horsemen," the Sheriff noted, watching over the curtain wall as the Constable called together foresters and soldiers. Amongst them was Gill o' th' Red Cap, the castle archer who'd made it into the semi-finals against Robin Hood. "Send word to block all major roads and see the minor ones guarded."

---

2   At this time Nottingham was still a town divided along ethnic lines. The older settlement on the natural ridge and the newer community with Norman allegiances that clustered in the castle's shadow had an uneasy peace. Each still had separate leaders and separate bylaws.

Mereward swallowed hard. "My Lord, the bandits may not use the roads. This Robin Hood doubtless knows the hunters' tracks and secret ways of Sherwood and…"

"Robin Hood is not alone!" snapped de Vendenal. "He has absconded with many others. Sir Richard at the Lee is an elderly man and his health is poor. His wife, Lady Mary, is given to having fluxions of the heart. Their old servant, Matilda's nurse, is still recovering from her public flogging. None of these can travel fast or far. All will require horses or cart which can not pass by unseen ways."

"Ah." The Castellan realised again that his new Sheriff had a formidable mind. Even now de Vendenal took chaos and disaster and plaited them into a plan.

"Hood also has wounded men with him. I stabbed the mercenary Scathlock in the leg. He will require treatment if he's not to bleed to death. Have bloodhounds take up the chase."

The Castellan nodded. De Vendenal turned back to Morgan of Shrewsbury. "Send word to Dunstan of Hucknall and his band of murderers. Loose them in the woods too. They may find what an armed column cannot. Offer them silver for any proven follower of Robin Hood, alive or dead–but tell them I'll need proof before handing over coin. A bounty of five hundred pounds on Robin Hood himself."

Mereward winced. "Five hundred…!"

"You haven't yet realised how serious this is!" the Sheriff hissed. "One moment of defiance by Robin i' the' Hood and the outer ward is wrecked and burning. Rebellion breeds rebellion. If this isn't crushed there'll be a dozen Robin Hoods attacking my tax trains by winter and a thousand outlaw scum raiding the villages."

"Five hundred, as you say sire," agreed Mereward hastily. "I'll have it cried.³"

"How do you think Prince John will respond to news of this?" De Vendenal growled. "What tale do you think Gisbourne will carry back to him? What of the real Marcel of Flanders, now presumably a captive of these wolfsheads? What of Canon Steven, who was replaced by an impostor? Less than three months since my investiture as Sheriff and the whole Shire is fallen into dissent and lawlessness. Well it shall not be. *It shall not be!*"

Screams came from down below as the archers loosed a volley at the looters.

The Sheriff allowed himself a small thin smile.

---

3   The standard method of distributing official news was through town criers, men of hearty voice who disseminated the news to waiting crowds with a shout of "Oyez! Oyez!"

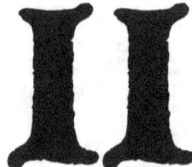

II

Robin Hood, Little John, Much the Miller's Son and David of Doncaster rode hard down the road to the West Bridge Ford - and Maid Marion rode with them.

It was a strange ride for the young woman, galloping beside the laughing bandit-king of Sherwood. Lady Matilda Fitzwarren had been changed by her brief encounter with Robin Hood weeks before. The outlaw had fanned the rebellion within her, awoken the rogue, taught her sense of natural justice that it could fight and win. With Robin she'd robbed the corrupt to feed the innocent. Apart from him she'd yearned for his smile. For him she had become Marion of the Greenwood.

Now she was beside him again and her feelings were complex and confused.

Robin had won a kiss. They'd wagered it in the dark fugitive hours after the young outlaw had stolen her from bandit camp captivity: a bet that Robin of Loxley was the best shot in England. He'd proved his claim at the Sheriff's archery butts. But more, the Sheriff had forced Sir Richard at the Lee to offer Matilda's hand as prize in that contest– and Robin had triumphed over all comers.

Marion wondered if that made her Robin's wife, his winnings, his Queen of May, or just some poor moth caught in the dazzle of his flame.

As she galloped down the road she didn't care.

"Is somebody going to tell me the plan now?" she shouted across at Robin. "I know that there were good reasons to keep me in the dark while the Sheriff could threaten my family but I'd really like to share the joke."

"Tell her, Rob," Little John advised. "She's one of us now."

Robin smirked. "It's not enough to get your folks out of the castle, Marion. The Sheriff's got plenty of men to chase after them and they can't melt away into the forest like my outlaws. So the escape's not over yet."

The horses clattered on the forest road then emerged from the treescape for a moment to track the river's course. The opposite shore was edged with small holdings, the perimeter of the city of Nottingham, but the water was too deep to ford.

"My mother and Constanza couldn't bear a long journey without a carriage or cart," Matilda recognised.

"Right. So we're going to deter the Sheriff's men from chasing them."

"By asking nicely?"

"Yes. Well that and having thirty archers lined up at the crossroads ahead where the Constable will be bringing his hunters."

Marion frowned. "You're going to kill lots of people?"

Robin shook his head. "I'm going to scare lots of people, and then they're going to chase us."

Marion looked at Robin and Little John.

"Us? *Us* us?"

"You wanted to ride with him," John reminded her.

A hunter's track took the main band of fugitives as far as the estate of Ruddington, a mere half-hour's hard ride from Nottingham Castle but enough to leave the injured Constanza gasping in pain and clinging to her pony. Loren de Weynold, Sir Richard's guard captain, was about to demand a halt before the old nurse fell off her horse when Will Stutely raised a fist and signalled for the party to pull off the road.

The grizzled old outlaw led them single-file through a thicket of ash and alder to a small clearing by a springhead. More of Robin's grubby band waited there with four fast carts. Three of the vehicles were already part-laden with heavy tree-trunks.

"What's this?" demanded Sir Richard at the Lee, anxious for his family's safety and unsure how to balance the pressing need for speed against the obvious problems of pushing his wife and servant too hard on horseback.

Friar Tuck dropped down from his own pony with a relieved wheeze. Perhaps the poor animal made a happy noise too as the fat friar's bulk lifted from her back. The tonsured monk gestured for Lady Mary Fitzwarren and her ladies to shift into the unladen wagon.

"The other carts will all head in other directions," Tuck advised them, "so any tracker will have to decide which of four sets of cart-ruts to follow. The horses will be ridden away cross-country. Our pursuers will have lots of choices."

Lady Mary walked stiffly to the indicated wagon. "What has this carried?" she sniffed.

"Best not ask, milady" chuckled Gilbert of the White Hand. "But we gave you the cleanest of the selection."

Young Aliss dropped off from her pillion position behind Captain de Weynold (although she'd been well content there clutching him around his chest and would have vivid dreams tonight) and hurried to attend her mistress. "What could those other carts have had in them that smelled worse than this?" she shuddered, not wanting to know.

Arthur a Bland told her anyway. "Best smells'll go in the other directions, o' course," the old poacher declared. "Trust a hunting dog to go after an offal wagon and a knacker's cart! [4]"

Will Scathlock pulled his own horse up to travel escort beside de Weynold and the three remaining soldiers of the old knight's guard. The mercenary was ashen and pale as he clutched the reins. The bandage on his calf was already crimson.

Sir Richard's youngest son, Adam, had been captive for many weeks in Nottingham castle. The gyves were still around his wrists. Gilbert had the young squire stretch the links across a log and severed them with an axe. Wan Adam managed not to flinch as the outlaw swung the blade.

Sir Richard wheeled his own horse round beside the cart carrying his lady. "Seems like young Hood planned well," he admitted.

"Oh, that's our Robin," agreed Tuck. "Always scheming. Sometimes his plots even work."

"Sometimes?" worried Lady Mary. Her youngest daughter had just ridden off with the madcap outlaw.

"More than you'd think," Tuck owned. "Anyway, here's where our company makes its first parting. What are we to do, lads?"

Gilbert leaped back onto his stolen mare with an easy panache befitting a former steward in an Earl's household. "We're taking the horses away over the fields, fast and furious, each in a different direction. When we're sure we're clear and free we make our way back to gather at the Major Oak."

Arthur a Bland twitched his tattered hood over his head. His washed-out rags blended well with the summer forest. "I'm back down the main road and scattering these caltrops," he rehearsed. He clasped a leather bag containing the wicked four-pronged foot-spikes that could lame a horse. Fast riders chasing outlaws would have to moderate their pace and watch their road if they wanted to avoid harming their mounts. "Maybe I'll stretch a rope or two across the path as well if I find places as suit. Then it's home to the Oak and a warm supper of coney or boar if I can find 'un."

---

4   A knacker recycled dead horses and other animals, often putting down old or injured creatures before stripping them for hide, bone meal, meat, and glue.

"And we're to flee with the carts," chipped in Riccon of Flintshire. "As far and fast as we can with the weight we're carrying to pretend we're loaded with folks. Then when soldiers draw close we're to desert the wagons and take to the woods, and so home by our own ways."

"Don't worry," Will Stutely comforted Sir Richard with a brown-toothed grin, "They're not our carts."

"What of us?" asked Alan a Dale. He and his new-won lady still rode a single mount and were staring at the preparation like new-borns with no idea of what to do next.

"You'll come with us," Adam urged. He and Alan had spent long nights in the darkness of the Sheriff's oubliette confiding their fears and hopes. Adam did not want to lose the friend he'd made in such desperate adversity. "We are comrades to the end."

"You're with Sir Richard and with me," Friar Tuck assented. "Stutely too. And Scarlet, I'll want you in the wagon for a while, so I can sew up that wound of yours. Never pretend it's not bleeding you dry. Don't make me knock you down to save your leg."

Will Scathlock was in enough pain that he didn't object.

"Move yourselves then," Stutely yelled at the outlaws. "And mind your woodcraft. Rob wants you all safe home and there's none of you I wouldn't mind seeing again to get my dice winnings, so take some care!"

"And thank you for your pains," added Sir Richard Fitzwarren, doffing his cap. "You have saved the lives of my family and have struck a blow against tyranny. It shall not be forgotten."

"That's going to be the problem," muttered Friar Tuck as they hurried on their escape.

Sir Guy of Gisbourne rode with Shankshard and the first pursuers. He'd dispatched his man Kinstain on a fast post horse to the Prince at Leicester. Now the vengeful black knight was at the forefront of the hunters who sought out Robin in the Hood.

"Slow down," the Constable warned him. "There'll be ambushes."

"We've six score men, and dogs as well," Gisbourne snarled. "What are you afraid of?"

"Of walking into a prepared trap like you did with the Prince's men last time you chased Robin Hood," snapped Shankshard. He didn't like the half-Moor knight. He didn't like his black horsehair hunting armour. He

"That's going to be the problem."

didn't like his full-face helm with the black mane attached to it. He didn't like the royal envoy's arrogance or prejudice or anything about him.

"At least I fought Hood," replied Sir Guy. "I hear that you were robbed blind by him of five hundred pounds of silver without even noticing it."

"The silver that was meant for your ransom after you were captured by the outlaw?"

"I escaped from the wolfsheads without need for ransom."

"Word is you did it by threatening the life of a goose-girl whom you swore not to harm, but afterwards left defiled and dead."

"She was a nobody." The black knight's tone was dangerous.

The Constable held his tongue and kept his peace. Sir Guy had the Prince's ear. It was further rumoured that Gisbourne had foresworn an oath to the Virgin Mary not to harm the goose-girl; Guy of Gisbourne was a black knight indeed.

The front-riders of the hunting party clattered over the wooden bridge at West Ford and chased along to the fork where the road branched to Radford and Edwalton. Shankshard gestured for a dozen men to peel off westward in case the escapees had moved faster than was likely. The Constable wheeled his main force to the right hoping to trap the slower refugees on the road.

Shankshard pictured the lay of the land and Robin's likely routes. Nottingham Castle sat on a ridge north of the Rivers Leen and Trent. The fugitives had made their escape across the Leen southwest of the castle. There were few crossing places back and they were guarded. That limited the outlaws to the woodland tracks south of the water.

The outlaws' known haunts were all north and east of Nottingham. Sir Richard's estates at Verysdale or Leaford also lay on the wrong side of the river. For Robin to reach the relative security of his forest hideouts he'd need to find a way round to them.

The ground was steeper beyond the castle westwards with fewer routes that a large party could take. The Constable had already sent men to cut off those roads. Shankshard and Gisbourne had swept east hoping to find the outlaws seeking an unguarded river crossing.

They were five minutes ride from Gamston when a hunting horn sounded from the woods. A flight of arrows sliced into the road. The lead riders reined their horses so quickly that the columns behind almost careened into them.

"Outlaws!" Gisbourne shouted, unnecessarily. Shankshard began to understand why Hood had nicknamed the black knight 'Brickhead'.

"Ready the dogs!" called Shankshard. "Men with long shields to the fore a-foot."

"Constable!" The call came from somewhere in the trees. "I heard you were looking for me!"

"Robin i' the Hood?" shouted back Shankshard. He could barely believe the wolfshead's audacity.

"That's him!" cried Gisbourne. "I recognise that arrogant peasant tone! Charge him now!"

"Hello, Brickhead!" called the outlaw. "How's the leg? Next time I'll shoot a couple of inches higher and hit your balls. Even the smallest target's no problem for me."

A few of the Sheriff's men exchanged little smirks. The black knight wasn't popular and that jibe was going to be common tavern fodder by tomorrow night.

"Give yourself up, Robin Hood!" called Shankshard. He didn't expect the outlaw to surrender but it gave his men time to lock shields and prepare to charge archers.

"That's what I was going to say to you, Constable. You know how many men I command in Sherwood. You're outnumbered and surrounded. Ask Brickhead how that worked out for him last time."

"He's bluffing," snapped Sir Guy.

The soldiers around him didn't look so sure. The archers had set their ambush where the forest pressed close to the road. At least thirty bowmen had loosed their shafts in unison to halt the hunters.

"I'm going to hang you, Robin Hood!"

"Doesn't that mean you've got to catch me first?" answered the young outlaw. "And doesn't that mean you've got to not be shot from your saddle? I've got an arrow pointed right at the eyeslit of your helmet. Want to bet I can't get it straight through there? Remember Harold at Hastings?[5]"

Shankshard kept his nerve. "I've brought enough men to take down your archers. Your men have to be close in forest this dense. Each might get a shot off, true, but once my men are at close quarters your bowmen have no chance."

"Don't talk with the wolfshead!" snarled Gisbourne. "Kill him!"

"You're confident of your troops, then?" Robin called. "William de Vendenal must pay pretty good wages that a man will throw his life away for

---

5   The last real Saxon king, Harold, died in the Battle of Hastings (A.D. 1066). Popular tradition had it that he received an arrow in the eye. Harold's fall led to the triumph of Norman invader William the Conqueror and the start of England's feudal age.

his Sheriff. And of course there'll be generous de Vendenal pensions to the widows and orphans of any man who dies today, won't there? I mean, why else would your men be willing to charge unknown numbers of outlaws on our own prepared territory?"

A nervous mutter ran through the ranks.

Sir Guy of Gisbourne's patience was exhausted "Enough of this!" he screamed. "Loose the hunting dogs! Sound the charge! With me!" He reared his horse and spurred it forward down the road.

Shankshard wanted to throttle the black knight, but Guy was the prince's envoy and had to be supported. He gestured to his lieutenants to bring their men in after Gisbourne and begin the shield charge.

Robin's broad-headed red-fletched arrow punched right through Gisbourne's shield and stopped an inch away from his breastplate.

The soldiers beat into the forest in good discipline.

There were no outlaws. Robin's merry men had all melted away as soon as they'd fired their first volley, while their leader kept the Sheriff's men talking.

Everybody heard the outlaw king's laughter. Robin and a small mounted party broke from cover and raced away up the road then across ploughed fields beyond.

"After them!" roared Gisbourne; and the chase began.

III

Lady Mary's wagon and its escort had progressed as far as the tiny hamlet of Wysall by the time the sun dipped below the horizon. That was signal for the last of the decoy carts to peel off and head west, setting its course for Radcliffe and Bingham.

Will Stutely bade the lads with him to light torches. The caravan continued moving through the night.

Scarlet's colour was better now that his wound had been properly treated. He'd insisted on taking the reins of the Fitzwarren party's wagon. "Someone's bound to report where we are to the Sheriff," he warned the bandits.

"Oh, there's plenty of reports as to where we are," Tuck promised him. "By now we're all over the shire. Robin's seen to that."

"Plenty of good descriptions, too," Alan a Dale promised. The minstrel had helped to brief the various grateful peasants and villeins that would bear tales of Robin Hood sightings. The outlaw would be robbing a butcher in Kneesall and wrestling an Ilkston potter, cheating at dice in Nutall, saving an infant at Foxhill, and a hundred other offences before tomorrow was done.

Sir Richard grumphed in appreciation of the tactic. "Seems that young Robin has thought of everything."

His son Adam edged his horse nearer to have private speech with the Knight at the Lee. "Father, I know we're indebted to these outlaws, but do you really think it right for Matilda to be off with their leader? I mean, she's a maiden without chaperone and…"

Sir Richard clapped Adam's shoulder. "I pledged Matilda's hand to the winner of that archery bout. The Sheriff forced me, yes, my word was given. If Hood comes and asks me for my daughter then I'll keep my oath and bestow her."

Adam glanced around at the outlaws moving through the night. "But he's a bandit. I mean, I don't want to be ungrateful. He got me out of a death cell. But Matilda…"

"Lad, I don't know what to think," the old knight cut him short. "Except that Matilda's grown to a woman these last few weeks. You saw her when she stole to your cell. How did she seem to you then?"

"Like a damsel inspired," admitted Adam, reluctant to praise his closest sister. "Or mad."

"Yes. That's what I saw too. And I've only seen its like elsewhere once."

"When, father?"

"When I saw Robin of Loxley at work."

Father and son kept pace quietly for a time.

"Your sister's on a hard road," Sir Richard admitted at last, "Yet I fear for her less tonight than I did when Prince John was our guest or when de Vendenal held her at Nottingham." He stroked his whiskers and mused. "I wonder why?"

The quiet talk was disturbed as Tuck called to the travellers. The wagon rumbled to a halt by a tiny smallholding. An earnest peasant waited with fresh horses for the wagon.

"Here's our next parting," Tuck instructed the party. "Stutely will take Sir Richard and Lady Mary back to their own estates by a roundabout route. Scarlet will go with you in the wagon. Robin's seen to it that word of what's happened runs ahead of you."

"And eventually I'll get paid," grouched Scathlock. His leg still hurt.

The fat friar went on. "I'll take Alan and Elaine with me. We've got business elsewhere. Young Master Fitzwarren can join us if he's for an adventure."

Adam and Alan exchanged surprised glances. "I'll go with Alan," the young squire agreed.

Elaine nodded mutely, still overwhelmed by the things that had happened on her wedding day.

"See you take care," Sir Richard told his son. "I'll expect you at Verysdale. It can be fortified better than Leaford if de Vendenal dares send men that far." The old knight didn't mention how his daughter would soon be in defiance of a royal summons commanding her to attend Prince John; that would bring more trouble down on the beleaguered Fitzwarren clan.

Father and son clasped hands. Lady Mary gave her rescued boy a kiss. "Don't be an idiot any more," she instructed him with motherly force. "I'm proud of how you stood your torment. Now be a man from it."

Even old Constanza had a few words of parting, but they were for Elaine of Loughborough. And private. "Now see here, Lady Elaine. I know the world's become a strange uncertain place for you, and you're clinging to that young troubadour because he's all there's left for you to cling to. But there's other choices still for you to make and no need to give yourself if you don't wish it. There are houses of God where you can be a bride of Christ rather than a bride of man. And I'm sure there'd be welcome and refuge for you with my Lady Mary at Verysdale."

Elaine bit her bottom lip. "My life has become unexpected and terrifying," the runaway bride admitted, "but I choose Alan. He's not only my final refuge, he's my first choice."

"Well then…" nodded Constanza, and bent her head close to impart certain practical advice which the young lady might find helpful on the nights to come. Elaine blushed bright red—and listened.

The cart moved on and the flaring torches of its outlaw attendants vanished into the darkness. Tuck led Elaine, Alan and Adam into the cramped warmth of the peasant hut. For one night at least Elaine would have no opportunity to try out Constanza's instructions.

At about the same time, Robin, Marion, John, David, and Much ended their long chase over field and forest at the water's edge. The wide expanse of the Trent rolled before them, dark and turbulent in the twilight.

"The horses have about had it," Little John warned. "And Brickhead's still coming."

"But his men are thinned out over half of the shire," said Robin Hood with a wink, "and just as tired as we are. Imagine how hard it'll be for them to swim their mounts across the river."

"Imagine how hard it'll be for us," objected Marion. "Robin…"

"No need," promised the laughing outlaw. He slid from his saddle and grabbed his ride's bridle. "Lead your horses this way."

The outlaws followed him single file along the thin towpath that ribboned beside the river. At a bend where the waters boiled a plank pontoon was suspended on two ropes across the river's course.

Robin covered his horse's eyes with a scarf. "Walk them over."

"Can John go last?" asked Much anxiously, eyeing the giant's bulk. Little John rode the largest of the horses too.

"Can I just hurl Much over there?" responded Little John.

Sounds of pursuit halted the jocularity. Robin pulled his steed across the groaning pontoon. It creaked alarmingly as the ropes stretched but it held.

"This is turning into a very unusual day," Maid Marion owned as she followed his lead. "A festival, a wedding, an archery contest, jumping off a castle, a hunt, and now drowning. You give me interesting times, Robin i' the Hood."

"I know you're easily bored, milady."

David of Doncaster crossed over without much difficulty. Little John had to push Much onto the temporary bridge.

"I can't swim!" panicked the miller's son.

"You grew up in a watermill," Robin's lieutenant argued.

"The water was three feet deep!"

"Well then, my advice is don't fall in."

Sounds of the hunters were closer. There was a crashing of undergrowth. A fierce hairy setter jumped from cover, snarling.

John knocked it away with his staff, but not too hard. He liked animals. The handler behind the hound backed away when he saw the grizzled giant. John didn't offer the same mercy to men.

"Cross over now," Robin called to the big man. The outlaw leader held his bow in his hands. The next pursuer stopped short as an arrow passed beneath his legs.

John dragged his mount across the logs that Robin's outlaws had set there only an hour before. The Trent was navigable so anything done earlier would have been spotted by river traffic.

The main force of the Sheriff's hunters arrived. Gisbourne spotted Robin Hood across the water and spurred towards the bridge.

As Little John made it to the other bank David and Much cut the ropes holding the pontoon in place. The current took the logs and the whole bridge disintegrated and was carried away downstream.

Robin placed another arrow in Gisbourne's shield, exactly where the last one had been.

"Across the river!" shouted Black Guy. "Swim your horses!" He couldn't follow immediately, because unlike most of the Sheriff's men's mounts his warhorse was fully barded and would need freeing from is heavy plate before it could follow.

The first man into the water toppled from his horse with Robin's arrow in his arm.

"In the time it takes for a man to cross I can kill him ten times over," the outlaw archer called. "Save your men."

Sir Guy was livid "Across, damn it! God's wounds, I'll gut any man who shirks!"

Another pair of the Sheriff's guards fell with flesh wounds from arrows.

"Go!" shouted the black knight of Gisbourne. "How many shafts do you imagine he has?"

"We knew this was where we'd cross," Robin pointed out. "My men left me a couple of spare quivers."

The soldiers halted again, disconcerted by the bandit's happy tone.

"All together!" roared Gisbourne. "Any man who doesn't want to be impaled on a spear by the morning will cross that river now!"

Even then it took ten or fifteen minutes to convince the soldiers to brave Robin's bow. By that time the fugitives had slipped away without farewells.

Much was elated as he trotted his blown mount along the track towards the hamlet of Colwick. "We did it! We got away from that horrible castle and that horrible sheriff and we're free!" He couldn't believe it.

"Don't jinx it!" snapped Little John. "You never say things like that till…"

The sound of racing horses echoed up the road from behind them.

"That'll be Shankshard," frowned Robin. "Sneaky. He anticipated us crossing the water and brought some men round by the Carlton road. Brickhead was just the diversion, though I doubt Black Guy knew it."

"Their horses sound fresher than ours," Marion pointed out.

"Good job we're very clever then," Robin replied. "Run!"

"Elaine?"

The former heiress of Loughborough was still awake in the fusty darkness, reflecting that this was not what she'd expected on the night of her wedding to the Sheriff of Nottingham. Lying on a straw mattress in a peasant hut was a pleasant relief.

"Alan?" she replied to the low whisper. She felt the minstrel's hand reach out and clasp hers.

"Are you alright?" Alan a Dale asked her, quietly enough not to wake the snoring Tuck or the exhausted Adam Fitzwarren.

"I think so. Better than I thought."

"This must be very strange for you."

"Yes. My whole life has become one of those ballads you used to sing to me."

Alan squeezed her hand. "We deserve a ballad, you and I. A song that everyone can sing and be happy for us." He paused a moment, then added in still quieter, more sober undertones, "That is, if you want to be with me. I'd understand if you didn't. Lady Mary said…"

"I don't want to be anywhere without you, Alan. I know that now."

"I talked with Adam," confessed the minstrel. "He's a good man, and noble. He promised me that if he could he'd offer you marriage. He's a younger son, but he's a fair…"

"Alan, if I wanted titles, wealth and power I'd be Lady de Vendenal tonight. I'm not. I'm Elaine of Nowhere, running for my life, hiding in a peasant cot. And I'm with you."

Alan stroked his lady's palm. Her skin was smooth and soft. "You've never experienced poverty, Elaine. You've never had to work, except for spinning and weaving and other noble pastimes. You've never been cold and hungry."

The lady caught her breath. "Alan, are you trying to get rid of me?"

"No! No, nothing like that. But I don't want to destroy you either. I love you. I'd die for you–I hope I proved that. I want you to be mine always and forever, just like in the songs. I want to write that song, and sing it full voice knowing every word is true. And I want to compose another one that tells how much I love you after fifty years together. But I don't want to lead you to tears."

Elaine closed her hand around his. "I think now that everyone comes to tears, whatever path they travel. When I come to mine, you are the man I want to wipe them away." She squeezed his hand. "Alan, when I saw you'd come for me today, at my wedding to that horrible Sheriff, it was the best moment of my life!"

"I'd like to give you better moments than that, Elaine, if you'll marry me. Will you? Be my wife, my love, my heart?"

"I will, Alan. That's all I want. I've given up everything else to have it. To have you."

Their whispers grew quieter and more private still, as they talked long into the night.

But when he was satisfied that the two young people had a proper understanding of each other, Friar Tuck stopped pretending to snore and allowed himself to snore in earnest.

"Not to nag you, Robin Hood, but those horsemen are closing very fast," Marion pointed out. "How far to Holme?"

Robin jerked his horse sharply left down a thin dirt track towards a ragged cluster of wooden buildings. "This is it," he said. "Holme rope ferry."

It was almost full dark now. Marion could barely make out the flat barge that bobbed at the water's edge. During the day the long ropes that traversed the Trent were harnessed to oxen to guide the platform from shore to shore. At night there was no sign of the animals nor the ferry handlers.

Little John led the way down to the tethered barge. The shallow boat rocked as he climbed aboard and examined the ropes.

Robin loosed an arrow in the darkness. The first of Shankshard's chase guards screamed and fell from his horse. The tumble hurt him worse than the shaft.

"Help me cut these cords!" John called to Much and David. The three men set to work on the mooring ropes and on the thick hawsers that guided the barge. Marion soothed the horses across the wide plank and picketed them on the ferry. It was a tight fit.

Robin fired again, three shots in rapid succession, then pelted down to the boat. "Time to go!" he suggested.

Constable Shankshard raced into view, flanked by link riders bearing torches. Another pair of Robin's well-aimed shafts sliced the brands out of their hands.

More men were behind the Constable, too many to hold off. One tried to make a shortbow shot from horseback but his arrow went far from the mark.

"Get them!" shouted Shankshard, spurring down towards the ferry.

Robin shot the Constable's horse out from under him then leaped onto the raft.

Little John heaved off with one of the punts, his massive strength sending the barge spinning away from the embankment. Without the guideropes the current quickly caught the flatbed vessel and pushed it downstream.

"Fend off the banks, lads!" John called to David and Much. "Try and keep us midstream. Marion, look ahead for sudden turns or hazards."

Robin stood at the stern, still loosing arrows to keep the pursuers in disarray. One or two tried to force their horses into the water, but the river caught the barge and speeded its passage. The soldiers were left behind.

Marion stood beside the outlaw leader. "We're not dead yet. Are you sure this is one of your plans?"

Little John snorted. "We're on a rickety barge meant for quiet hauls from bank to bank, speeding downriver in pitch blackness, trying to guess if we'll be wrecked before we sink. It's absolutely a Robin Hood plan."

"We're away and clear now," Robin told them. "We can leave the river anywhere we choose. Shankshard and Gisbourne will have to check every possible place. We'll set the horses loose a few miles into Sherwood and go on foot after that, and then nobody will find us. We'll be at the Major Oak by tomorrow night."

"Isn't that jinxing it as well?" worried Much.

Robin splashed water at him. "When I say it, it's a done deal," he replied.

IV

The Sheriff was waiting in his solar when the searchers returned in small crestfallen bands the following morning. Shankshard, Captain Aelstan, and Mereward the Castellan were particularly nervous as they eyed Morgan of Shrewsbury's crudely stitched face.

"Let us summarise," suggested William de Vendenal, his elbows on his writing desk, his fingertips arched. "Yesterday, a brigand trickster and many of his followers infiltrated a castle on detailed watch for him. He kidnapped my bride. He assaulted me. He then escaped said heavily-guarded castle over the parapets by rope-drop while the wall watchmen were all observing the games and subsequent riot in my outer bailey. He spirited away an entire family of elderly and sickly hostages from a secure tower and vanished into the forest. Then they all disappeared. Is that correct?"

The Sheriff's retainers exchanged nervous glances. None of them were willing to make the first response and risk their master's ire.

De Vendenal turned to his disfigured bodyguard. "Morgan, are you in pain?"

"Yes, my lord," admitted the man who'd felt the Sheriff's crop.

"Would you like to share that pain with others?"

"Very much, my lord."

The Sheriff turned back to Shankshard, Aelstan, and Mereward. "I ask you again: is my summation correct?"

"Yes, sir," admitted Shankshard, straightening his back. "But…"

De Vendenal's stare focussed on the Constable. Aelstan and Mereward edged away from Shankshard.

"But?"

The Constable swallowed. "But you were taken in by Hood's disguises too, my lord. He stood as close to you as we are now, and you spotted him no more than we did."

Mereward and Aelstan shifted further away from Shankshard. Mereward might have excused himself because yesterday he'd been given specific duties; he hadn't been told not to accept ransom for the Fitzwarren boy. Aelstan could have argued that his troops were deployed as the Sheriff had ordered to keep control over the festival crowds, not to prevent unauthorised exit via some absurd nigh-impossible rope trick over the back wall. Neither spoke.

The Constable stood his ground.

The Sheriff eyed him. "Hood fooled me too," he conceded. "Shankshard, you speak the truth."

The Constable exhaled, surprised to be alive.

De Vendenal pondered. "We all made errors yesterday. Mine was in underestimating Hood and Lady Matilda–his Marion. I'll have to avoid that error next time."

Morgan of Shrewsbury shifted angrily, disappointed not to be able to carve up the Constable–today.

"Next time?" ventured Captain Aelstan.

The Sheriff rose from behind his table. "There will be a next time. Soon. Already Gisbourne's toady Kinstain is riding to the Prince. When Lackland hears of today's farce, of the taking of his man Marcel of Flanders, of the detainment of a canon of York, he'll be bound to act. After that mess with Sir Guy only weeks ago he'll have to shore up his authority. The court already sniggers behind John's back, at a time when he seeks to displace the men King Richard left in authority over England. He cannot allow Hood's actions to go unanswered."

"Prince John will return here?" Mereward the Steward worried. The castle's resources were still recovering from the last royal visit.

"More likely Soft-sword[6] will send some of his thugs. Probably a lot of his thugs, so that Gisbourne can go on another rampage. I suppose I'll be expected to foot their bill."

Captain Aelstan looked gloomy at the idea of keeping hundreds of foreign mercenaries in order, especially if they swaggered under the Prince's banner.

The Sheriff stared out of the solar window across the inner ward. Tired horses and exhausted men were still returning from their wild goose chases around the countryside. Hood had been prepared.

"Lady Matilda Fitzwarren is still under royal summons to appear be-

6   Youngest and weakest of the old king Henry II's five sons, Prince John inherited the least of his father's estates and wealth. His nicknames were "Lackland", referring to his poverty, and "Soft-sword", an insult about his battle skills. By 1190 he had already been King of Ireland and lost his throne to rebellion. For all that, when Richard I took the crown of England John was his only surviving legitimate brother, well positioned to displace the stewards Richard left to govern during his crusade and take control of the kingdom.

fore Prince John," he said. "If she does not then she is committing treason, and all who aid her. Her brother Adam left my custody without official discharge, another offence to the King's law. Her family are conspirators against the Crown and accessories to the crimes of outlaws. And we know where they live."

Mereward was glad to be able to prove his usefulness. "Sir Richard at the Lee has a number of holdings across Yorkshire and Derbyshire. Of these, the principal ones are estates and a manor at Leaford and an older fortified house at Verysdale. There's a keep at Anston but it's further north and partly ruined."

"Sir Richard will head for Verysdale," predicted the Sheriff. "It's further from my reach and easiest to defend. That's where we'll find him."

"I don't know that we've enough men and resources to take a fortress by siege," warned Captain Aelstan. "I mean, we'll try of course but…"

"I don't want the fortress taken," snapped the Sheriff. "Why would I want that? I want Sir Richard pinned down, starving, sending for help. I want his dear daughter Marion to call for aid from her wonderful Robin Hood. Then when the outlaws stick their necks out away from their forest sanctuaries I want to stand back and loose Gisbourne's ravening thugs."

"Ah," understood Shankshard. "Two problems eliminate each other."

"Have arrest warrants drawn up for Sir Richard and Adam at the Lee," de Vendenal commanded Mereward. "Give Fitzwarren two days to be sure he gets to Verysdale before you set Gisbourne after him," he ordered Aelstan. "Hang whatever prisoners you took yesterday, guilty or innocent," he told Shankshard. "And bring me my absconded bride's father."

Beside the great cross in Nottingham's corn market, Gill o' the Red Cap and a band of soldiers in the Sheriff's livery offered a silver half-coin to men who would swell the Sheriff's guard.

"Step up, lads!" called Gill, the Sheriff's finest archer, who'd made the final six in yesterday's contest. "There's good silver here for any man as will make his mark to serve his shire! There's food and lodgings, new clothes and good ale. There's rich pickings to be had and all for a bright lad who knows his chances. And all the girls like a man in uniform!"

"All the girls like Robin i' th' Hood!" a wag shouted from the market crowd.

That raised laughter. "Ooh! Give me a merry man any day!" called out one brazen hussy.

"Give me two!" shouted another.

"None of that!" warned Gill. "Now roll up! This is a fine chance for a young man looking to make something of his-self. The new Sheriff's going places…"

"Without his wife!" someone mocked.

"You watch your tone if you don't want to join them as is hanging from the castle walls," Gill warned. "Now our new Sheriff, he's hard but he looks after his own. He pays well and he doesn't grudge his men a bit of sport. If you're a bold fearless lad then this is the life for you!"

"Unless you can join Robin in Sherwood!" snorted a cynic.

"Until Robin in Sherwood finds you, with a bow in his hand," cat-called another.

Gill gestured for a couple of men to push into the crowd and seek out the hecklers. There was a chorus of jeering.

A huge, lumbering man shouldered his way through the throng, not minding who he shoved aside. He stalked up to the guards and glowered down at them. "How much does it pay?" he demanded.

Gill looked up at the rogue. The brute had a confident sneer and the air of a man who'd been travelling for a long time. "Ninepence a week and board," he offered the newcomer. As the big man glared down at him he added. "A shilling if you're experienced."

"I'm experienced. What'd I be doing?"

"Whatever you're told," Gill answered harshly.

The big man worked a sliver of meat from his teeth with his tongue. "You're going after bandits. After Robin Hood?"

"It's likely. Sheriff intends to see him dead."

"They say Hood runs with a giant called John of Hathersage, near as big as me. Little John."

"They say right," Gill admitted curiously. "Why?"

"I want to meet him," answered the big man. "One of us'll be alive afterwards. Will you pay me till then?"

Gill o' the Red Cap looked the stranger up and down. The big man had scabs on his knuckles where he'd been fighting and speckles of blood on the outside of his tunic. "You'll be paid, and a bonus if you break Little John, I don't doubt. What name shall the clerk put in the book?"

The big man cracked his knuckles. "Reynold. Reynold Greenleaf. Bigger than Little John."

Sir Guy of Gisbourne rode back to Nottingham hours after the other searchers, still in a foul mood, and with blood on his knife. He threw the reins of his black stallion at one of the stable hands, cuffed another to the ground with his steel-studded gauntlet, and stalked up to see the Sheriff.

He slammed open the door to the Sheriff's private solar and interrupted a conference with Mereward and his tax collectors. "De Vendenal!" he called, "You let Hood get away!"

William de Vendenal put down his goose-quill and turned to the taxmen. "You may go," he told them. "You too, Mereward. Make sure those letters seeking passage of arms[7] are off to the northern barons today."

"My lord." the Steward responded, bowing before hurrying out with the tax gatherers. He diplomatically closed the door on the Sheriff and the black knight.

De Vendenal leaned back in his chair. "You have something to say, Gisbourne?"

"Hood has escaped. You had him right here, right in this castle, surrounded - and you let him get away!" All Sir Guy's furious searching and the pain he'd inflicted on random serfs in the villages he'd passed through hadn't found the outlaw.

"You are telling me things I know, Gisbourne. What's your point?"

"My point? My point is… is that you are responsible for this farrago, this massive failure! The outlaw who injured me, who kept me chained naked amongst pigs, has walked free again. He's laughing at you, de Vendenal. He's laughing at me!"

"Anything else?"

"I've sent word to Prince John. He'll know everything about this. Everything. He'll know where to lay the blame. You, de Vendenal, you are supposed to be the Sheriff of Nottingham, and you allow this!"

"Any more?"

Gisbourne swept the papers and cups off the Sheriff's desk in a high temper. "More? How can you be so by-the-lady calm when you've done this? Don't you know what situation you're in?"

"You mean, five heartbeats and three words away from having you taken out and flayed as a lesson in manners?" asked de Vendenal calmly. "I am, as you say, Sheriff."

"And I'm an envoy of Prince John of England! You can't touch me!"

The Sheriff held his eye. "Would you bet your life on that? Will you?"

The black knight paused. The Sheriff hadn't even raised his voice but

---

7   A legal agreement to bring an armed force over the territory of another nobleman without hindrance or penalty.

there was something in his face that daunted even Sir Guy of Gisbourne.

"It doesn't even have to be official," de Vendenal went on. "You might just vanish. A score of men would give oath that you left the castle whole and well. Then the outlaws must have caught you while you were unwisely rampaging through the countryside damaging my villeins. Who knows what indignities and torments they inflicted upon you before finally cutting your throat?"

Gisbourne stared at the Sheriff in disbelief. "You wouldn't dare."

"Your messenger Quimper Kinstain is delayed on the road, Sir Guy. Everyone has to be searched and questioned in our hunt for Robin i' the Hood. My own ambassador will be reaching Prince John before yours with a more measured account of events. He will, of course, remind his highness that you alone had seen Robin Hood up close before he came to Nottingham, and it was you upon whom we relied for his identification to spring our trap. *Did* you spot him, Gisbourne?"

"He was disguised. Who would have expected that kind if brazen boldness?"

"You were told to look for a disguised man," the Sheriff reminded Sir Guy.

Somehow the situation had changed. Without raising his voice, without rising from his chair, de Vendenal had the bully pinned. "I want Hood dead," Gisbourne demanded. "I want Matilda for Prince John."

"Then we have areas of mutual interest," summarised the Sheriff. "Let us work on them and avoid any more unpleasant discourtesies. I have a low tolerance for them. Do we understand each other, Sir Guy?"

"We do."

The Sheriff stared at the black knight one last time. "Then you may go," he said at last.

An unruly huddle of disreputable offenders slouched in the darkest corner at the *Sign of the Crow*, the nastiest tavern brothel on Pilchergate. Constable Shankshard stepped over a bravo who lay passed out drunk in a pool of his own urine and approached the leader of the gang.

Dunstan of Hucknall had been a condemned man once, suspected but never proved of murdering infants for pleasure. The new Sheriff had remitted him in exchange for his service; de Vendenal had need of seasoned murderers who'd go to places and do things that his regular guards could not.

Dunstan looked up through a heavy hangover. The child prostitute he'd been gripping during the night had somehow worked free and escaped while he slept, doubtless hoping to avoid more hurts. He'd find her later and prove otherwise. For now he dragged himself to a sitting position and belched at the Constable. "Yeah?"

Shankshard looked down his nose at the stinking mercenaries. "Your Sheriff has a job for you."

A few of the cutthroats chuckled cynically but Dunstan feared the Sheriff's icy malice. He hauled himself to his feet. "What is it?"

A few other freed murderers began to stir. Ned of Newark noticed the tall man standing silently behind the Constable. "Who's your big boyfriend?" he called.

Shankshard ignored the lout and addressed himself to Dunstan. "You heard about yesterday? The outlaws got clean away. The Sheriff doesn't want it so clean."

Dunstan of Hucknall nodded. "So what do we do?"

"The Sheriff wants a little blood let. Some of Hood's people. So Hood knows things are serious."

"You want us to go into Sherwood and chase Robin Hood in his own country?"

"No. You're to find one or two of his people away from the rest—men or women, doesn't matter—and make them die slow and bloody. Then leave them for Hood to find."

The cutthroats liked that. "What's the fee?" demanded Dunstan.

"Apart from not having your necks stretched as you deserve?" Shankshard spat. He had little time for criminals even if he was instructing them. "There'll be five shillings each for every proven kill. But see they're Hood's people. I'm not paying for just any slaughter of whoever you decide to butcher."

"But if we do butcher some peasant lass or lad," asked Dunstan slyly, "can we say as we're Robin Hood's men to those as watch us?"

Shankshard didn't answer that. He turned to indicate the big man he'd brought along. "Here's another to go with you. This is Reynold Greenleaf, who wants to kill Little John."

"You likes a big boy then, do you, Constable?" mocked Ned of Newark.

Reynold turned to the loudmouth, moving fast for so large a man. He caught Ned by the neck and dislocated first one arm then the other. As the cutthroat screamed, Reynold dropped him to the ground and deliberately shattered each of his kneecaps.

The big man looked at the other suddenly-sober mercenaries. "Anyone else got any questions about me?" he growled.

Ned was still screaming so Reynold kicked his head to render the cripple unconscious.

There were no more questions.

"Then get on with your work," Shankshard instructed Dunstan.

Sir Edward Lambert, the Knight of Loughborough, came to audience with the Sheriff in a state of high agitation. His concern was such that he brought with him his whole retinue, including his wife Lady Hilda and his son and heir Artus.

He bustled in with a crimson face and went on the attack. "Lord Sheriff, my daughter…"

De Vendenal cut into the intended tirade with icy calm. "Ah yes. Your daughter. My intended bride. The runaway. That is what I want to discuss."

The Sheriff's tones warned Sir Edward to moderate his own voice. "She was carried away by ruffians. Carried away from her own wedding!"

"She ran off, Sir Edward. With your minstrel," de Vendenal corrected the knight. "She jilted me and escaped to be an outlaw whore."

Lady Hilda forgot that her role was to stay silent and passive in this meeting of men. "She was led astray," she wept.

"Was she?" the Sheriff pondered. "I wonder. I wonder what your intention was in proposing this alliance to me in the first place, Sir Edward?"

The Knight of Loughborough gestured to his son. "It was a good match for you and it secured a good position for Artus amongst your officers." He changed from bombast to wheedling. "It still could be, if the girl can be found."

"I doubt she's fit now for a decent wedding," the Sheriff sneered, "if ever she was."

"A more generous dowry…" suggested Sir Edward.

The Sheriff cut him short. "Her dowry is forfeit, for breach of contract. But of more interest to me, Sir Edward, is whether this whole marriage agreement was part of some larger plot, a conspiracy to make the Lord High Sheriff of Nottingham look a fool and thus discredit the royal Prince who confirmed him in that position."

Sir Edward blanched. "My lord, no!"

"Because that is my suspicion," de Vendenal went on. "Treason, from one who plots against the Prince of this realm. Which of John's enemies bribed you to this farce, Sir Edward? Ely? Durham?[8] One of the great Barons who wants to undermine the Prince's authority?"

"My father would never do that!" blurted young Artus. He still wore his new livery of the Sheriff's guard. "We are your loyal allies!"

"Really? Because I have information that you plotted this with Elaine and the minstrel all along. My men have been questioning your daughter's maid Jenet all night. She has made full confession."

Lady Hilda winced at the torments the frightened teenage servant would have undergone to make whatever statement the Sheriff desired.

"That's nonsense!" argued Sir Edward. "Nobody can believe the screamed confessions of a tortured child."

"I do." The Sheriff rose. "Sir Edward Lambert, I arrest you on suspicion of high treason, and your son and wife with you. You will be held in close confinement pending my investigations, until I am satisfied of your guilt or innocence."

"No!" the Knight of Loughborough shouted, surging forward, but Captain Aelstan and the castle guard were already waiting to seize the prisoners. The entire Lambert party were grabbed and dragged from the chamber.

"You can't do this!" wailed Artus; too late his sister's warnings about the Sheriff rang true.

De Vendenal returned to his desk and picked up his quill. "Interrogate the retainers," he instructed Aelstan. "I want full confessions from all of them before they die. Make sure the stories match up. Dates and times can be very convincing evidence."

"Yes, sir," saluted the captain of the guard. "And the Lamberts?"

"Lodge Lady Hilda in her tower for now," the Sheriff decided. "Make sure she had access to a dagger should she decide to open a vein. As for Sir Edward and his annoying brat, I believe the oubliette is now vacant."

"Yes sir. Will they be fed?"

"Dead men need no food. I believe sickness will take them before their charges are heard in open court. Mereward, see that my stewards manage the Lambert estates until such time as their eventual ownership is deter-

8   King Richard left England in the charge of two Justiciars, William de Mandeville, the Earl of Essex and Hugh de Puiset, the Bishop of Durham. When de Mandeville died he was replaced by the ambitious William Longchamp, Bishop of Ely, who was already the Lord Chancellor of England and master of the Tower of London. Longchamp and de Puiset soon fell out and took arms against each other. Prince John worked to undermine both and gradually seized power from them.

Things had worked out better than he'd hoped. The Lambert fortune was his.

mined. The revenues are to be added to my account."

The Sheriff leaned back and smiled his thin smile. Things had worked out better than he'd hoped. The Lambert fortune was his and he'd not even had to marry their insipid child.

Things were looking up.

V

Marion lay beneath a spreading chestnut tree and watched Robin
Hood sleep. She liked to see his face like that, stripped of guarded
cunning, innocent like a little boy. She loved the scheming canny
rogue he became in the daytime–she was willing to admit that to herself now,
if not to the world–but she loved him more knowing that beneath the mask
he was a hopeful child.

The morning sun was shining through the leaves already, dappling Robin
and Marion with light and shadow. They were alone; John, David, and Much
had all separated from them late last night to confuse further pursuit. Marion
leaned over and kissed Robin because she could.

The outlaw woke as a mischievous pair of lips covered his and a wicked
tongue flicked into his mouth.

"Are you taking advantage of me?" he demanded, shying away and pulling
his bedroll up to cover his chest.

"Idiot!" Marion laughed. "That's supposed to be my line."

Robin wondered why him holding Marion in his arms all night without
trying to take her would define him as 'a perfect gentleman'. Every gentleman
he'd ever met would have had the girl's skirts up and be riding off whistling
by now. But Marion was different from Robin's former lovers, and she wasn't
ready. She was worth the wait.

He had no objection to her kisses, though. "Be gentle with me," he begged
her, resuming his supine position beneath her.

Marion kissed him with a tenderness that set him tingling from head to
toe.

"So what are we now?" Robin asked her at last. "You and me?"

Marion's unbound red hair spilled down over his chest. It tickled him as
she moved. "I don't know, Robin. Together, I think. You won my kiss in our
archery wager, and I'll be paying that off for quite some time."

"The longer you wait the worse the interest gets," warned the young outlaw.
"Regular instalments are best."

"I'll keep that in mind. And you won the archery contest, where the prize was more than just a golden arrow." The gold-plated trophy had been con-cealed safe in Marion's bodice at some point, but Robin had managed to retrieve it.

"Wasn't there a lady's hand offered to the winner, too?" Robin recalled. "And other parts, maybe?"

"That prize was never formally bestowed by the Sheriff," Marion pointed out. "Although the rules judges are considering the matter and will let you know when they reach a decision."

"What rules judges?"

"That would be me."

Robin rolled Marion over so now she was on her back and he leaning down to kiss her. "Is there any way I can bribe or persuade the rules judg-es?" he wondered.

Marion fended him off with a half-hearted push. "The judges will take their own time. In the meanwhile your prize is going to keep your wander-ing hands out of *there!*" The last words were delivered with a squeak and Robin got a boxed ear.

"Just establishing the situation," grinned the young archer. His smile was infectious.

"Establish it with your hands somewhere else. Not *that* somewhere else."

"So we're not up to verse twelve yet," Robin noted.

Marion tried to fathom that comment as she relaced her bodice. It somehow always came loose when she cuddled with Robin Hood. "Verse twelve of what?"

"Ah, yes," Robin said, a little nervously. "It seems there are a number of alehouse ballads circulating about you. About you and me, actually. About us kissing. And things."

Marion's eyebrows arched. "Indeed."

"That archery contest, people somehow knew beforehand what it was all about. Wagers and champions. Rumours from the revels where they crowned you May Queen and we danced. Country people draw country conclusions."

"You're saying that they're singing of my sluttishness in taverns from York to Lincoln?" Lady Matilda of Leaford and Verysdale demanded.

"Well, people know that I'm in love with you, that I want you."

Marion felt a flutter in her breast that was nothing to do with Robin's wandering fingers. "You're *in love* with me?"

Robin caught his breath. "Did I say that? Did I say that out loud?"

"Oh dear. And Robin Hood is famous for never getting caught."

The young outlaw dropped his head in shame to Marion's bosom. "Well, I've been caught now. Yes, I love you. I love how you make me feel. I love how you make me think. I love how you talk to me and listen to me. I love that you see things in me that I didn't even know were there - and then you make me become them. I love how you care about everybody you meet, that there's nobody doesn't matter to you. I love how you believe that the world can be made better—and must be. I love how you make it summer when I see you, and how the whole world stops when you kiss me. And that's only the beginning, Maid Marion. I find new ways of falling in love with you every moment I think about you. And I think about you all the time."

Marion's lips formed a little O.

"What about you?" Robin asked her anxiously. "Do you love me?"

The maid smiled at him, rubbing her fingers across his cheek. "I'll let you know," she teased.

"Did you sleep well, Lady?" Alan asked Elaine worriedly as she appeared from her ablutions. Tuck and Adam Fitzwarren were packing the mules and horses for the day's ride.

Elaine realised that despite the hard straw mat and the unfamiliar surroundings she had slept well; the best since she'd first gone to Nottingham Castle. "I feel like a new woman!" she realised.

"Will the new woman ride with me?" Alan asked her. "I quite liked the old one, but if the new one's even better I'm willing to give her a try."

"That's minstrels. They're fickle. They proclaim undying love until the next set of petticoats flounces by. Everyone says so."

"The only woman I ever want is with me now. If she's ready to blossom like a rose in summer then I'll be happier than ever. But I want no other rose," Alan assured Elaine.

The lady looked at him half-sceptically. "Poets."

"My muse," replied Alan. Later he'd sing her the song he'd composed when he thought her lost forever, but privately; that was not a merry tune for a summer's ride.

The young couple had come to the horses. Adam was eager to assist his friend's suit. "Alan does love you, Lady Elaine. He spoke of nothing else when we were imprisoned in the Sheriff's donjon. You were the one bright moment in his dark hours."

Elaine remembered that Alan had already proved his devotion. "I could be his muse," she conceded with a little unladylike wink at the minstrel.

Alan helped her onto her mount. "Where are we going?" she asked.

"Loughborough," replied Friar Tuck. "Your father's house."

Elaine panicked. "What? I can't go back! I won't go back! I want to be with Alan!"

"Then you'll need clothes and possessions, won't you?" the fat friar pointed out. "And perhaps a dowry?"

Adam whistled as he caught on. "We're to relieve Sir Edward of his treasury while he's away in Nottingham. And none will question us because the daughter of the house is with us and the house's minstrel with her!"

Alan a Dale and Elaine exchanged startled looks then burst into laughter. "I'm an outlaw's woman now!" she exclaimed with a delighted glee.

"Tuck," called Alan urgently. "There's a chapel at the manor. Marry us!"

Friar Tuck rode on, smiling.

In the deep forest an ancient stump cross rose from the tangled turf. Robin led Marion across the clearing and showed her the old dolmen.

"Nobody knows how long it's been there," he told her. "Some say it was set by the Romans. Others believe its older still, one of the waystones the elder people used to raise in sacred places."

Marion ran her hand over the weathered rock. Her fingers found faded indentations, eroded carvings of cups or spirals.

"They say Sherwood's haunted by ghosts and fairies. This is one of its secrets." Robin said. "The country folk still creep out here sometimes when they want babies. They lay fruit and flowers and then they... lay."

"Well don't you get any ideas, Robin Hood," Marion warned him. "I don't need a wolfshead baby."

The outlaw shook his head. His mood was more pensive, less flippant here. "I just wanted you to see it. There are worlds within Sherwood, Marion. There's falls where the water crashes down to make rainbows. Secret glades where the animals are tame enough to touch. Old straight tracks and hidden caves and trees big enough for a man to live in. There's an ancient eagle that can look at the sun without being blinded and a white hart that only a true king can catch."

Marion watched Robin as he stood in the dell, where the sun shone down on his yellow hair and made it golden, where the shadows of the leaves danced around him like a cloak. *He is Sherwood*, she thought, *dazzling and maddening and so deep behind his concealing canopy.* The idea made her pulse quicken.

Robin went on. "There's a rock with a bell on it. They say that if you go there at the dark of the moon and pull the chain a voice asks if it's time yet for the sleepers to awake. There's a sunken village that only rises every ten years. There's a salmon the length of my arm that can sing the future. There's a bear that was once a man and an ancient mound where the Fair Folk hold court at midsummer."

"And you've seen all this, have you?" asked Marion, half sceptical, half wanting to believe.

Robin shrugged. "Does it matter, if you want it to be true?" he wondered. "Have you ever seen justice? Or people getting what they deserve? Or true love? But we tell the stories as if they were true, until…"

"Until they become true," Marion understood. "So what is Sherwood's magic? The Sheriff's men fear it. The peasants respect it. You somehow… you use it."

Robin raised his arms and gestured to the trees around him. "Every story, pretty much, is about a journey, isn't it? One way or another, it's a journey. And every journey takes you through the woods, the dangerous woods with their secrets and surprises. It's going into the woods that changes you."

Marion remembered old Constanza's tales. "It's dangerous to stray from the path."

"But that's when the adventure starts," Robin smiled. "You know that, right?"

"There are outlaws in the woods."

"And a rare white hart that can only be caught by the true king." He moved over to Marion and embraced her. "Do you know the real reason we haven't made love yet?"

"Because I still have a dagger?"

"Because I've won your kiss by becoming Robin i' the Hood and I've won your hand by taking up the people's cause as your champion, but I haven't yet caught the hart that confers and confirms my rule. Your heart, that is. There's still something left for me to do before you're ready to be caught by me, full and forever."

Marion was pressed up against the old stone, its ancient carvings at her back. Sherwood wheeled around her, vast, powerful. Robin held her close, the forest lord chasing the people's queen. "What else must you do?" she heard herself asking.

"When it comes we'll know," said Robin Hood. "Then we will be together in Sherwood and it will be ours."

They kissed then in surety of that time to come.

And the forest waited.

The Steward of Loughborough was uncertain about letting Lady Elaine into her father's strongbox in his absence, but she claimed to have his key and his goodwill and she was the daughter of the house. Elaine herself seemed very excited, babbling something about additional funds needed for dowry and to bestow her brother Artus.

The fat clergyman who escorted her and the young squire of good breeding helped convince the Steward. Sir Edward's minstrel was also present, adding to the verisimilitude of the mission. Alan had often ridden messenger for his employer in the months of his service to the Lamberts.

"We had word that yesterday was your wedding," ventured the Steward.

"It was a wonderful occasion," Alan a Dale promised. "So much better than the usual dull affairs. Everyone said so. They'll be talking about it for years."

"The Sheriff's probably exhausted by now," Tuck added, waiting until Lady Elaine was out of earshot forcing the treasure box. "He had a very busy wedding night."

Adam Fitzwarren hadn't really caught on to the idea of bandit banter yet, but he made an effort. "The flowers were lovely."

Elaine emptied out the strongbox's plate and silver into a thick burlap sack. She left behind the deeds and charters, which were worthless to sell, and chose from her mother's jewellery those pieces to which she felt she had an honest claim. Elaine's family had done her wrong and she was leaving Loughborough forever but she was not willing to return misdeed for misdeed. It was one thing to take away a fair dowry that was her due–at least by some means of reasoning–but she would not rob her family of more than it could afford.

"How is Master Artus faring in the Sheriff's service?" the Steward ventured.

"His armour is very shiny," answered Alan. "He's the same as always, otherwise."

"Men who meet the Sheriff of Nottingham learn quickly," added Adam.

"But then it's often too late," muttered Tuck to himself as he helped lift the sack across one of the horses. He turned to the Steward. "And now I'll need to use your chapel. I promised I'd conduct a sacred office while I was here. Lady Elaine, Alan a Dale, lead the way to the altar, please."

"Robin! Robin i' the Hood!" The camp guards were the first to shout greetings at their leader's return.

The laughing bandit strode out of Sherwood as if he'd been taking a morning constitutional, and he led Maid Marion to the Major Oak.

The watchmen had all been with Robin against Gisbourne at Minsthorpe Wood; they knew the Saxon-haired girl already. The other denizens of the outlaw village abandoned their domestic duties and gathered round the couple.

Ros of Waltham dropped a wicker basket of laundry and rushed over to hug the young woman. "Well now! This is what we've been missing, milady!" she cried. "Someone as can keep that young rogue in check!"

Robin looked over his shoulder to see what rogue Ros was talking about.

"And glad I am to be here," Marion confessed, hugging Ros back. "How's little Tad?"

"Walking right sturdy now," the peasant woman answered, pointing over to where her last surviving child was playing in the grass with some carved wooden blocks. "John had him pull back his first toy bow last week."

Tad heard his name, looked over, then toddled rapidly to Marion on sturdy legs. He looked much stronger and healthier than the last time she'd seen him.

The others of the camp gathered round to greet Robin and meet his lady. The newcomer was surprised to realise that her arrival had been awaited with much anticipation.

"May I present to you the Maid Marion," Robin said to the women and children that had accumulated at camp since Robin's men had set up there.

A cheer rose from the assembly. There were thirty or more people Marion didn't recognise gathered to welcome her. "Hello," she said, a little shyly.

"They all want to meet the legendary Marion," Robin teased her. "I hope you're feeling legendary enough to cope?"

"At least as legendary as you, Robin Hood," the maiden replied, sticking her tongue out at him in a fashion that would have outraged her mother.

"And I daresay a good deal humbler."

"I'm humble," Robin pouted. "I'm the best there is at being humble."

Canon Steven's angry shouts cut across the banter.

Ros glanced over to the captives. "I was thinking of gagging that one," she frowned.

"Maybe later," Robin promised her. "Marion, come over and meet our guests."

"Now I'll tell you about marriage," Friar Tuck said, standing before the altar where Alan and Elaine held hands and Adam stood watching. "I could recite you that long Latin ceremony again but you both heard it yesterday. Instead I'll tell you something else."

The young lovers only stared into each other's eyes.

"Our Lord Jesus went to a wedding[9]. It was back before he was famous, before his ministry had hardly begun. It was a family wedding, and his mother Mary was there. Jesus turned up with his new disciples and, maybe because of that or maybe not, but the wine ran out at the wedding feast. Now that was a shameful thing to happen, a bad omen for the bride and groom. Enough to spoil a happy wedding day and maybe the marriage after it."

Alan and Elaine were startled enough by this unconventional sermon to turn to the friar.

"So Our Lord's mother asked Jesus to do something about it. Christ replied that his time hadn't come yet. It wasn't in God's plan to start his mission at some little country wedding. But you know mothers. She just bade the servants listen to whatever her son told them. She knew her lad pretty well."

Adam nodded his head ruefully. He knew mothers.

"So Jesus changed his plan, God's plan. He had the servants bring the big man-high jars that held the water to pour out for washing and he turned all of that water into rich wonderful wine. When the head steward tasted it he was amazed that they'd saved the best drink till then. And the wedding was saved and the ministry of Our Lord had begun."

Tuck clasped Alan and Elaine's hands together.

"Now after that Jesus healed lepers and cast out demons and made the

---

9   The account is found in *The Gospel of John* 2.1-11. Tuck's gloss is inspired by William Barclay's definitive 1955 commentary *The New Daily Study Bible: The Gospel of John*, volume 1, ISBN 0-664-22489-X

blind see and even raised people from the dead–all sorts of amazing miracles. But I take great comfort in the fact that Our Saviour was willing to change the universal plan to get a humble couple off to a good start in life, just because he was asked to. It means even my silly prayers and yours might have a chance. It shows that Our Lord understands how a man and a woman can want to cleave together for life and why it's important. It means when I say these words that God really will bind you two as one for all of your days, and no going back. So Alan a Dale, Elaine of Loughborough, in Jesu's name: do you want to be wedded to each other?"

"Yes," breathed Alan.

"I do," confessed Elaine.

"Does anyone object?"

"Well, there's the Sheriff," noted Adam, honestly.

"Does anyone here object? Anyone who's not a sour scourge on humankind with an appointment awaiting him in the firepits of the eternal abyss as soon as Rob gets him?" Tuck amended his question. "No? Then by Christ Jesu I bind you two as man and wife. What God has joined together let no man put asunder. Amen!" He made the sign of the cross and clapped Alan on the back. "Kiss your bride, lad!"

Adam turned aside to allow the newlyweds a private moment. He saw Tuck chugging at a wineskin he'd somehow picked up from Loughborough's stores.

The friar chuckled. "I thought it was water. Must be another miracle."

Canon Steven was not in a good mood. Ros and the camp women had allowed him to almost pick his way loose from his hemp bonds before they'd come and renewed them, laughing at his frustration. Even his fellow captive, Marcel of Flanders, had joined in the joke.

"Let them 'ave their laugh," the Prince's man told the livid priest. "Soon enough they will weep when his highness' wrath falls upon them."

Canon Steven was still promising damnation when a cheer rose up from the outlaws around the cooking fire. Marcel strained to see what was happening. "So, Robin 'ood has won his lady," the Frenchman realised. He found he couldn't disapprove.

"Kidnapper! Robber! Blasphemer! Gallows-bait!" shouted the Canon.

Robin and Marion joined them under the shadow of the great oak that dominated the clearing. Robin introduced the lady to the prisoners bound there.

Canon Steven wasn't interested. "I demand you release me at once!" he screamed at Robin i' the Hood.

Robin squatted down beside him. "Why?" he wondered.

That caught the priest off-guard. He spluttered in confusion as he tried to change his speech in mid yell. "What? You must release me because I am a man of God, a servant of Christ whom you have blasphemously…"

"You're a priest?" Robin asked him, straight-faced. "Really?"

"I am Canon Steven, of the Arch-Diocese of York, appointed to the…"

"You don't look like a priest," Robin told him. "Where's your robes? Where's your breviary and beads? Where's your fat money purse?"

"You stole them from me, you robber!" screeched the Canon. "You will hang for your crimes! You will burn in hell!"

Marion knelt down next to Robin to examine the bound prelate. Marcel watched her appreciatively.

"He might be a priest, Robin," the maiden admitted. "I mean, he's poor. He *might* be honest. Has he done charitable things? Has he shown grace and faith and love to all around him? Has he forgiven his enemies?"

Robin leaned in closer to examine the Canon's choleric-red face. "I don't know about the forgiveness part," he admitted. "He might be able to turn the other cheek. He's got a lot of cheek. And jowl. And belly."

Marcel suppressed a snort of amusement.

"You will not mock me! I am a man of importance!" cried Canon Steven. "You have robbed me, tied me, left me to be tormented by those hellion sluts…"

Robin shrugged. "Let me tell you, there's plenty of fellows would be happy to be tormented by those hellion sluts. But don't worry. Word's sent to York to get you back there. You'll be on your way, poor if not honest or charitable, just as soon as Archbishop Geoffrey pays your lodgings-bill for your time with us."

"My bill? I'm captive here, fed peasant slop while…"

"Yes, fed. And watered, and sheltered, and protected from the dangers of the forest. It all costs, you see."

"It's a shame you tried so hard to ruin my father," Marion accused the Canon, staring into his eyes. "I might have pitied you else."

More than Hood's banter, more than Ros' contempt, Marion's condemnation caused Canon Steven to tremble. She held his eye for a long time, not speaking.

Finally she rose up and shook her skirts. "Keep him out of my sight, Robin," she said.

Marcel of Flanders would have clapped had his hands been free. "Lady Matilda," he acknowledged, "The Prince was right to desire you."

"Oh, everybody desires Marion," Robin assured him. "She's very desirable. Fortunately she's also humble. She says so."

"But she is not for you, peasant," the Frenchman warned. "Prince John 'as sent for her."

Marion flushed red. "And Prince John can go and…"

Robin clasped her round the waist and pulled her to him. "Marion has a problem in answering the Prince's summons."

"I certainly do!" snarled the daughter of Sir Richard at the Lee.

Robin cut off her further angry remonstrance with an unexpected kiss. Then he grinned at Marcel of Flanders. "I'll explain. The beloved and saintly Lord High Sheriff of Nottingham–a charming man whose beard in no way looks as if a scurvy rat has died and decomposed upon his chin–kindly put on an archery contest and promised a golden arrow and a red-headed lady to the winner. You may recall that you were making your way to the match when you were waylaid by forest bandits?"

"I recall it well," admitted Marcel sardonically.

"Well, I've always wanted a golden arrow and a red-headed lady so I went along to Nottingham to try my luck. And behold! Here's a rather nice gold-dipped arrow, although I reckon it wouldn't shoot very far, and an even nicer Saxon-maned heiress. I won them fair and square and now they're mine."

"Says you," warned Marion, pushing him off. "Just you recall what happened to the last outlaw chief that tried to do me a mischief."

Robin took a step backward and bowed to her. "Anyhow Marcel, according to both the Sheriff and to Lady Matilda's father, this refreshingly fierce young maiden is now mine to wife. Her version of events may vary, of course, but that's women for you."

"I'm not going to wed you, Robin Hood, just because you happened to saunter out of a castle with me!" scorned Maid Marion.

"*Saunter?*" Even Robin was outraged at that description of his feats of yesterday.

Marion chuckled to have scored a point back, and tweaked his nose.

"Well, whatever happened yesterday, I've got the lady here with me, Marcel. And she's mine to wed, which I think creates an interesting legal position regarding her summons to Prince John."

Marion caught on. "Oh! Yes! If I didn't attend Weaselly John's summons when I was in my father's guardianship then Sir Richard Fitzwarren would have been responsible in law and could be charged for treason. But now Robin has rights to me so he's to blame if I'm not yielded up to Lackland!"

Robin nodded. "I'm not a lawyer–I'm not that dishonest, I'm only a forest bandit–but I reckon that means that neither Sir Richard nor his family can be blamed for Marion's absence. She's been removed by her legal guardian and she's held whether she wills it or not by the outlaw king of Sherwood." He folded his arms triumphantly and looked down at Marcel. "And that's how it is."

Marion linked her arm with Robin's. "That's how it is. Robin has carried me off. I'm helpless in his clutches. As long as he stops clutching when I tell him to."

"I'm very good at choosing my clutches," Robin promised her. "I'll demonstrate later."

"See?" Marion appealed to Marcel. "I'm absolutely stuck. Pass on my regrets to Prince John that I'm not able to attend him. Otherwise I'd have come to court and given him what he needs. What he so very much needs."

"We're letting you go," Robin told Marcel of Flanders. "You'll be escorted blindfold back to the road so you can tell the Prince how it is with Marion."

"Prince John will hunt you to your death," the Frenchman promised him.

Robin unslung the bow from his shoulder and strung it. He selected six arrows from his quiver and set them ready on the ground. The people in the camp watched. Without any other sign, Robin seized up shaft after shaft, sending them thrumming into the knot on a distant ash tree. All the shots hit within a circle no bigger than a penny.

Robin looked back at Marcel and his eyes flamed. "Not every forest creature is safe to hunt," he warned. "Tell Prince John that as well."

VI

Prince John, Count of Mortain, Lord of Ireland, was shorter than his famous kingly brother, barrel-chested with dark red hair and a prominent hooked nose. He enjoyed fine clothes and jewels and wore his best even in private. His thin ring-bedecked hands had bitten nails.

He was most dangerous when he was disappointed.

"Bring them in. All together," he ordered his man Rothmere.

While he waited he laid out a series of parchments on his desk, unstoppered a bottle of squid's ink, and sharpened a new quill.

Rothmere returned with three worried men. Lewis of Newark wore Nottingham's livery. It was he who had galloped in first with the Sheriff's account of the debacle at the wedding. Quimper Kinstain affected court finery, his choice of cut and style subtle tribute to Prince John's royal influence. Sir Guy's messenger had brought a different account of the fateful archery contest. Marcel of Flanders was clad in the Prince's own colours. He'd ridden in late last night with news of Sherwood's defiance.

The three stood before the Prince's desk like guilty choir-boys, each well aware of Lackland's mercurial tempers.

The Prince laid his hand over a parchment pile on his writing table. Unlike many noblemen he could read and write well and kept a private library. He spoke without any preamble or greeting, without even looking up at the men before him. "I have here correspondence from the Archbishop of Canterbury," John said quietly. "It concerns his interference in my marriage to the Count of Gloucester's daughter last year. You may recall, or you may have heard idle tongues gossiping, that the Archbishop has declared our marriage null for reasons of consanguinity, Isobel being my second cousin, and he has placed our lands under interdict. I must now cozen and bribe the Pope to overturn Canterbury's absurd objection. This makes me irritable."[10]

---

10   The political marriage between John of Mortain and wealthy Isobel of Gloucester was allowed by Richard the Lionheart in the hopes of buying his brother's loyalty while away on his crusade. Isobel was between 9 and 15 years old at the time of her marriage. Baldin of Forde, Archbishop of Canterbury from 1185, Britain's sen-

He shifted his hand to another set of documents. "What about this? My genius big brother set two men to rule England while he went off to smite Moors. Hugh de Puiset decided that being Bishop of Durham wasn't enough. He bought himself the Earldom and the Sheriffship of Northumbria and became one of the twin pains in my backside who think to hold England from my rightful control. He has annoyed my bastard half-brother Geoffrey, the Archbishop of York, who believes that the Bishop of Durham is his subordinate. Both of them have complained to the Pope. Again."

Another scroll. "De Puiset's fellow Justiciar, William de Mandeville, had the courtesy to die. But then the Lord Chancellor William Longchamp, Bishop of Ely, master of the Tower of London, gave Richard £3,000 to become Mandeville's replacement. It is hard to say which Justiciar dislikes me most. Fortunately they like each other no better. This letter is an account of Longchamp's intention to arrest de Puiset and confiscate his castles, earldom, and hostages."

Prince John still kept his gaze down on his desk. "Our dear Lord Chancellor seems very busy. He's everywhere. He's in London, promising the city the right to elect their own Sheriffs and bill the Exchequer for it. He's in York, putting down the riots that massacred the Jews. He's in Wales, chasing Rhys ap Gruffyd while the marcher lords cheer and applaud him. He's parading round like a king with a huge retinue of retainers and festival animals to the adulation of the people.[11] And where am I?"

John looked up and his gaze was venomous. "Where am I? I am in Lincoln, getting letters from Geoffrey, Archbishop of York, refusing me support because his canon is held hostage by forest men. I am in Lincoln, hear-

---

ior churchman, objected to the wedding because it broke the laws of consanguinity. Catholic canon law prohibited marriages within "the fourth degree of relationship" - third cousins - from at least the year 1215. Isobel and John were both great-grandchildren of Henry I and therefore second cousins.

Beyond the time of our present narrative, Baldin died before 1190 was over. Pope Clement III lifted the interdict on the couple's estates and allowed them to remain married but forbade them to have sexual relations. This did not prevent Isobel from bearing John five children. It was John himself who eventually had the marriage annulled for consanguinity in 1199 shortly after becoming king of England. He kept Isobel's lands.

11   This is a somewhat shorthand and biased summary of English politics in 1189 to 1190, the first year of Richard's absence on crusade. The two Chief Justiciars who were supposed to hold power did indeed quarrel. Longchamp, who replaced original Justiciar de Mandeville after de Mandeville's death, successfully suppressed de Puiset. Before 1190 was done Prince John and Longchamp were engaged in military operations against each other.

ing that I must dispatch troops to put down revolt in Nottinghamshire because my idiot envoy Gisbourne couldn't ride down a few bandits. I am in Lincoln, a laughing-stock because my chosen champion surrendered to wolfsheads and was impersonated as part of a plot that shamed me before the holiday crowds. I am in Lincoln, bereft of funds because my new Lord Sheriff of Nottingham is unable to make good on the financial obligations he accepted when he weaselled his way to receiving that important and lucrative office from me. And everywhere there is paper, and treaties, and letters. And *nowhere is there action!*"

Prince John slammed his hand down on the table. The ink-pot danced.

"I wanted Sir Richard at the Lee destroyed. I wanted the Barons to tremble at what I could do to them if they crossed me. I wanted pretty little Matilda Fitzwarren squirming and sweating in my bed, willing or not, no matter to me. I wanted Geoffrey to come in line and help me hammer de Puiset and Longchamp into oblivion. I wanted England to be mine!"

The three men ducked as John hurled his ink-pot at them.

"My lord…" began Kinstain, but Lackland cut him short.

"Do you know what isn't written on paper?" Prince John snarled. "They don't write down the tavern-songs they are singing, right here in Lincoln. They don't write down the ballads of Robin Hood and Maid Marion. They don't need to. Everybody knows the words! They know he 'robs from the rich, gives to the poor'! They toast him and cheer him and they *laugh at me!*"

Marcel of Flanders fell to one knee. "Your highness, I can find 'eem. Allow me to take some men and make good my error. I can comb Sherwood Forest and bring you Robin 'ood's head."

Quimper Kinstain interjected. "It isn't another hunting party that's needed, my Lord, led by a soft trick-shot. Sir Guy of Gisbourne sends for a thousand men, armed for war, to reave the shire and teach them to fear your might. That will send the message to your Barons that you are not to be crossed, and to your Sheriffs too."

While Marcel was reacting to Kinstain's dismissive description of him, Lewis of Newark stepped forward. "Great prince, I have some counsel from my Lord Sheriff of Nottingham, if you will allow it," he offered.

Lackland glared at him. "All I want from de Vendenal is order in his shire and my money."

"Those things you can have my lord, and more besides. My Lord Sheriff recognises your anger and understands its reasons. That is why he bade me ride here directly and tell you how he proposes to make amends."

Prince John silenced Kinstain and Marcel and leaned towards Lewis. "Tell me."

"Sire, everything you wanted to accomplish can still be achieved. My Lord Sheriff has expended his own resources to make it possible for you. He can make good all your losses, in gold and men's respect, and far more. He will send officers to arrest Sir Richard at the Lee and his household at their stronghold of Verysdale. He expects the Fitzwarrens to resist. He expects to have to pin them in a siege, and has lent soldiers and machines to your man Sir Guy for that purpose."

"Enough to take a castle?" scorned Marcel, his Norman accent becoming stronger as he lost his temper.

"No, sir. Not even enough to prevent a messenger sending for help from Sir Richard's daughter's suitor, bold Robin of Sherwood. The Sheriff intends to draw Hood out of his forest fastness to where he can be caught. And then he hopes that you will send an overwhelming force to take Verysdale, Sir Richard, his daughter, and the outlaw all. Leave nothing behind and give all your enemies the most miserable deaths you can devise. Avenge Archbishop Geoffrey and gain his gratitude. Let Longchamp and de Puiset learn to beware."

Kinstain considered this. "The Sheriff will buy Sir Guy his army?"

"My Lord de Vendenal is the Prince's most loyal subject and would not stint to support him in this action," replied Lewis.

Prince John sat back in his chair, worrying his jagged fingernails. "It might work," he mused. "It is bold. They'll say it's bold. It might just work." He looked up abruptly at his man Rothmere. "Get these three out. I have to think."

Reynold Greenleaf emerged from the farmer's cot wiping blood from his knuckles with a tattered scarf. He tossed the rag back through the door and kicked the flimsy wicker trap shut to hide the interior.

"He told you?" asked Dunstan of Hucknall.

The big man nodded. "I know. You can burn it now." Then he had a second thought. "No, wait! If Robin i' th' Hood's men are hard by there's no point giving them a bloody warning beacon. Leave it be. Let's get on."

"What did the serf say?" demanded Dunstan. He noticed that now Reynold had wiped his hands they were undamaged. The blood had all come from someone else.

"Woodbarrow. It's about five miles north. A fat friar went through there yesterday with two lads and an old woman on a hand-wagon. He left a brace of partridges for the widows and orphans. Probably left the widows with more orphans on the way, if his reputation holds true."

Dunstan looked at the motley gang of cutthroats that he'd scraped from the Pilchergate stews. Gill o' th' Red Cap had appealed to the brave young swains that swaggered along Nottingham's main streets and dreamed of adventure and glory. Dunstan's men wanted rape and pillage and a licence to destroy.

Thirty-two of them slouched along the road, sullen, mostly sober now they'd drained the last of the sack. The child-murderer had kept them off the roads as much as he could. He didn't want it obvious that the raiders had set out from Nottingham. Robin's merry men lived in Sherwood's heart, and it would be easier to blame atrocities on them if Dunstan's reavers first struck there too.

The killer considered that capturing Robin's fat friar would be an ideal way of fulfilling Constable Shankshard's mission. The tavern tales mentioned many of Hood's bold outlaws, but chief amongst them were Little John and Friar Tuck. Dunstan quickly sketched out a suitable scenario that concluded with leaving the skinned monk's pelt nailed to the door of Woodbarrow's chapel. That should get Hood's attention.

He glanced back at his band. He knew they were grumbling already, missing the sport they'd been promised, eager for prey. He'd have to give them blood and flesh soon or they'd turn on him. Only the presence of Reynold Greenleaf had kept them in order so far; they all remembered what had happened to Ned.

The fierce hairy giant fascinated Dunstan. There was a terrible discipline in the big man's movements. His eyes were never still. Despite his bulk he walked silently. His whole focus seemed to be on finding his rival John of Hathersage.

Dunstan hoped that they could take Little John alive, if only for the pleasure of watching a blood-match between John and Reynard, to see them maim each other.

Ferret Wen raced back from scouting ahead. He'd found the track that the farmer had confessed to Reynold. It cut along a natural ridge, shielded on one side by thickets of gorse. The reavers shifted to single file and followed it.

Dunstan kept right behind Reynold. The giant was an excellent meat shield. "You never said why you've got such a mad on at John Little," Dunstan ventured.

"You never said why you murdered all those little girls," growled back the big man.

"I never said I did that."

"Difference between you and me, Hucknall. I'm not ashamed of anything I've done to people."

Dunstan scowled. His best carving blade was right there, strapped to his left wrist. "I'm not ashamed or afraid."

"Then why did you kill them?"

"Because I wanted to. I liked it."

Reynold nodded. "That's more like it. Face up to your deeds. Be a man."

"I am a man," warned the child-murderer. "As good as any. Better."

"Did you ever manage to kill someone who wasn't an infant?" Reynold's sneer betrayed his contempt and stung Dunstan.

"I've killed plenty. More than you. I gutted that old knight's servant on the London Road–the old knight they say is Maid Marion's father."

"Was he armed?"

"Does it matter? The lackey begged after I carved his face. He died screaming. The old man wept."

The giant didn't reply. He strode on along the track.

"So you and Little John?" pressed Dunstan, his curiosity piqued.

"We knew each other as kids. We learned to fight together. We loved the same girl. Now he's what he is and I'm what I am. But we both face our enemies when we go after them." Reynold turned round suddenly. He jammed his seven-foot quarterstaff hard into the turf. "And that's all I have to say about this. We should move along quietly now."

The reavers moved with deadly intent towards Woodbarrow.

More than twelve hundred people travelled in Prince John's royal procession, the mobile court that travelled the country with its would-be-ruler dispensing justice and collecting tithes. The cost of maintaining the household was too great for any one place to sustain it permanently. A two-week visit could deplete even large castles of a year's food and drink. Smaller venues were indebted for years to sustain the lavish celebrations of their Prince's progress.

Lackland's stay at Lincoln was coming to an end. Already the wagons were being packed for tomorrow's departure. Three hundred carts carried everything from wardrobes and wine-baskets to furniture and concubines. The courtyard was heaving with activity as the Prince's household packed up the gifts and gold he'd collected on his stay and made ready to leave.

The Tattooed Woman was still in her cell, though. She wouldn't be taken to her cage until the very last moment. She tended to upset the other creatures in the Prince's menagerie.

Nobody knew how old the Tattooed Woman was. Some said she was a Moor, that she'd been a great beauty won in the last crusade and brought slave to England. Others doubted that she had ever been young or was ever born of human mother. Certainly now the tiny bony hag was wrinkled and sour, her ink-blotched limbs and face as stained with liver spots as with ornate interlocking body art.

She sat cross-legged as always in an inscribed circle intersected with a magic triangle that she'd filled with Greek script. John knew enough to make out the Arabic formula *abracadabra* written out on each of the three sides of the magic diagram;[12] some claimed the word was Aramaic for 'create as I say'. A pair of obscenely fat toads crouched beside the Tattooed Woman as she jerked back and forth.

A guard preceded John into the cell. The Tattooed Woman was manacled with iron to bind her powers but the Prince didn't trust her. It was said that she fed her toads with her blood, giving them suck on her withered dugs, and that she licked their backs to see visions of far off things.

The Prince squatted down, careful not to soil his finery on the filth that littered the dungeon floor. "Can you hear me?" he asked the Tattooed Woman.

Yellow eyes flicked up and found him.

"I've come for advice," John said. "There's a man. An outlaw. They call him Robin i' th' Hood. He's caused some trouble in Nottinghamshire and Yorkshire."

The Tattooed Woman looked down to the dirt she'd been studying. The remains of some small animal, a mouse or vole perhaps, had been torn open and scattered around the circle she occupied.

John went on. "We're leaving Lincoln tomorrow for York. I need to get the city on my side—and maybe my half-brother. He's Archbishop of York and he's bound to demand what I'm doing about some fool canon of his

---

12   This kind of magic triangle, in which the word 'abracadabra' is written on each successive line with one more letter omitted from the beginning and end, is first recorded in Quintus Serenus Sammonicus' the 2nd century *Liber Medicinalis* or *De Medicina Praecepta Saluberrima*. Physician to the Roman Emperor Caracalla, he prescribed this magic triangle as a means of curing malaria.

that the forest men have captured for ransom. I need to know about this Robin. Should I take him seriously?"

The Tattooed Woman grubbed in the dirt, cackling and whistling to herself.

"Should I take him seriously?" the Prince repeated. He raised the whip he'd brought with him to threaten the witch.

The crone ignored him, muttering as she fingered the entrails of the animal she'd dissected. She tasted her thumbs and looked up just as the Prince had raised his lash to strike.

"The Hooded Man is more than you," she said in thickly accented Norman French.

Prince John froze. "What?"

"The Hooded Man is more than you. His story is stronger than yours. He will be remembered."

"What does that mean?" John demanded, colouring with anger. "Speak, you devil-woman!"

"The Hooded Man will be remembered till the end of time. You will be remembered because of him."

Her filmy eyes seemed unfocussed but they terrified the Prince. "I'll kill him!" he promised.

"The Hooded Man chases the May Queen as you do. Only one can catch the hart."

Lackland's brows furrowed. "Speak clearly. Robin Hood pursues Matilda at the Lee, is that it? He carried her off from Nottingham, as he stole her once before. But I have commanded her to come to me or I shall destroy her family."

"Who catches the white hart–or the pure white hind–catches England's heart," snickered the Tattooed Woman. "If the Hooded Man catches it you will be nothing."

"What's that mean? Will I be killed? Murdered?"

"Worse. You will be reviled. Forever." The Tattooed Woman pointed at the Prince. "Forever."

John hit her with the whip until she bled and blubbered on the floor but she would not change her words.

After an hour the Prince stormed from her cell and called for Lewis of Newark and Quimper Kinstain. He had an army to dispatch.

Dunstan's reavers arrived at Woodbarrow as the dusk gathered. A light rain dampened the ground, muffling their approach, driving the serfs and peasants of the little village to indoor tasks.

Ferret Wen scouted and reported to his chief. "Six cottages, no more. Perhaps twenty men and near as many women. I saw no babes. Perhaps there was famine?"

"Do they suspect anything?" asked Dunstan.

"They're keeping a watch, but not for us. There's a man with a torch watching the Southwell road at the other end of the village."

"I'll take him," said Reynard Greenleaf. Nobody argued.

"How strong are they?" Dunstan asked Ferret Wen. "What arms?"

"I saw none. I take it they have a strict lord. We're not far off Bestwood Park. That's a forest enclosure. Weapons might be forbidden them."

"We'll take them by surprise anyhow," Dunstan told his men. "Take 'em alive. More fun that way." He looked over at the ramshackle collection of wooden sheds. "There'll be children there somewhere," he promised himself.

"First I'll take that guard," Reynard said. "I'll be back." The giant vanished between the trees with a speed and stealth that belied his bulk.

Dunstan turned to his cutthroats. "Listen well, lads. We're here for word of the fat friar and the cart with the old woman on it. That's what we have to bleed out of these folks. Save taking your fun till we've got what we need. And if any asks, say we're Robin Hood's bravos."

"But then we get our sport?" one of his thugs checked.

"Whatever sport you fancy," promised Dunstan. "We'll burn this place when we're done. One survivor's enough to tell the tale."

Reynold returned as swiftly as he'd departed. "It's done," he said, "but there's riders coming up the road."

Dunstan frowned. "Who? How many? Of what rank?"

"Couldn't see. It's too dark. Couple of horses maybe, or a horse and an ass. Could be what the guard was on lookout for."

Dunstan turned to his men. "Range out. Cover the road. Cover the village green. Mark each cottage door so none can leave. Surround the travellers unseen and wait for my word."

His reavers shifted off to take up station. Dunstan gestured for Reynard and a couple of others to stay with him.

The hoof-beats were audible now, slow steps of a horse walking with a donkey or mule beside it. Mount and rider came into view, and a youth afoot leading a tethered pack beast.

"I am Marion of the Greenwood. Surrender. Or die."

Dunstan peered through the almost-night at the cloaked figure on the mare. "Is that a woman?" he breathed.

A moment later his question was answered. The rider slid from the saddle, landed gracefully, and drew back her hood to reveal a coil of Saxon-red hair.

Dunstan grinned unpleasantly, slid his sword from his belt, and stepped forward. "Halt! Make no move!"

Woman and youth turned to face the murderer. Their mule was laden with heavy sacks of grain and vegetables for the people of Woodbarrow. The boy fumbled for a knife-belt but the woman restrained him.

Dunstan led Reynard and the others out of cover and approached his prey. The girl was young and comely, a very fair prize. "Who are you?" the child-killer asked her.

The woman didn't shy from him. She fixed him with the imperious glare of a descendant of princesses. "I am Lady Matilda Fitzwarren of Leaford and Verysdale, daughter of a knight of the Cross, Sir Richard at the Lee," she answered, "But some name me Maid Marion."

Dunstan's blotched face screwed into a sinister grin. "Well now, that's much better than killing a fat friar!" he gloated.

Marion did not back down. She took a step towards the reavers and she commanded them: "I am Marion of the Greenwood. Surrender. Or die."

VII

Alan a Dale had grown to be a connoisseur of manors. A wandering minstrel earned his living and stayed alive by reading the character and mood of his potential patrons' houses. Before Alan's tenure at Loughborough he'd lived a troubadour life, drifting from feast to feast, finding shelter and work where he could amongst the estates of Leicestershire, Warwickshire, and Northamptonshire. So as he rode up to Verysdale with his new bride and the youngest son of that household he looked around with keen interest.

They arrived near sunset, when long shadows stretched eastwards and a light breeze stirred the long grass in the harewoods. Down to their right a patchwork swathe of ploughed fields clustered along the snaking River Wharfe. The irregular strips were mostly planted with barley, wheat, and oats. Rows of cabbages and root vegetables squashed into any available gaps. A third of the furlongs lay fallow to allow the land time to recover from previous harvests.

The village estate straggled along the Huddersfield to Harrogate road. A crenellated house with smoking chimneys dominated the ridge above, with clear lines of sight in all directions. The walled manor was of old local stone, not fashionable but secure.

"There it is!" Adam Fitzwarren told his friend. "If you think this place is crumbling you should see our manor at Anston."

Elaine sat sidesaddle in front of Alan, her arms wrapped round his neck as if she'd never let go of him. She squirmed pleasantly to get a better look at their destination. "What do you make of it?" she asked her new husband, knowing he'd have appraised it already.

"It's not in such bad shape as Adam thinks," the minstrel judged. "It's old and a bit rundown but it's defensible. And it looks like there's been some hasty repairs done. Look at those new wooden screens above the gatehouse. And some timber's been newly felled on the approaches."

Alan looked across the peasantry's carefully-delineated ribbon-land holdings. Unusually, the narrow fields were empty of serfs. No beasts grazed the commons.

"Word was sent ahead that there might be trouble," Adam remembered. "Kent is steward here. He knows his business."

"What else, Alan?" Elaine pressed. She loved to hear him talk.

"Well, it's a good manor. I mean a good place to live. The farms we passed were cared for and neat. The houses of the village are well tended. This isn't a lord who squeezes his tenants. Not a lot of animals about though. I wonder if they've been moved for safety?"

"Kent's the cautious sort," Adam admitted. "There's grazing in the manor forecourt if it's necessary to shift the herds there."

"The keep's clean and there's no carrion birds at the midden heaps," Alan went on. "That's a good sign too. It means the owners keep things in proper order. There's less chance of sickness." He squeezed his bride. "All in all, if I was back in my wandering days I'd judge this a good prospect for a few nights stay with a chance of a modest purse at the end of it."

"Only a modest purse?" Elaine teased him. "I thought you were good."

"This isn't a rich estate, love. It's a pleasant manor but not a wealthy one. Nobody leaves here with a bulging purse, but always with some coins and a full belly. That's a result."

Adam was interested in his friend's assessment. "Father says there's an unwritten contract between the people and their lord. They support him and he serves them. That's the feudal pact. Sir Richard tries to maintain it. His neighbours think him soft–but they wouldn't dare say it to his face."

The riders descended the ridge track to the main road. All the cots were closed up, their movables gone. Porches were stripped of baskets and pots, of all the usual accoutrements of daily life. No children played in the sheep meadow. There was no sign of life at all.

"Perhaps father and mother got here before us?" speculated Adam. "We did have to detour a terrible long way to cross the Trent where there were no Sheriff's guards. And of course having to stop for twelve hours every night so two newlyweds could creep off to a haystack delayed us quite a bit."

Elaine blushed and giggled and snuggled Alan tight.

"I reckon they probably have got home," the minstrel considered. "There's not many villages would decamp everybody on the say-so of a steward. Sir Richard's taking no chances."

"Would the Sheriff follow him here?" Elaine worried. "It's a long way from Nottingham."

"To get you back?" Alan guessed what was worrying her. "He won't want you now. I've ruined you. I'll keep ruining you again and again until you feel safe."

His bride blushed more, but she didn't object to the plan. She was look-ing forward to meeting the nurse Constanza again. She had additional questions.

The fortified house was built on a natural rise, where steep banks jutted from a forested hill and a stream ran along one side. A curtain wall that served as the rear of the manor itself dominated the tallest ridge. Towers marked the north and south corners of the enclosure. The manor's top floor was a gabled wood construction with windows of horn under a sloped slate roof. Sir Richard's arms, a phoenix *or* rising from flames proper[13], fluttered atop the gate.

"Where is everybody?" Adam puzzled, squinting up at the sunset-sil-houetted castle.

Elaine pointed to the steep track that curved to the manor house. "There's someone! Isn't that Will Scarlet?"

Alan and Adam saw the mercenary too, riding hell-for-leather down the slope, waving his arms. His voice drifted over the distance at last: "Ride, you by-the-Lady fools! Run!"

Alan turned his head the other way and saw horsemen closing on them from the harewoods. "Adam!" he called warning.

The three travellers spurred their horses along the manor approach. A dozen riders ranged out behind them, closing fast. The pursuers wore the livery of Nottingham Castle. Two archers nocked horse-bows.

Elaine gave a little squeak then forced herself to be silent. Matilda Fitz-warren wouldn't panic or scream, Elaine was sure of that.

When Scarlet saw Sir Richard's son and his companions were alert to the trouble he slowed his mad charge. Although the riders were still far off, Will had a sword in his hand and looked ready for trouble.

Adam spurred his mount up the incline. "Come on!" he called. The ap-proach track curved around behind the castle then turned sharply left to a small gatehouse. Up close the youngest Fitzwarren son could see defend-ing archers concealed behind the crenulations.

Alan and Elaine followed slower. Their horse had to carry two. A black-

---

13   This heraldic description refers to a golden phoenix rising from natu-ral-coloured flames. Heraldic etiquette prevents metallic tinctures from ever being placed next to other metals, and coloured (non-metallic) tinctures ever touching other colours, but furs and 'proper' or natural colours can touch either. The phoe-nix rising is the actual arms of the Fitzwarren family and was first recorded by her-alds in 1215, a mere 25 years after this narrative. Of course, Maid Marion was also identified by Elizabethan playwrights as Matilda Fitzwater or Fitzwalter, daughter of Baron Robert Fitzwalter who led the Magna Carta revolt against King John, in which case the arms on display over Verysdale may have been different.

fletched arrow whirred past them. They were in range.

Adam reached Scarlet. "It's the Sheriff!" he called to the professional soldier.

"Really? I'd never have guessed," spat Will Scathlock. "They got here a couple of hours ago. We think they're a vanguard. Keep moving."

Another pair of arrows curved towards Alan a Dale. These came closer. The archers were finding their range. An arrow arched back from the walls of the castle, but at that distance it was no more than a warning shot. Inside the keep some sergeant would be berating his man for wasting a precious shaft.

Scarlet waited while Alan and Elaine laboured up to him. "Keep going," he told them. "I'll be with you shortly." He waited on the path to see if any of the soldiers would be stupid enough to brave the embankment. None was.

Alan recognised Loris de Weynold at the gate. Sir Richard's guard captain waved him through.

Sir Richard at the Lee himself stood in the animal-filled inner yard, armed cap-à-pie in ancient crusader armour. He looked across as his son Adam rode through the portcullis in good order and raised his visor in a nod to Alan a Dale and Elaine.

"Welcome to Verysdale," he said, without any hint of irony.

The great steel portcullis lowered into place with the groaning of ropes and a metallic creak. Verysdale's thick iron-bound doors closed and were barred.

Elaine breathed a sigh of relief.

Grooms came forward to attend to the newcomers' blown horses. Will Scathlock dropped heavily from his mount, favouring his wounded leg, biting back a soldier's oath. Adam embraced his father. The old knight clapped his son on the back and chided him for his late arrival.

Elaine looked round the wide crowded courtyard. An encampment of makeshift tents had been set up at one end, where the refugees from the village made the best of their enforced stay. An outdoor kitchen supplemented the bakery, scullery, buttery, and slaughterhouse that were ranged along the southern wall of the green. Lady Mary Fitzwarren turned from organising the women at the stew pots and moved over to welcome the newcomers.

"Hello mother," Adam greeted her, and kissed her cheek. "It looks like I'm still causing you trouble."

Lady Mary touched his face. The long weeks he'd spent in the Sheriff's oubliette had made it thin and pale, but there was a maturity there that she hadn't seen before. Adam had become a man. "You won't cause any more trouble for this family, Adam Fitzwarren," she told him. "You will cause trouble for our enemies."

Alan a Dale swept a full courtly bow at the lady of the manor as she turned to him. "Milady, I thank you for admission to your castle. I regret not having the opportunity to formally greet you at Nottingham–events somewhat overtook us, I fear–but I am Alan a Dale. Here is my wife and the lady of my heart Elaine, whom you know."

Lady Mary looked at the young couple. Elaine of Loughborough had changed from her wedding finery and wore a well-made riding dress taken from her trunk at Loughborough. It was grubby and stained now from hard travel and outdoor sleeping, but the girl wearing it was radiant and alive.

Elaine curtseyed nervously to the lady of Verysdale. She wasn't sure whether she'd be welcomed here, or how. After all, she'd turned her back on her family and her father's wishes, had absconded with a fair portion of her father's plate and treasure, had eloped with a mere minstrel and ruined herself as a woman of quality. Lady Mary could easily turn her back on the fallen girl and cast her out of doors as a worthless slattern. The runaway bit her lip and reached her hand out to clasp Alan's without even realising it.

The minstrel bowed again. "My lady, we travelled here with your son. He hoped that we might find hospitality here, a respite from foes and fury that are too great for such as us to survive without aid."

Lady Mary addressed Elaine. "What is this bard to you?" she questioned.

Elaine blushed and glanced at Alan. "And it please my lady, he is my husband," she confessed. "The fat friar wedded us." She swallowed hard and found her courage. "I love Alan and I will not be parted from him."

Alan's hand tightened around Elaine's. "We are together," he agreed. "If we are not both welcome here then we shall both depart, despite the wolves at your gate. Better danger and death than separation and solitude."

"He came for me," Elaine told Lady Mary. "When I needed rescue, when I was going to be destroyed, he came for me. He saved me from a life of torment with William de Vendenal. Can you understand what that means to me?"

Lady Mary's eyes strayed across the yard to where Sir Richard was questioning Scathlock on what he'd observed beyond the walls. She remembered back, before the thinning white hair and the wrinkles, before the limp and the stoop, to a bold young knight who'd quested for his heart's desire. "I understand," she told Elaine. "You are both welcome at Verysdale. Even if Alan had not given solace to my youngest son during dark days of imprisonment, even if you had not braved the Sheriff's dungeon with my wayward daughter to bring him comfort..." She smiled at last. "Well, I understand that Alan a Dale is an accomplished minstrel, and it is too long since these halls had music and laughter."

Alan bowed again, more jocularly. "I will be glad to try my new instrument, my lady," he promised. The Sheriff had broken his last lute. The young bard did not mention how or where on his travels he'd managed to acquire another one.

Lady Mary turned back to Elaine. "Constanza will find you somewhere to sleep and clothing better fitted for daily wear, child. Look to her for instruction in your duties. You may find it hard to fit in at first, for your upbringing has suited you to one station and you have chosen with your body to take another, but there is honour and reward in being a good wife to a good musician. Moreover you are my daughter's friend and confidante–or is that co-conspirator?" The lady of the manor looked to the walls where the men of Verysdale stood ready with bows. "You shall attend me with Constanza and Aliss. When siege comes we shall have much to do ordering the survival of this stronghold."

Elaine knew, at least in theory, of the preparations and hardships that entailed. An unpleasant worry nagged her. "I have heard it said... that is, it is taught that good military doctrine requires that a fortress under siege first expels all unnecessary people–the old, the children, all women. [14]"

Lady Mary shook her head. "Perhaps that is what they teach. But Sir Richard at the Lee holds it his duty to defend those who cannot defend themselves. He will protect all who look to him. And what man will not fight the harder to defend a wall if that wall protects his mother, his wife, his sweetheart, his daughters?" The lady of Verysdale patted Elaine on the cheek. "As I say, my dear, we women shall have much to do ordering the survival of this place."

---

14   As late as the 16th century siege on the royal castle at Ludlow the entire female population of the castle was cast out defenceless to survive as best they could so that limited resources could be reserved for the fighting defenders. Even the women of the royal family were abandoned to flee for safety or sue for mercy from the attacking soldiers.

Adam was across the yard with Scarlet, de Weynold, Kent the Steward, and Sir Richard at the Lee. The old knight wanted to know the number and quality of the Sheriff's men that had chased his son.

"They were outriders," Scathlock told. "Lightly armed, on fast destriers. Scouts and a vanguard, I'd say."

Loren de Weynold frowned. "A vanguard supposes a larger force behind. If there's enough of them that they're putting out a screen…"

"De Vendenal's serious, yes," concluded Sir Richard. "It means he's coming after us in force. Probably needs to show Weaselly John Lackland that he's not as big a fool as young Hood made him look."

"How big a force?" Adam worried. Verysdale was a strong fortified manor but it didn't really have the capacity of a full castle to resist a prolonged and determined siege. The site included a great hall, private rooms for Sir Richard and his family, and a ramshackle collection of domestic and industrial lean-tos, enclosed behind a thick wall protected by gatehouse and two stubby towers, but those fortifications were designed to hold off raiders just long enough for relief to come from neighbours or nearby garrisons. Verysdale couldn't hold forever against an army in the field, especially one with royal authority.

"Big enough," Scathlock guessed. "Whatever mistakes the Sheriff made on his wedding day he's not a fool. He'll send force enough to do the job, whatever that might prove to be."

"What do you mean?" Adam was still new to war.

Captain de Weynold explained. "There are three possibilities. He might send scouts, just to spy and intimidate. From what Scathlock says there's more than that. He might send a punitive force to burn the crops and farms, to do damage while we're penned in our stronghold unable to stop them. That's our best hope. Burned fields can be resown. Ruined hovels can be rebuilt. It costs and it makes for a hungry winter but that's all. Or it could be worse."

"He wants the castle?" Adam said.

De Weynold nodded. "If it's Sir Richard he's after, or you, or his runaway wife and the churl who stole her–or perhaps Lady Matilda herself–then he'll send enough men to pin us here until siege equipment can arrive. Then he'll overcome our walls by sapping or bolts or casting fire and take his revenge."

Scarlet fingered his sword-hilt. "He could do all of that, aye. But they'd still have that forest at their backs as they charged. That makes them vulnerable."

Sir Richard understood the professional soldier's meaning. "There's no army willing to take the field for us against the Sheriff of Nottingham save one: an army of masterless men in Sherwood Forest."

"That's it. An army of a forest lord, the only fellow that's ever wiped the smirk off Nottingham's face. A sworn band that follow Robin in the Hood - and the lass who inspires him."

Adam still had trouble thinking of his sister as the queen of Sherwood. "Matilda? Our hope is that *Matilda* brings her Robin Hood to save us?" The young nobleman thought again. "What about Lucas? Or Greystoke?"

Sir Richard frowned at mention of his second son and his son-in-law. "I've already written to them, of course. No idea if the messengers got through. They might not come anyway. De Vendenal mentioned threats he'd sent to Lucas and to Anne's husband, warning them of the cost of supporting me against the Prince. I suspect Mark never got his letter either, or else it's following him all the way to the Holy Land. In any case there's not much chance of help from the family."

"Send me," Adam volunteered. "Father, you know Lucas. He might ignore a herald but he can't ignore me. Same with Greystoke. And I can visit the Barons too. They have no love for Lackland or his Sheriffs."

Sir Richard considered it. "That's dangerous work, Adam. You'd have to creep away by night and ride like the wind. Get to York, perhaps, then send messengers to our cousin FitzWalter in London[15], maybe to FitzPeter[16] and Norfolk[17]. Then bear messages personally to Matilda and Lucas. Kent can

---

15   Lord Robert FitzWalter of Dunmow Castle, Essex and Baynard's Castle, London, (d.1235) is another historical character who has become entangled in the Robin Hood legends as a kinsman or father of Maid Marion. Historically he led the 1215 Baron's Revolt that forced King John to sign the *Magna Carta* and then warred to enforce the new charter of rights upon the king.

16   Geoffrey Fitz Peter (c.1162–1213) was an advisor to Chief Justiciar Hugh de Puiset and an occasional critic of Prince John. He was probably one of the powerful men John hoped to cow with his treatment of the Fitzwarren clan. Fitz Peter later became the first Earl of Essex.

17   Roger Bigod, 2nd Earl of Norfolk, (c. 1144/1150 - 1221), was another signatory witness to the Magna Carta, as was his son by his wife Ida de Tosny. Ida had formerly been the royal ward and mistress of King Henry II and was also mother of one of his recognised bastards, William Longespée, 3rd Earl of Salisbury. Bigod was one of the best-connected barons of the age, powerful enough to dispute with kings and popes and survive. He is of an age to have gone to war together with Sir Richard at the Lee.

draught something for you."

"Alan a Dale has a very fair hand, I gather," Adam offered. "And a fair tongue and a courtly manner if he'd ride with me."

"It's risky," de Weynold warned. "By now that vanguard will have set watch for riders."

"Not as risky tonight as tomorrow," judged Scarlet. "The noose is going to tighten round this place every day. You want messages out you do it now."

Sir Richard Fitzwarren's frown deepened. He needed to think.

A shout from the tower warned him of the plume of smoke rising from the east. The soldiers were burning the village.

Elaine found Aliss at one of the great hall's high slitted windows, staring down at the valley below where black fumes billowed from the burning cottages. The young maid turned, startled, and curtseyed nervously when she saw Sir Edward Lambert's daughter.

"No need for that," Elaine assured the girl. "I gave up being a noblewoman when I ran away from my lord."

"I suppose," Aliss said. She didn't sound too sure of it. "That was very romantic. Like something in the songs."

Elaine smiled. "Alan tends to make everything like that. And of course we got sucked in to the maelstrom that seems to swirl around Robin Hood."

"My mistress Lady Matilda, she ran off with the bandit. Or he carried her off. Twice." Aliss sounded shocked and envious.

"From what I've seen those two carry each other off. If Alan drags me into ballads, then Robin and Matilda–Robin and Marion–they drag each other…"

"Where?" wondered Aliss, eagerly.

"Into legends."

There was movement behind them in the hall. Labourers began to lay down fresh rushes on the floor and to shift the benches from the wall. The great chandelier wheel was lowered on its ropes so a boy could renew its thick tallow candles. Serving girls brought pewter goblets and clayware in preparation for the evening meal. The great hall was the heart of the manor, in turns dining room, workplace, and sleeping chamber for most of the inhabitants of the fortified house.

The domestic bustle reminded Elaine of the daily routines of her own family's manor at Loughborough. Verysdale was not so grand–indeed, it was rather run down compared to many great houses, since this wasn't Sir Richard's principal seat–but it had the same rhythms and sounds and smells.

Elaine wondered how her family were dealing with her elopement. She wondered if her mother had wept. She wondered what would become of her maid Jenet.

Long shafts of evening light through the west windows painted the wooden chamber with gold, making the dust motes shine. The hall's warm industry was in stark contrast with the deadly predations of the troops that now gathered in the valley's shadow.

Aliss' gaze was pulled back on the columns of smoke rising from the remains of Verysdale. There was movement in the pass, men and horses, more than before. Elaine had overheard Captain de Weynold report that enemy reinforcements had arrived.

"I wish I were in a ballad or a legend," Aliss confessed. "Anywhere but here, really."

Elaine understood her fears. "It's my first siege too. It's only natural that we worry."

Aliss swallowed. "I'm not brave. I'm not important. I'm just a by-blow some visiting lord left on my mother." She leaned closer and spoke confidentially. "When the wolfsheads kidnapped my lady I was so scared they would take me too, but Lady Matilda wouldn't let them. I was afraid all the time when we were at Nottingham castle as well. But this is even worse."

"We have strong walls and strong men to guard us," Elaine comforted the maid.

"I heard Will Scathlock talking–that soldier they call Scarlet? He said Verysdale couldn't survive a proper long siege. What'll happen to us when the Sheriff's soldiers break down the gates and get in?"

"We shall fight to the last and we shall die before dishonour," Elaine assured her.

Neither of them had heard Constanza waddling up behind them. "Before we all die on our knives maybe we could get a bit of work done?" the old nurse demanded. "It's not my first siege nor my second and I can tell you that there's chores and duties all the same. There's well water to be dragged into butts to quench fire-arrows. There's bedding to be cleaned so that plague doesn't blossom. The common folk need guidance about how to go on inside castle walls, where to graze their animals, where to dispose of their night soil, when and what to cook and so on. There's a thousand things need doing and it's our job to help Lady Mary see they're done."

Aliss jumped down from the window, looking guilty. "I just wanted to see, Constanza."

"And now you've seen. Pray you don't see them any closer up, my girl. And if you do then remember a blade can save you from dishonour two ways. Don't point it at yourself if you can point it at a man. Now run on and make sure the laundry-girls are properly organised for all the extra work. I need a word with Lady Elaine."

Aliss scampered off. Elaine waited until the old nurse had lowered herself painfully onto one of the long benches that lined the wall.

"So you're a woman wed," Constanza said at last. "Wed and bedded?"

Elaine felt her cheeks redden. "Yes, and it please you. Thank you for your advice. It was very... helpful."

The old nurse chuckled. "There's some things every bride has to know. There's other bits its more fun to work out for yourself. But it's not all haystacks and mattresses, lass. There's other parts to being a wife."

Elaine's hands strayed down to her belly. "I don't know that I've quickened yet. It's only been…"

"Not that, although that trial and blessing might come. No, there's another hard test for a young bride that I think might be upon you."

Elaine's heart skipped a beat. "What?" she asked nervously.

"I heard you in the courtyard today, as you clung to your love. Never parted, you said to my Lady Mary."

"I love Alan. I'm his wife."

Constanza nodded. "Aye. And bound by God to cleave to him for life, I pray. But there comes a time when every good wife has to send her husband forth and she stay behind. That's the hard test you face, sooner than I'd wish."

Elaine shook her head. "We're under siege. Alan's staying here. We can't leave."

"*You* can't leave," agreed the nurse. "But Alan's a useful fellow. They say he's run envoy for your father, and he knows his court manners and his writing. He's more use riding out than entertaining the hall."

"Then I'll go with him."

"No, my dove. He'll be riding hard and fast, with Master Adam if I read my Lord's moods right, though Sir Richard yet doesn't know he'll choose so. Your Alan will be riding for his life, and no time to bring along a lovestruck bride." Constanza smoothed her fingers across Elaine's pale cheek. "A wife, a strong wife, a true wife, she's got to let her man go and be a man.

You've got to send your Alan to war, maybe to his death. Love him, pray for him, fast for him, yearn for him–but let him go."

Tears prickled Elaine's eyes. "So soon?"

Constanza caught her in big fat arms and pulled Elaine's head into a bosomy embrace. "Go and tell him you love him. Tell him he has to go with his friend. Tell him he'll be riding to save you and to save us all. Then find a quiet corner out of the way and make him a warm farewell. That's what you need to know about being a wife today, Elaine Lambert."

Constanza held her until the tears had passed.

The smoke had cleared for now. In the deepening dusk the watchers on the towers could still see lines of soldiers passing along the road below the fortress. Scarlet estimated there were over a hundred men down there now.

Sir Richard stood on the gallery above the hall. Bustling servants below strained to accommodate so many unexpected guests for dinner. People and dogs swarmed everywhere.

Lady Mary brought the rolls listing the hundred and sixty-three men, women, and children inside Verysdale Manor. There were thirty-two men deemed capable of fighting and eleven boys to support them. Of the fighting force, Sir Richard deemed only seven as competent shots or swords.

Kent brought the supply legers. The cellars of Verysdale were well stocked with food for a siege of six weeks, longer if rations were lessened; but it was too early for the harvest so the fields still stood with grain, a storehouse for the invaders. There was a delicate calculation to make about when to slaughter the animals in the yard. Too soon would destroy the livelihoods of the smallfolk who relied on them, too late would deplete feedstock and add to the castle's troubles.

Loren de Weynold presented an inventory of arms. Sir Richard handed out ancient chain shirts and what polearms and blades he had. Bows were in good supply; the Knight at the Lee tended not to enforce hunting laws too severely on his land. He would have preferred more barrels of arrows.

"We weren't ready," Sir Richard complained to Lady Mary when they had a quiet moment during the ordering of the stronghold. "We should have been more prepared."

"Who'd have thought it would come to this, Richard?" his wife asked. "When should you have foreseen it? When Lackland flirted with Matilda at Leaford? When she repelled him with force from her bedchamber? After Adam's absurd tragic duel with young de Loris? When you went to sue for clemency from William de Vendenal? When the Sheriff's murderous thugs assaulted you on the road from York? Or during our confinement in Nottingham Castle? Exactly when do you think you should have turned around and looked to the fortifications here?"

"I don't know," the old knight confessed, "but sometime. Now we're defending a keep that hasn't been properly maintained, with far too few trained defenders, with limited arms, without aid or ally. Our treasury's depleted. Our family's scattered. Matilda…"

"Matilda is fine," Lady Mary insisted. "The Good Lord knows I've worried about that girl, about her waywardness and her forwardness, but my! Did you see her in Nottingham Castle? Did you see her face down de Vendenal? Did you see her at the archery match?"

"I saw her," Sir Richard admitted. "And I saw her with Robin Hood."

Lady Mary tilted her head to admit that a bandit son-in-law wasn't perhaps everything she'd hoped for from her younger daughter. "I saw a young woman in love with a young man. A good man, I hope." She squeezed her husband's arm. "There's something to be said for being foolish and loving a good man."

Sir Richard touched his fingertips to her hand. He nodded. It was enough.

Below the lord's gallery the commons were gathering for their supper. Torches on the walls set shadows dancing across the high roofbeams. The regular staff of the house jostled for bench-space with the villagers who had swelled the company. There was some good-natured banter but mostly people were nervous; many present had seen the smoke of their burning homes.

Adam Fitzwarren was making himself useful directing the stewards who laid out the feast. The youngster's fresh, easy manner raised spirits and quieted discord.

Sir Richard looked at his youngest son, trying to make a choice. The boy had just survived a long incarceration. He was untested and hot-headed. He was desperate to do something to make up for his part in the Prince's plot against his father.

"You have to decide," Lady Mary prompted the knight.

"I have to decide," agreed Sir Richard. He limped down the stairs that connected gallery to the main floor of the great hall.

Adam saw him descend and came over to him. "Have you made a

choice, father? May I ride out with Alan and raise help against the Sheriff?" he asked, trying not to sound too eager.

Hungry for action, Sir Richard thought. I was young once.

"A mission of this importance requires a knight as envoy," the old crusader said at last.

"Father, you are too…" Adam blurted before he could stop himself: too old, too ill, too tired from your ordeals, he's wanted to say. Instead he bit his tongue.

"A knight, I say," Sir Richard at the Lee insisted, "not a callow squire boy."

Adam cast his eyes down. "As you say, father," he accepted, struggling to be obedient.

"Kneel down, Adam."

The young man's jaw dropped. He fell on one knee. Sir Richard drew his sword, the one he'd carried at Acre. It was heavy and notched by Saracen blades.

"Gather close!" the old knight called to everyone within earshot.

The hall was full. Kent the Steward, Constanza, Aliss, the whole household and the many villagers waiting at table for the trenchers to be passed round pressed forward and formed a ring.

They waited, confused, worried, bothered by the strange circumstances that had trapped them there, looking to their lord.

Sir Richard addressed them. "This is a hard time and a troubling one. The enemy's at the gate. At a time like this a man needs his son. The people need their lords. Their knights. So I'm making one."

Alan and Elaine appeared from a side door, hand in hand, looking dishevelled.

The old crusader gestured to the kneeling Adam. "By regular custom this lad would go into the chapel and stand vigil all night, praying to be worthy. But he's spent many dark hours in a deep cold place of late, thinking and talking to God, I'll warrant. He'd be clad in new white linen to show his purity and honour. Well for that he'll just have to show such virtues in better ways, by what he does rather than what he wears. And he'd have two sponsors…"

"I'll stand for him," offered Loren de Weynold. "And Scarlet's not a knight but he's a strong man at arms." Scathlock nodded.

"Well then, so," agreed Sir Richard. "Point is, it's not the fasting or the ceremonies that make you a knight. It's your heart and the promises of your heart. A knight made on the battlefield is as much a knight as one made in a palace. Maybe more of one." He turned to the young man knelt before him. "So, to the charge: Adam, my son, to be a knight you have to know this. A knight is true, to his word, to his comrades, to his lord, and most of all to God. Never traffic with traitors. Respect women, give them no evil counsel, defend them against all. Abstain and fast when holy days require it, hear Mass and be generous to Christ's church. Use your strength and valour for good not ill. Do you swear to all of that?"

Adam Fitzwarren nodded his bared head. "I do. I swear it by Jesu."

Sir Richard smacked his sword flat onto each of the young man's shoulders. The colée almost toppled Adam but he kept his balance.

"Then by the knighthood conferred on me by Henry, King by God's grace, I confer on you the order of knighthood. I dub thee Sir Knight. Arise, Sir Adam at the Lee! Arise and make me proud."

VIII

arion stood at bay. Dunstan of Hucknall and his bravos surrounded her and Much, swaggering and leering.

"I don't believe you're in any position to make demands, Maid Marion," Dunstan said. "In fact this is when you should start begging and pleading."

"As Willem Crowe begged and pleaded?" demanded the queen of Sherwood. "Yes, I know who you are, Dunstan of Hucknall. You and your thugs murdered Crowe and Paul and Florian and robbed my father."

Dunstan paused. He was not used to prey who did not act like victims. "I did," he replied. "And now I have you."

Marion shook her head. "You are a foolish savage murderer, Dunstan. Do you think it chance that I arrived here tonight at the moment you were to raid Woodbarrow? Do you think I have not been hunting the men who murdered my family retainers? *Do you think I came alone?*"

Dunstan realised that the movement in the shadows was not only his men. There were other shapes, stealthy and silent, and while Marion had been speaking they had crept up on the concealed reavers.

Then the cottage doors opened and more men emerged. They were not the peasants of the village, and now each was armed with blade and bow.

Reynard rushed forward, seized Marion, and placed his hands around her throat. Dunstan approved.

"Hold, bandits of Sherwood!" the reaver chief called. "Stay your weapons or my man snaps this wench's pretty neck!"

Most of Dunstan's men were already on the floor. The outlaws backed away and left the rest alone.

Dunstan bared his teeth. It might have been snarl or smile. "Now, let's see who we can flush out. Are you there, Robin in the Hood? Come on out, cur!"

A young tow-headed man with bow and sword emerged from the darkness, clad in hunting leathers dyed Lincoln green. "You called?"

"I have your woman," Dunstan pointed out.

Robin shook his head. "No. The big fellow, he has my woman."

Dunstan glanced at the giant. "Reynold Greenleaf? He's mine. He's come a long way to find and kill your Little John."

Robin sized up the big man. "He's ugly, I'll give him that," the outlaw admitted. "No uglier than John of Hathersage, mind."

"Let's see about that, Hood. Bring out your enforcer and see how he measures up to mine."

Robin Hood shrugged. "Right then. If you insist. Little John?"

Reynold Greenleaf stiffened. "Yes, Rob?" he replied.

"You can let go of Marion now."

The giant released the maiden with a grimace of apology for his rough deception. If he hadn't seized her then Dunstan might have. Marion was without fear and had strayed too close to the murderer.

"Now!" called Tuck from the darkness. The outlaws from the shadows and the outlaws from the cottages moved as one and pinioned the reavers again. Robin's men were not gentle and this time no bravo escaped capture.

Much kicked one of the raiders flanking Dunstan in the shin then downed him with a punch he'd practised with David of Doncaster. A backhand slap from Little John sent the other thug flying. Will Stutely knelt on the stunned marauder with a dagger to the thug's eye. The old bandit had removed his disguise as the serf who Reynold had supposedly tortured for the information that had led the reavers here.

That left Dunstan of Hucknall alone, backing away from Maid Marion. She had never once taken her eyes off him. Her stare was implacable. "You stay away from me!" the murderer warned. "You don't want to cross me!"

Robin breathed in sharply. "Oh, Dunstan, I think that she does."

"I have questions," Sir Richard's daughter agreed. "I'm interested to know what your orders were when de Vendenal sent you after my father. Did he tell you to kill the others or was that of your choosing?"

Dunstan looked around him for escape but there was none. Woodbarrow had been cleared of all bystanders. It was entirely populated by the men and women who dwelled in Sherwood with Robin Hood. Dunstan's rough band had gone down hard, surprised by the forest outlaws; many of the reavers were bruised and bleeding. Ferret Wen had made it almost into the woods before Robin had placed an arrow through his knee.

"I'm not 'frit of you!" Dunstan sneered at Maid Marion, even as he backed from her. "Nor of Robin in the Hood!"

"That can be fixed," Robin promised him, unsmiling. "Answer the lady."

"The Sheriff of Nottingham will see you all dangle!"

Reynold Greenleaf–Little John–stepped forward. "Leave him to me Rob, Marion. It's me who's had to put up with him these last days, hearing him boast and laugh about all the bad things he's done. Bad things to women. Bad things to little girls and boys." The giant rounded on Dunstan of Hucknall. "I'll stand for them."

Robin glanced at Marion. She nodded.

Dunstan's eyes widened more. He gripped the dagger and short-sword in his hands. "How can you be Little John? You said you wanted to kill him?"

"It was a fib," Robin explained. "We're outlaws. We do that sometimes."

"You attacked my father and his men, Dunstan of Hucknall" accused Marion. "You intended harm to the villages of Sherwood. Of course Robin Hood was going to get you for it."

The pinioned reavers began to realise their fate. It was too late for them to struggle.

Dunstan struck with no warning of his intent. His blades flashed out at John of Hathersage, striking for the throat. Little John was ready though, catching the sword on the edge of his quarterstaff, wrapping his massive fist around Dunstan's knife-hand.

Little John twisted and the child-murderer's wrist splintered.

Dunstan howled and backed away, still holding his sword out defensively while cupping his broken hand. A stream of obscenities flowed from his mouth, meaningless, mindless, as if the darkness in his soul had been uncorked to spew across the world.

The giant moved as fast as Dunstan had. He struck the blade from the villain's hand and planted one steel-shod quarterstaff tip right between Dunstan's legs.

The murderer folded over, wailing. John picked up Dunstan's fallen sword and snapped it over his knee.

The marauder tried to rise but could only manage a half-crouch. He dragged another blade from his tunic, a wicked gutting knife that was still crusted brown from former use.

John snarled and broke Dunstan's other wrist.

Robin tried to turn Marion away. She shook her head and watched as Little John demolished the murderer. It was her duty to see justice done.

"I'll confess!" screeched Dunstan of Hucknall, huddled in a ball of agony on the floor just like he'd left his victims. "I'll talk! It was the Sheriff what told me when he set me loose. Don't harm the old man much, he said, but you can have the others. Bring me the treasure and you'll be rewarded! Go into the forest and kill Hood's men, he told me. Burn and ravage and call yourself Hood."

Robin glanced at John for confirmation.

"That last part's true," the big man affirmed. "I was there when the Constable gave his instructions."

Ferret Wen squirmed in the grip of David of Doncaster. "We was only following his orders!" he bleated. "It was Dunstan did that stuff, not us!"

"I've heard all of 'em at their cups, Rob," Little John said. "All of them proud of the evil they've done to folks. Murderers, the lot of 'em. That's why the Sheriff wanted them. That's why he turned them loose."

"Loose on his own people," Marion scorned.

Robin frowned. "Loose on my people. What would your father do to them, Lady Matilda?"

Marion looked Dunstan in the face. "He would hang them," she replied. "Hang them, Robin. Hang them high."

Dunstan broke then, broke and pleaded for his life.

"Ros, take the women back to camp," Robin said. "John, Will, have these brave child-killers up to the crossroads on Hunger Hill. Tuck, if any of them want to cleanse their souls then hear them if you can stomach it. Will, send word to the people of Woodbarrow that they can come home now. Compensate them for the rope we're taking."

The reavers all began to beg then.

But Marion went with Robin to the gallows crossroads and saw them dead.

Sir Richard waited until it was fully dark, then longer so that whatever enemy lookouts had been posted might grow careless, before he signalled for the sally port to be quietly opened. The small door within the larger one was designed to allow just a few men to slip out without the noise or danger of opening the main gate.

Sir Adam and Alan a Dale were ready, dark-cloaked on horses with muffled hooves. Elaine clung to her husband until the last moment, trying hard to be brave, terrified that she'd never see him again. Lady Mary made her farewells to her son, straightening his hood as if he were a small boy again.

Scathlock slipped through the low door and looked around outside,

Dunstan broke then, broke and pleaded for his life.

sword in hand. "Looks clear," he whispered back.

De Weynold glanced up at Verysdale's irregular towers. Atop the taller and older south tower were three of his seven competent archers. The others were ranged on the roof of the gatehouse itself.

Down the slope where the gradient tapered out there were almost a score of watchfires, ranged to cover as much of the manor's perimeter as they could. It was impossible to tell how many eyes watched the castle. There was no way of knowing if the attempted departure had already been spotted.

Alan and Adam led their horses through the sally port. Sir Richard handed Adam the document scrip that contained letters to family and allies, with a purse of as much gold as remained to the besieged knight; in fact it was the gold given him by Robin Hood. He clasped his son's wrist in a warrior's handshake and touched him on the shoulder: a soldier's farewell.

De Weynold ushered the old knight back into cover of the castle, but Scarlet remained at the port and watched as the young men led their horses down the track. Adam knew this place well and remembered a short cut that a horse could just manage which circumvented the guarded path.

Over at the watchfires somebody passed in front of the flames.

Alan and Adam were invisible now, beyond the range of Scarlet's night vision. The soldier hoped that meant they were equally hard for enemy watchmen to see. He judged that by now the two young men must have reached the turnoff which Adam believed would allow them to avoid the Sheriff's camp.

Scarlet waited to be sure there was no hue and cry. Then he slipped back inside and reported to Sir Richard that the escape might just have worked.

The villagers of Woodbarrow returned by night, worried what harm might have happened to their homes and property. They found two likely lads guarding a heap of supplies that would make the peasants' winter a lot more comfortable than they'd expected.

"This is from Robin Hood," said Much proudly, "with his thanks."

"You're to share it properly, says Lady Marion," added David of Doncaster.

Their welcome was warmer after that. The young men helped to lift the hams, root vegetables, and grain sacks to places where their lord's steward wouldn't notice them. It was heavy sweaty toil but the villagers worked with a will.

Afterwards Much and David were allowed to slump on a haystack in one of the barns and rest for the night. A couple of Woodbarrow girls brought them flagons of small-beer.

"You're with Robin Hood, then?" asked Cedony with a certain shy curiosity.

Much nodded.

"And you caught them rogues as were going to murder us all in our beds?" noted Malkyn. She was a couple of inches shorter than her sister, but bolder.

"It wasn't that hard," Much told them. "They weren't looking for us."

David cut him short. "It was quite dangerous though," he told the girls. "There was a bit of fighting. But we won. You're safe."

"With you here?" giggled Malkyn. She plumped down next to David to sip his beer.

"We had Robin with us," Much explained to Cedony. "And he had Marion."

"We saw Maid Marion," the village girl admitted. "She was very pretty."

David was a city boy. He knew a thing or two. "You two are very pretty," he said.

"I thought all outlaws were supposed to be scarred and ugly," teased Malkyn. "I don't see any scars. Maybe you're not really outlaws?"

"I have scars," David promised her. "You just have to go looking for them."

Malkyn giggled. "They say wolfsheads will tell a girl anything to get into her skirts."

David raised an eyebrow. "What would you like to hear?" he asked.

It occurred to him that Much was shy and might need a bit of help getting Cedony to soften. He turned to put in a good word for his friend.

Much and Cedony had already vanished down into the straw and appeared not to need any advice at all.

He turned back to Malkyn, reached for her, and hurried to catch up.

Sir Guy of Gisbourne returned from his round of the sentries and dismounted from his coal-black destrier. Rulf Blakehelloc rushed over to report.

"Sire, we've heard back from the watchmen. Two riders left the manor an hour before midnight. They cut down to the river and swam their horses across."

"Any word on who it was?" demanded the black knight.

"No sire. It was very dark. But they were on good horses so they were probably on official business, not deserters. You left orders that any men leaving tonight should be allowed to run away."

"How else can word be sent to Robin Hood to race to the rescue?" growled Gisbourne. "But that's all that escape now. Next men to leave the castle get their horses shot out from under them and they're brought to me for torture. Send the word."

"Yes, sir!" Blakehelloc helped his master shrug off his heavy new shield and laid it on a stand outside his tent. "There's a couple of other matters. Word's out that there's a siege here. We've had messages from a few of the neighbouring estates, mostly assurances of their fealty to the Sheriff."

"What about the rest?"

"Expressions of concern. Not everybody's happy to have an army camped hard by. A few seem to genuinely care about the knight of Verysdale."

"Note which ones they are and send men to burn a few of their fields," Sir Guy commanded. "Next time their messengers come bleating send them home without their tongues and ears. They'll soon learn."

"We're getting some mercenaries turning up as well, wanting to join in. A few of them look useful."

"Take on the ones worth keeping and chase the rest off. But set watch on the newcomers. I don't want any of Robin Hood's men sneaking their way in as spies."

Blakehelloc nodded. "About that, sir. One of the mercenaries claims to actually know Hood and most of Hood's men. Says he could point them out if he saw them."

That piqued Gisbourne's interest. "Who is he?"

"A lanky streak calling himself Black Dane. I wouldn't wonder but he was once a wolfshead in Sherwood himself."

"I've heard of him. I'll see him tomorrow and decide if he's any use."

Blakehelloc paused. "We've also found some peasants, sire. You told us to range out until we discovered people. There were a couple of farmsteads out in the forest a long way off the track."

Sir Guy smiled grimly. "They're here?" he asked.

"They're kneeling in the stockade, sir."

The black knight strode across the battle camp to where a new-made ring of staves around a pit formed a makeshift prison. Three families, more than twenty people, were confined inside the wooden circle.

Gisbourne inspected the cowering captives. He pointed to the youngest of the women. "Take her to my tent. Tomorrow she goes back with the others and I want them all crucified on scaffolds within sight of Verysdale. Outside bowshot range. I want no mercy killings from the archers on the walls. See they take all day to die."

Blakehelloc swallowed hard but nodded. Sir Guy was not a master to cross. "Slafot! Evalgast. You heard our lord. Get to it!"

The cruellest men in Gisbourne's army set to their work with a will.

Gisbourne was already thinking about other things. "Also tomorrow set the men to pull down that chapel in the village. I want Sir Richard to watch that too. And then dig up the graves around it and throw the bones to the dogs." He laughed for joy at the siege he was planning.

And at the end of it he'd get to kill Robin Hood!

Little John stared at the campfire. Tuck came and sat beside him. He thoughtfully broke off a portion of chicken leg and passed it to the big man.

"I'm not hungry," John told the fat friar.

Tuck wolfed down the morsel himself. "Executions put some people off their food," he admitted. "Weak stomachs."

"Nobody could accuse your stomach of that," the giant admitted with a trace of his usual good humour.

Tuck finished his food and hurled the bone onto the fire. "Some of them made good ends," he judged. "But I heard their confessions. All of them deserved to die."

"I've no doubt of that," Little John said. "I was with them for days. I'd have knotted ropes for the lot of them myself. The world's cleaner without them in it."

"But?" prompted the monk.

"But it was hard being Reynold. When Robin planned it I thought it'd be a lark–fooling the Sheriff again, spying on his plans, setting up whoever he sent after us. I thought I could play the merry game like Rob does."

"You didn't like even pretending to be one of them," Tuck understood.

"I really didn't. Half the time I wanted to punch them and the rest of the time I wanted to punch myself."

Tuck patted him on one huge arm. "Well that's good. I often want to punch you too but you're so damned big. But really, I'd want to punch you a lot more and I'd like you a lot less if you weren't unhappy about your mission. You were uncomfortable playing the murderous bully. I'd say that reflects rather well on you."

John snorted. He'd not thought of it like that.

Robin and Marion joined them at the fire, hand in hand.

"So you decided to be his lady, then," Little John said to the knight's daughter. "We all thought Rob was crazy. Well, we still do."

"I'm thinking about his offer," Marion answered, sitting down close enough for Robin to hold her. "He's hunting me. I just haven't decided whether to get caught."

"Well watch out," warned the giant. "Rob's a good hunter." He sneezed into his hands a great snort that sounded a bit like "Clorinda!"

Robin thumped him on the arm.

"I'm going to have to hear about this famous Queen of the Shepherdesses sometime," Marion considered.

"But not tonight," said Robin Hood hastily. His face sobered. "It's not really the time for jests, is it?"

Tuck knew that the forest of hung men was in the young outlaw's thoughts. "You did what you had to," he advised. "You chose to be the people's lord. Sometimes that requires doing the people's justice."

"And it shouldn't be easy," Marion told him. "It should hurt. It should make us think. Killing should never be simple, even execution." She hugged him close.

Little John looked at the couple and wished he could let them have peace. Instead he spoke. "There's things you need to know, Rob, Marion. More stuff than I had time to pass to Will when I was supposed to be roughing him up. Things about Marion's father and Elaine's father."

Marion looked up sharply. "What?" she demanded.

"Well, as to Sir Richard at the Lee, it looks like the Sheriff isn't going to let him go. He's sent Gisbourne with soldiers to chase him to Verysdale."

"How many soldiers? Verysdale is fortified."

"Enough to pin the people there while more forces can be sent," Little John appraised. "De Vendenal's not letting this pass, Rob. Meanwhile he's arrested Sir Edward Lambert and his whole household. He's thrown them all into his dungeons without mercy or comfort."

Marion caught her breath. "Elaine's mother? In those vile cells?"

"They left her a dagger. I'm sorry."

"Sir Edward is a knight. He has rights!"

Little John nodded soberly. "He's not expected to come out alive to claim them. That Morgan of Shrewsbury, the Sheriff's hound, he set to work on the serving lass Jenet. You'll guess that when they'd finished with her she'd confessed all kinds of treason from her master. That's how they've condemned the Lamberts."

"And the Sheriff's confiscated their wealth," Robin guessed.

Marion bit her lip. "He's destroyed them. Destroyed them all, for revenge and profit!"

Tuck crossed himself.

Little John told the rest. "Rumour is that both the Sheriff and Gisbourne have sent to Prince John for license to take Sir Richard and come chasing you, Rob. I mean seriously, with hundreds of soldiers to get the job done right."

Robin and Marion exchanged looks.

"What have we done?" Marion asked, dismayed.

"What we had to," Robin answered. "What's come after shows we were right to start this." He turned to John. "Well, it was worth sending you as Reynold, anyhow. Even if it hadn't brought us Dunstan and his stinky crew we needed to know how bad it was with the Sheriff's plans."

"Did you know it was going to turn out like this when you saved me?" Marion asked, subdued and unhappy.

"I knew it'd probably go like this when I stood up to the Sheriff for the people's sake. Now William de Vendenal is tightening his grip, it seems." Robin gazed into the fire. "We'll have to squeeze back even more."

"What have you got in mind?" Little John asked warily.

A wicked smile crossed Robin's face. He looked up. "Something amazing," he promised.

IX

ir Gerold of Kilington rode unhappily in his saddle. Last night he'd feasted at Pontefract Castle, where he had a slight family connection with the Lords de Lacy who held that powerful fortress, but the fish course had disagreed with him, making it difficult to travel in full armour. His men were beginning to snicker at each break where he had to scuttle into the bushes, assisted by his squires.

An unseasonable downpour had turned the roads into mud, slowing the progress of the train he escorted. Even now it slithered rather than rolled down Longbull Hill, the oxen holding back rather than pulling the two heavy carts that carried arms and pay for the Sheriff's men at Verysdale. Swearing sweating soldiers were plastered with slime as they struggled to keep the wagons under control.

Sir Gerold began to regret the detour that had diverted them to enjoy the pleasures of Pontefract. It had been refreshing to spend a night safe behind thick walls, but Robert de Lacy's youngest daughter had ignored him. His tokens to her had been returned unexamined. Now the final hill before the water crossing was proving difficult and delaying.

It was well into the hours of *none*[18] before Sir Gerold could see through the canopy of trees to where the silver coil of the River Aire snaked east-west across the landscape. The side track the caravan had followed joined again with the straight old Roman route now called the Great North Road, or by its

---

18   In a time before clocks were commonplace the day was divided by the eight "canonical offices", the periods of religious observance ordained by Catholic doctrine. After the night-time periods of vigils, matins, and lauds (whose names and times varied with the ages) came prime (6am), terce, (9am), sext (12pm), none (3pm, rhymes with 'bone' and is confusingly the origin of our word 'noon'), vespers (sunset), and compline (before bed). The daytime offices were used to describe the time, so the period of none would refer to the period between the observance of sext prayers at 12pm and the observance of none prayers at 3pm. This means that our present narrative is taking place a little before three in the afternoon.

Saxon name of Ermine Street[19]. From there the highway trailed down to the bank of the wide deep river and the ramshackle collection of huts that passed for a village at the ferry point.

Sir Gerold had been warned to be careful. Captain Aelstan himself had briefed the knight on the precautions he was to take carrying a pay chest and an arms wagon through the depths of Sherwood. The train was protected by four-score men-at-arms who would thereafter join the siege at Verysdale and a third of them were archers. A pack of six fierce hunting dogs were leashed by their handlers ready to be loosed. The knight of Kilington, his two squires, and three other soldiers were mounted.

Sir Gerold sent scouts ahead to turn out the huts. Two older men and two younger ones, a wife and child and an adult daughter were rousted from their work.

The oldest man shuffled forward, tugging his forelock. One of the lads came with him, steadying him as he walked. "Good day to ye, good sir knight," the ancient called out fawningly. "You'll be wanting river passage then?" He eyed the wagon train hopefully, calculating his fees.

"I'll need to cross, yes," said Sir Gerold, "on the Sheriff of Nottingham's authority." That meant no payment.

"You'll have to speak up, sir," the young man told the knight. "He's deaf."

"On the Sheriff's authority!" Sir Gerold yelled. "The Sheriff!"

"The Sheriff," the young man repeated for the older. He mimed a long pointy nose and a chain of office then did a pantomime of a snooty official marching. "The Sheriff of Nottingham!"

"Enough of this," Sir Gerold sniffed. "Prepare to convey my men and carts over the river."

"For free?" asked the younger man unhappily. "That'll be about six journeys. We'll be all day at it."

"Then you'd best begin or be whipped to speed you," the knight snapped. He looked at the distant shore where a wooden jetty jutted into the water. "Take me across with the first of my men. I want to check the area."

"Eh?" asked the ancient.

"He wants to check," the youth bellowed. "He's going over first."

The old man looked confused. "Without the ferry?"

Sir Gerold ignored the local yokels and ordered his men. "Bring the wagons down to the water's edge. I'll cross first with a quarter of our

---

19   This route, which is largely the same path as that now taken by the modern A10, A1 and A1M roads from London to York, was a major Roman artery but its Roman name is lost. The Saxons called it 'Earninga Straete' after the Earningas tribe who occupied some of the southern lands through which it passed.

strength. Naisen, you come with the second crossing and I'll return back. Third crossing we bring the gold wagon. Fourth crossing it's the arms. Then Guillaurme and the rest of the men in two more journeys. And keep a good watch at all times. We're beyond Robin Hood country now but vigilance is still important."

The river passage began. The old man grumbled constantly about his fees but he and the other three bargemen shepherded the first twenty soldiers and made them sit in balanced rows on the wide flat barge. "If we turn over then swim for the nearer shore," the other older man advised them. He had a Lincolnshire twang to his voice and he walked with a limp. "If you've armour or weapons on you then drop 'em, or you'll sink like a stone."

"What if we can't swim?" worried one soldier.

"Then drown," the elder advised. "You'll learn how to do that soon enough."

Once at the other side of the Aire, Sir Gerold posted a picket and made a quick recce to check for hidden outlaws. As an additional precaution he loosed the hunting dogs, but they found nothing. By the time the second shipment of soldiers arrived he was confident enough to leave things in Naisen's hands and return to the guards on the south bank.

Things were still in relatively good order, although there was a shrill argument as the goodwife protested to an uncaring sergeant that his men had stolen a skin of ale from her stores. If such a thing had been taken there was no sign of it now that Sir Gerold had returned.

It took longer than the knight would have liked to coax the oxen aboard the barge. They had to blindfold the beasts and uncouple them from the cart, then have their handlers lead them on, coaxing them personally. That left the soldiers to manhandle the wagon onto the boat. The vessel lowered alarmingly at the weight of the chest.

"I don't like this," the deaf old man complained. "Two frightened beasts and a laden wagon? Better to take them in two trips."

"It's getting late already," Sir Gerold objected. He didn't want the sun to set while he had his guards divided on opposite banks of a deep fast river. "Put your backs into it."

The younger man beckoned to the women. "Maggie, Ros, come with us and help keep a hand on those oxen. We can't afford to have them stamping around." The women came aboard, one still leading her toddler, and took up position beside the carters.

Sir Gerold made to ride aboard as well but the old ferryman winced. "Not the horse as well, my lord! Please! You and them four soldiers is bad enough!"

The knight relented and handed his horse off to his squire. "Keep a sharp watch," he warned.

The boat rocked away from its mooring and the ferryman paddled it out across the stream.

The young boatman looked at the receding bank. "You've brought a lot of men with you, my lord," he observed. "Is the Sheriff that scared of Robin Hood now?"

Sir Gerold didn't like the boy's tone of insolence. "The Sheriff is a cautious man. We fear nothing."

"Really? 'Cause I heard the Sheriff cried like a baby when Robin Hood battled him in Nottingham Castle. I heard he wet his breeks."

The knight's face darkened with anger. He reached for his sword. "How dare you...?"

At that the four boatmen each swung an oar and knocked a soldier into the water. The women each put a knife to the carters' throats.

"I heard that Robin Hood was really really scary," the young man said with a grin, pointing his oar at the knight. "And really clever as well. And did I mention handsome?"

Sir Gerold realised that he was trapped on the river with Robin Hood and his merry men.

"You're badly outnumbered and wearing armour," Maid Marion warned him. She and Ros of Waltham were still holding the ox-handlers tightly, preventing any resistance. "Proper fitted armour, sir knight, not chain shirts you can ditch like those poor idiots who just got spilled into the water. If you go over it'll be the death of you."

Arthur a Bland looked over at the flailing men in the water and tossed them a plank to float on. "I warned 'em about falling over," the Lincolnshire poacher said.

"I thought we were supposed to push them in?" puzzled Much the Miller's Son.

"Don't be foolish," Marion advised Sir Gerold. "We don't want bloodshed here. We've had enough of that." The row of gibbets on Hunger Hill a week before still haunted her dreams.

"I could stand to see another rich lordling drown," Will Stutely admitted. Now he wasn't stooping the old outlaw looked lean and dangerous.

"If you're going to do something stupid then do it," Robin advised the stricken knight. "Otherwise lay down your sword and yield."

"Please," Marion asked him.

It was the unexpected courtesy that broke Sir Gerold of Kilington. He reversed his blade and held it out hilt first to the lady.

"Put it on the deck, please," she asked him. Marion was not a fool.

On both shores the soldiers had spotted that something was happening. Robin produced a bow from the gunwale and sent off a half dozen warning shots at the hopeful archers on the banks. "Time we were rowing, lads," he said to his men. "The current will take us downriver faster than they can follow us. At least that's the plan."

"And Robin's plans never go astray," Marion sighed.

"Can you swim?" Arthur a Bland asked the carters. They shook their heads.

"Where are you from?" Robin asked them.

"Algerthorp," one replied. "Sir."

Robin moved closer so he could speak to them quietly. "Well, lads, you've got three choices. You can jump into the water and try for the bank; maybe Arthur'll find you another plank to hold to. You can get tied up and left when we reach shore and steal your cart. Or you can join up and be men of Sherwood with me. Which is it?"

The carters conferred hastily, then answered. "Sir, I'm a family man. I can't abandon my Daisy and our bairns. I'd like to be tied up please. Norris here's a youngster and there's not much future for him with me. Maybe he'll have better luck with you."

"Norris?" Robin checked.

The younger carter nodded.

"Right then." The outlaw lord turned back to the older ox-handler. "Listen, we'll be taking your cart and animals. But there'll be a secret purse to compensate you for your trouble." He glanced at the treasury on the cart. "It's not like we're going short."

"Thank you, Robin Hood. So the stories are true."

"Maybe up to verse twelve," Marion said severely.

Arrows flew across the water but not too close. Robin fired again, taking one of the archers in the arm. "It's not like I didn't warn them," he said.

Much and Stutely disarmed and tied the knight. Sir Gerold sat disconsolately in the stern of the barge, watching his men recede along the riverbank. "The Sheriff will kill you," he told the outlaws.

"He'll have to do better than he has so far then," Robin replied.

The boat carrying the soldiers' pay was caught in the river's flow and vanished off beyond the soldiers' sight.

Turstin Guillaurme suppressed pangs of panic. At sixteen the younger of Sir Gerold's two squires had little experience of leading two score of grizzled fighting men. Now his master had been carried away downstream and the more experienced Naisen Renouf was trapped across the water with no way back.

He turned to his sergeant but didn't know what to say.

"Best we send Oswolt on horseback to follow 'em, sir," the veteran prompted. "Detach ten of the lads, say, to chase with him as best they can, all with orders to return at nightfall. We'll pitch in here, set out a screen, place a watch, wait for them on the other side to find another boat."

"Yes, that's good," agreed Turstin. "Those are my orders."

"Thought they would be, sir. I'll tell the lads."

Turstin regarded the forest with a sense of foreboding. What had seemed a formidable guard force had been halved by one simple trick. A quarter of the men remaining to him had been detached to hunt for his kidnapped lord. A mere thirty soldiers did not comfort the young squire as he worried about protecting the wagon of weapons bound for the Verysdale siege.

The miserable day dragged on with intermittent showers and an early evening gloom. More travellers arrived at the ferry crossing and were dismayed to find the boat gone. A coalman with a loaded wagon shared Turstin's bandit fears. A tinker and a pardoner squatted down together to dice while they waited for the situation to change. A lorimer[20] arrived with a pair of mules loaded with harnesses, followed by a colporteur[21] who tried to sell the squire a religious tract. A courier to Castleford had no patience and turned aside to take a longer track west. A rich milliner from Peterborough as much as accused the squire of deliberately losing the barge. A blind mendicant-friar with an idiot boy to guide him tried to calm the conflict. Turstin ordered them all to be shepherded away from the wagon to a single area where they could be watched.

As the sun vanished behind the forested hills the young squire ordered that torches be lit and decided on an inspection of his men. He and the sergeant were both appalled to discover that most of the troup was insensible. The stolen ale-sack lay empty beside the sleeping guards, its drugged contents all too effective. No amount of kicking would rouse those men before morning.

At the discovery there was a loud whistle from the camp where the other travellers were confined. A dozen arrows from the treeline landed in the ring of firelight around Turstin and the sergeant-at-arms.

---

20   A smith specialising in the small metalwork of horses' harnesses such as bits and bridles.

21   A merchant of holy books

"Lay down your arms!" came a voice from the darkness.

Turstin drew his sword.

Another arrow landed right between his legs. "Don't be a fool, lad," warned the giant at the treeline. From his size and his sheepskin Turstin knew it must be Little John.

The squire looked around to judge his options. He had a dozen remaining men in a fit condition to fight. The outlaws had a least that many archers trained on them.

The blind beggar-monk was led up with his hand on the idiot-boy's shoulder. "Let me speak to them," the mendicant pleaded. "There's no need for violence."

"Get back," snapped the young squire. He made to push the monk away. The idiot-boy's fist crashed into the side of Turstin's helmet like the wrath of God.

And that was all Turstin remembered of the fight.

The barge might have lasted longer with the proper boatmen steering it, but it was all Robin and his men could do to keep it from shipping too much water before they banked it downstream somewhere near Haddlesey. Further on the river ran past a Templar manor anyhow, where there was more risk of being seen.

Once Sir Gerold was blindfolded as well as bound the carters were willing to help coax the oxen ashore and recouple them to the gold cart. They were surprised when Robin and his men didn't load the metal chest onto the wagon but instead heaved on a heavy pile of river rocks.

"You're going to be left tied at the nearest road," Robin told the ox-drover who'd claimed a family. "Stutely and Norris will take the cart and leave a goodly trail heading north. When there's fear of capture they'll abandon the wagon and melt into the woods. Join us back at camp, Will, in your own time."

"What about the treasure?" puzzled Norris, unused to Robin's Byzantine plans.

"That's coming back on the river with the rest of us," declared the outlaw with a wink.

"Hear that, Tad? We're going for another ride on the lovely boat," Ros cooed to her infant son. "Isn't this a nice day out on your first job as one of Robin's band?"

Robin continued his instructions. "While they're chasing that rock-filled wagon we'll be heading south where there are villages in need of a little charity. Or a lot of it, actually." He had the bandits bail as much water as possible then steadied the chest into the centre of the barge.

Captured Sir Gerold went with the boat too as Robin pushed off and let the current drag them back out midstream. From there it would be a haul to ground again on the southern shore.

"Watch out for yourself, Will Stutely," Robin called across the water.

"Oh, you know me, Rob. I'll keep my head down," the old bandit called back. "Try not to get yourself hanged before I'm home."

Will Stutely watched the barge halfway across the river then gestured for Norris to load his bound mate onto the cart. They goaded the ox-team to haul the wagon over the rough ground until it joined a country farm track, then followed the road.

"You know Robin in the Hood well, then?" Norris ventured.

"Since he first ran into Barnsdale Forest ahead of the watch," the old outlaw agreed. "I taught him everything I know. But not everything he knows."

"Is he everything they say?"

"I don't know all they say. But if they say he's a good thief and a good man and as fine a bandit king as ever was then I'd say yes. You picked the right leader to follow."

Norris nodded slowly. "I think so," he agreed. Then he slammed his ox-goad into the side of Stutely's head, felling the old man with a single blow. "It's just that Robin's not that leader," he told the unconscious bandit. "I'm the Sheriff's man."

Robin piloted the river barge by lantern-light into the snaking waterway marshes known as Eggborough Ings[22]. Here tall grasses and floating clumps of vegetation obscured the boat. Much and Arthur used poles to navigate through the narrow channels until they found a dry landing.

"Take our guest a little way up the bank," Robin told Marion and Ros. The women and Tad guided the blindfold knight away over the squashy ground. He couldn't be allowed to hear Robin and Much holing the boat to sink it and the gold into the shallow water at the river's edge. It would be easier to conceal the treasure in the marsh and send for it later than try to

---

22   Ings is the Yorkshire name for water meadows and marshes in the Humber floodplain.

convey it while being hunted. Few would be able to find one spot again in that winding water meadow, but Arthur a Bland was amongst them.

Sir Gerold tried to convince Marion and Ros to release him, first with threats and then with promises. "You are a high-born lady, Matilda of Leaford," he cozened at last. "Your actions have set the Sheriff and the Prince against your father to Sir Richard's destruction. Surely you must see that your best recourse now is to release me and surrender yourself?"

"You clearly don't know de Vendenal and John Lackland," Marion replied. When the knight was far enough from the waterline she allowed Much to remove his blindfold.

"What are you going to do with me?" Sir Gerold demanded of Robin Hood when the outlaw caught up with him.

The young outlaw appraised his prisoner. "What do you reckon the chances are that the Sheriff will ransom you? Good? Fair-to-middling?"

The knight's face fell. In his short time in office William de Vendenal had not established a reputation for generosity in the well-being of his vassals–or for forgiveness of those who failed him.

Robin patted him on the back sympathetically. "Don't worry. We'll take you deep into the forest, give you some breakfast, take your purse and goods as payment, and send you on your way. Whether you go back to Nottingham's up to you. You might want to think of this as a chance to find new employment."

"My manor's at Kilington. I hold it of Sir Jonas of Botsford and he from Sir Roger de Bully. I'm levied to the Sheriff as part of my knight's fee." [23]

Marion was disdainful of his whining. "A knight is a knight because of his honour, not his estates. If you put your wealth and security before your duties doing right to God and man then you deserve to serve de Vendenal."

They pushed on without speaking to the hamlet of Hensall, where Riccon Hazel waited for them with horses.

Turstin awoke when someone slapped him hard across the cheeks. A large dirty palm stifled his cry of protest.

---

23   A knight's fee was a parcel of land sufficient to support a knight, his squires, and all the industry and agriculture required to maintain him; the word fiefdom is derived from it. However, grants of land to lords came with a provision that the lord would equip, pay, and deliver a certain number of knights and men at arms to the service of the granter, usually for up to 40 days per year. The great barons were expected to render quantified amounts of military aid to the king, or to pay scutage (a cash equivalent) for each knight's fee they owned.

"Keep quiet or I'll throttle you," said the man leaning over him.

The young squire fell silent, terrified. His assailant lessened the pressure on his face.

"I'm taking my hand away now. Make any noise and I'll break your skull. Understand?"

Turstin nodded the best he could. The constriction was removed from his mouth.

The squire blinked, trying to cope with the darkness all around him. He could barely make out glimpses of night sky above the black tree canopy.

"Listen carefully," the man who'd woken him said. "You were captured by Robin Hood's men. They took you and all your soldiers, using trickery like they always do. That blind monk was really Friar Took. His boy was David, a champion boxer from Doncaster. No wonder he took you down like a sack of turnips."

Turstin recognised the source of the throbbing in his head. His dented helmet was gone, along with his armour and weapons.

"They also got your supply wagon, with the weapons on it," his captor went on. "But I stole it back."

The squire didn't understand. "You stole it? From the thieves?" He'd thought himself a prisoner of Robin's band.

"I stole it and I stole you. Wrung three necks to take down the guards then walked the oxen out while everybody slept. It was too risky to try and take on the lot of them. I'm strong but not stupid."

As Turstin's night sight came to him he realised that his companion was a big man. "Who are you?"

"Reynold Greenleaf. A Sheriff's man, like you and your lord. Bigger than Little John, that's me."

"You took the wagon?" Turstin's headache wasn't helping his comprehension.

"Sneaked it away. There was no way to free your men. I could only get the guards on the cart and drive it away while the rain masked me. But I can't move it easily alone so I grabbed you to help me."

Turstin sat up. He could dimly discern the shape of the ox-cart and its important cargo.

"So listen," said Reynold. "You came here from Pontefract, right? You know the road back there, to the castle? If we can get this wagon there before the bandits catch us we'll be heroes. The Sheriff will shower us with silver."

"Heroes?" That made Turstin perk up. A minor squire slinking back after his lord was captured by wolfsheads could expect shame and distain, perhaps even flogging and dismissal. A heroic squire who grasped victory from the jaws of defeat and returned triumphant having saved William de Vendenal's arsenal might have a very different future.

Reynold saw that the boy had caught on. "We have to move fast. They'll find the downed sentries soon and there's no better trackers than Robin Hood's men. Little John's with them and he'll be closer to you than you'd wish. Can you walk?"

He didn't wait for a reply but hauled the squire to his feet without even straining. Turstin wondered if the leather-clad mercenary really was bigger and stronger than Hood's famous giant.

Reynold bundled him onto the ox-cart and slapped the animals to set them going. "Just remember the way the best you can," he said.

Turstin vowed to try his hardest. "Where did you come from?" he asked the big man. "You weren't with our caravan."

"I was sent with some cut-throats to chase Hood in Sherwood. It was a stupid idea from the start. The outlaws ambushed us, cut down damn near everybody and hung the rest. Only I fought my way free. But I couldn't go limping back to Nottingham empty-handed, so I followed them to see what they'd do next. And you know what they did next."

"You'll be welcomed back by my Lord de Vendenal after this," Turstin assured the mercenary. "You'll be famous."

"First we have to get to Pontefract," said Reynold Greenleaf grimly. He spurred on the ox-team and pushed them through the dark.

The siege had been laid for a week before Sir Guy of Gisbourne elected to call for parley. The delay was unusual; it was customary for the blockade to be formally announced and for negotiations to take place between the two sides. Sometimes the attacker would grant free passage for visitors or non-combatants to leave the fortress. The long line of rotting corpses on scaffolding just beyond bowshot of the manor house showed that the black knight observed none of those courtesies.

Quimper Kinstain acted as Gisbourne's herald. Sir Guy's factotum had returned only yesterday with news of Prince John's benefice. Now Gisbourne knew that he need only pen up his prey long enough for a royal force to arrive with enough men to utterly overwhelm battered Verysdale. Kinstain rode to negotiate a conference wherein Sir Guy could impart that news to Sir Richard at the Lee.

The meeting was conducted at a distance. Neither side trusted the other. Sir Richard and Captain de Weynold stood at the sally port ready to duck for cover, Sir Guy and Kinstain fifty yards away with man-high shields to guard them. The conference was not convivial.

"Richard Fitzwarren," Gisbourne began, deliberately omitting the knight's title, "You've broken the Sheriff's law and committed treason on the crown. You're harbouring a fugitive from justice, namely your treacherous son Adam, and you've denied a royal summons from Prince John himself to send him your daughter Matilda. Your lands and honours are all forfeit and you face destruction and death."

"Guy of Gisbourne," spat back the old crusader. "Blasphemer, oath-breaker, murderer, and worse. What harm had those innocent serfs done that you tortured them to death on those railings there? Most of them aren't even tenants of mine."

"Why should I care? Fear is a powerful weapon in war, and now your castle stinks of it. Those mewling weaklings who tremble inside know what I'm going to do to them. They know they've no hope. You've doomed them all."

"Bold words from a false knight!" retorted Sir Richard. "You're a brave man with an army at your back."

"And you're a brave one hidden behind a wall. Next time I won't just make you lick the shit from my shoes, I'll make you swallow it as I squat over you." Gisbourne sneered contemptuously at the old knight. "Are you waiting for Robin in the Hood and his outlaws to come and save you?"

The Knight at the Lee tried to mask any reaction but Sir Guy read his face. "You are, aren't you? The Sheriff was right. He said if we let your messengers get away they'd lead Hood and your slut of a daughter back into our trap."

"Trap?" repeated de Weynold, worried. The whole defence of Verysdale was based around surviving until relief came.

"Of course. Hood is invisible in Sherwood. He'd be very hard to catch and kill. But the woods are thinner here and there are forces coming that he does not know of. Enough men to comb this forest and look up every tree." Gisbourne laughed contemptuously at the manor's defenders. "You didn't think we'd come all this way for you, did you? Or maybe you thought the Sheriff wanted to flay his runaway bride and draw and quarter her minstrel boy? Well we will, but mostly we'll have Marion for Prince John's pleasure and Hood for my revenge."

Sir Richard clenched his fists. "Hood's made a fool of you before. Let's hope this time he kills you."

"He's a peasant boy. I'm a knight, trained since childhood to kill peasants like him. Or were you going to stand as his mighty champion, old man? Shall we have a single combat here and now to see who wins the siege?"

De Weynold restrained Sir Richard. "He's goading you, sire. Let me answer his challenge."

Sir Richard saw the glint of smugness in the black knight's eye. He knew it was another trap, a means of depriving Verysdale of a valuable defender. "A battle of honour requires both sides to have honour," the old crusader spat. "Have you anything else to bark, Gisbourne, or have you spat your venom for today?"

Sir Guy shrugged. "I've always got more venom for miserable has-beens and cowardly pretty boys like you two. Anyway, here's what I've come to tell you. Three weeks from now all your people are dead."

Fitzwarren tried to control his reaction. "Three weeks? What do you mean?"

"I mean that by Lammas[24] there'll be a royal army knocking on your

---

24   1st August or the "Gule of August" was the feast day of St Peter, which the *Anglo-Saxon Chronicle* calls "the feast of first fruits". Lammas is derived from "loaf-bread" and the day was usually celebrated with a harvest festival.

door, old fool. And I guarantee that thereafter there will be no man in your fortress walks out unmaimed, no woman unraped, no stone left to show that this was ever anything but a miserable barren wasteland. I mean that you'll be up there on my scaffold beside those peasants, watching me cut slices off your son and your wife. I mean that I will give you an end so awful that generations from now men will tremble when they hear of it. Is that clear enough?"

It was hard for Sir Richard to maintain his calm in the face of such naked malevolence. "What terms do you offer?" he asked. He was willing to surrender himself to save his people.

"No terms," Gisbourne told him. "This isn't a negotiation. It's a declaration. I want you to know what's coming. I want all your people to know what's coming. I want you to lay awake dreading your end and knowing that you've led your daughter into a trap. I want you to understand the price of defying my master, and then I want to charge you that price in humiliation, pain, and blood." He flicked a mocking salute at Sir Richard at the Lee. "I'll be waiting."

"Come back inside, Sir Richard," Loren de Weynold advised as the black knight marched away. Fitzwarren was trembling and clutching his chest. "Robin Hood may yet prove cleverer than that evil knight."

The old man judged differently. "Hood could possibly have chased off Gisbourne and his marauders, if they weren't expecting him. But nothing can defeat a royal army, nothing that can be mustered in time. Hood is leading his men to death. His men and Matilda."

He didn't say any more, but both he and his captain knew that they'd just heard their death sentence.

The Sheriff of Nottingham rode into Pontefract Castle with a small army at his back. Well over a hundred men, half of them mounted, had accompanied William de Vendenal north to the fortress of Baron Robert de Lacy. Amongst them were the Sheriff's Constable Matthew Shankshard, Guard Captain Aelstan, and Morgan of Shrewsbury, de Vendenal's brutal bodyguard.

After all, the Sheriff of Nottingham was visiting his predecessor.

Pontefract Castle was a building site. The older wooden fortifications were long gone, replaced by a donjon tower, high curtain walls, and a lavish set of outbuildings. Now the rich, powerful de Lacys were adding another chapel, an improved gatehouse, and a stylish long gallery in the continental fashion.

William de Vendenal reigned in his envy. Nottingham Castle was every bit the fortress this place was but it did not have so pleasant a plateau on which to rest, nor such spacious graceful layouts. The first de Lacy had come to England with Conqueror William and the family had prospered and grown in power ever since. Of course they could afford the best. Even old Roger de Lacy's politically required withdrawal from office, when King Richard's Sheriff of Nottingham made way for Prince John's appointee, had been astute and well timed. De Vendenal was still clawing his way up to the place that Robert de Lacy and his sons occupied through the fortunes of their birth.

The Baron of Pontefract did not come out to greet the Sheriff. The old man was of advanced years, being then almost ninety; or he may just not have wished to meet the parvenu William de Vendenal who had replaced him. Nor were Roger's heir or grandson present to make any formal welcome. John de Lacy had shipped with the Lionheart to Palestine. Roger de Lacy was in York, at nineteen already a rising star at Prince John's court[25].

De Vendenal in turn almost ignored the greetings of Pontefract's steward, leaving Aelstan to deal with the man in the matters of stabling fifty horses and accommodating six score of hungry soldiers. The Sheriff demanded and received access to a guesthouse and took command of a secure chamber in one of the castle's nine square towers.

At last he was settled behind a writing table with a glass of mulled wine by his hand. "Bring them in," he ordered Morgan of Shrewsbury

The scar-faced enforcer passed the word. Very quickly Shankshard ar-

---

25   Records for the time of Richard's crusade are incomplete but suggest that Roger de Lacy received his role as Sheriff of Nottinghamshire and Derbyshire about the time that the Lionheart was preparing to depart for the Levant. His appointment was presumably another precaution to limit the power and influence of Prince John. However, one William de Wendenal or de Vendenal succeeded to the post almost as soon as Richard had left the country, while the ageing Roger de Lacy astutely retired to his other extensive holdings with his fortunes unscathed. His crusader son John de Lacy had departed with Richard and was probably already deceased by summer 1190, the time of this narrative, but word of his death in Palestine had not yet reached England. Roger de Lacy II, the original Roger's grandson and heir, went on to be one of Prince John's (later King John's) greatest supporters and gained fame for defending Château Gaillard, Normandy, against King Phillip II of France. This second Roger's son, John de Lacy, born in 1192, eventually became the first Earl of Lincoln and was one of the signatories of the *Magna Carta*.

       Some scholars have suggested de Lacy, rather than de Vendenal, as the "original" for the Sheriff of Nottingham in the legends of Robin Hood.

"I saved the cart!" Turstin blurted.

rived with the pale squire Turstin Guillaurme and the giant Greenleaf.

De Vendenal pointed at the trembling young squire. "You first. Tell me what happened."

In the days since his hurried night arrival at Pontefract the boy had been called upon to tell his story many times. Fearsome Reynold Greenleaf had helped him stitch together a coherent account of the fateful Aire crossing, one that detailed the errors that Sir Gerold of Kilington had made and minimised any culpability on the squire he'd left behind. Turstin stammered out his testimony under the Sheriff's penetrating stare.

"So you sent a rider and ten men after the gold?" de Vendenal said when the story was told.

"Yes, my lord. They had not returned when the bandits attacked."

"You did not, for example, send the rider to the royal fortress at Tickhill, a mere seven leagues away, where a garrison might have been turned out equipped to search for my stolen treasury? Or to Doncaster, to seek aid from the burghers?"

Pale Turstin became sheet white. "I… no. My Lord."

"In fact you sat down on your arse and waited for outlaws to attack you," the Sheriff suggested. "Why didn't you take your men and follow my stolen treasure along the river bank? Both you and Naisen Renouf had strong forces that could have ranged both sides of the Aire, hunting. Instead you did nothing while your men drank themselves to insensibility."

"My Lord, it's not so. We… I did my best. I posted sentries and tried to keep order and…"

The Sheriff cut him short. "You did nothing. You got yourself blindsided by a bandit friar in disguise. You got yourself tied like a hog. You gave a wagon full of good arms and armour to rebels and wolfsheads."

"I saved the cart!" Turstin blurted.

"Did you? Did you really?" De Vendenal pointed to Reynold Greenleaf. "You now. Start with Dunstan of Hucknall."

Little John felt a prickle of sweat on his back. The big man wasn't used to feeling nervous, but the mere presence of the Sheriff was doing it. He wondered again why he'd let Robin talk him into this wild deception. It had seemed like such a clever idea when the laughing outlaw had suggested it. Now it seemed like suicide folly.

"And it please your grace," the giant said, bowing awkwardly, "I joined up with your men to chase down Robin Hood's band. I wanted to find that Little John, on account of scores between us, and…"

"I didn't ask your life history," snapped the Sheriff. "I asked about Dunstan. Get on with it."

Little John nodded. "Well, sir–sire - my lord. Um, your grace..."

De Vendenal's lip curled into a snarl.

The giant sensed his peril. "I went with Dunstan's band from Nottingham north into Sherwood," he said quickly. "We trailed up through Thugarton, mostly keeping out of sight. Dunstan didn't want anyone knowing where we'd come from. He wanted folks to believe we were Robin Hood's men when we started harming folks."

De Vendenal looked to Shankshard. The Constable gave a confirmatory nod that this was in line with the orders he'd agreed.

"Eventually we caught a peasant who'd seen a fat friar with an old woman on a cart with a pile of food. We thought it might be that Tuck they say runs with Robin Hood and maybe the old wife of the knight that escaped from Nottingham."

The Sheriff wasn't impressed. "And you didn't think it might be, say, a trap?" he asked the big man.

"Sorry, no. Not then. I questioned the man myself, beat him bloody. He wasn't lying. By the end he'd have sold his own mother to stop getting hit. A trap it was, but not one that he knew about."

De Vendenal seemed satisfied with that. "Carry on."

"The trail led us to Woodbarrow, a tiny place east of Bestwood. We didn't know that the outlaws had cleared out all the villagers and replaced 'em with their own people. We thought we were taking them unawares. Instead..."

"Instead the wolfsheads ambushed you and took you down," accused the Sheriff. The long line of hanged men had been found on Hunger Hill. Word had spread quickly of the price marauders paid in Sherwood and of what befell such men as hunted the forest king.

"Aye," said Little John. "They made fools of us. I can't even say that I'd have done much different than Dunstan if I'd been in charge. Watched the place for a bit longer, perhaps, but nothing more. Robin Hood set a grand trap and we slunk right into it."

"Except for you," Shankshard noted.

The giant shrugged. "Oh, I was in it alright," he confessed. "Only difference is I don't trap easy. I was at the back when t'others went in, so I wasn't surrounded when the outlaws fell on us. It was pitch black and confusing, a rough melee, and I'm good at them. They hadn't expected somebody with my size and strength. I downed a couple of them at least–permanently I hope–and fled off into the forest."

"And Hood's outlaws did not track you?" the Sheriff asked sceptically.

"'Course they did, my lord. Chased me for two days. I've never had to work so hard to lose a tail. They've got some by-the-lady good trackers on their side, I'll give 'em that." He dared to look de Vendenal in the eye. "But I'm better."

The Sheriff gave no sign of his thoughts. "So you got away. What then?"

"I didn't just get away, my lord. I turned the tables on 'em. I followed them as had followed me. I tracked them back to their band."

"To their camp?" asked the Constable eagerly. "Where?"

"Not their camp. They were on the move, the lot of them. I wasn't going to get close enough to count 'em. I just trailed them up the North Road to see where they'd go. I was still hoping for Little John."

"They were proceeding to their rendezvous with my gold," presumed the Sheriff.

"Aye. I know that now. But then all I knew was they'd ambushed some soldiers by the Aire ferry. So when it got dark and stormy I got closer, saw they'd got a wagon–hoped it was treasure–and decided I'd be having that back."

"You managed to sneak a laden ox-cart past bandits who could track you through deep forest for two days?" the Sheriff questioned.

"They were busy with the merchants they'd caught. There were only three guards on the cart. I cut their throats and walked it off. And you know why."

De Vendenal was surprised for the first time by that statement. "I do?"

The big man nodded. "If I'd come back here with nothing, to report abject failure, Dunstan's execution, and naught else you'd have hung me high. If I'd run, well, there's not many places where a big fellow like me can hide. And I could hardly join Robin Hood's merry men, could I? So I had to do something to make up for Woodbarrow, no matter the risk. Right? So I grabbed what I could back from the bandits and pulled the boy out with me to help and ran for my life." He faced the Sheriff's stare. "Have I done all right?"

De Vendenal paused for a moment to consider, then made a tiny nod to Reynold Greenleaf. "You're the only one to emerge from this sorry mess with any scrap of credit." He tossed a purse over to the giant. "I reward competence." He turned back to Turstin. "I punish incompetence. Morgan, take our brave squire to the yard now and personally administer thirty lashes. Make sure it leaves scars to remind him to be more diligent in future."

"My Lord!" protested the boy, terrified. Morgan of Shrewsbury cuffed him to silence and bundled him out.

Little John waited uncomfortably. The Sheriff finished his toddy and sorted his correspondence. Youthful screams came from the courtyard outside.

"Any sign of Sir Gerold of Kilington yet?" the Sheriff asked Shankshard.

"No, my lord. Most of the men the outlaws captured have found their ways back from the various wilderness places where they were loosed, but either the outlaws have him still or he's fled fearing your wrath, probably seeking sanctuary in some religious house. The merchants have all complained to you of their losses but I sent them on their ways. The outlaws are richer by a milliner's wardrobe, a load of saddles, some religious texts, and a wagon of coal meant for the Abbess of Whitby."

"Seize Kilington. Have Gerold cried as a traitor to King Richard. Take what compensation you can from his estate. If he has a wife or mother then lock them in the pillory. When the other squire appears give him to Morgan to discipline as well. Dock the wages of the soldiers who lost my gold and give every fifth man ten lashes. I want it known that I am not happy about this."

Turstin's screaming ceased. Morgan returned alone, coiling a bloody whip back at his waist. He gave Reynold Greenleaf a nasty grin.

"You have seen some of Hood's bandits," the Sheriff said to Little John. "Would you recognise them again?"

The big man shrugged. "Happen a few. They were dark-cloaked and hooded and dressed in green to hide well in the trees."

The Sheriff turned to his Constable. "Bring in the others."

Little John waited again. His back was sweaty now under his tight, unfamiliar leather shirt. The Sheriff was clever, too clever. Maybe Rob could spar with him, but for the first time in his life John of Hathersage felt out of his weight class.

The giant didn't recognise the two men who entered dragging a third with a bag over his head. One stranger was young and lean looking, the other middle-aged and wider. The captive between them was old and bony and his rags did not conceal the livid scars of his recent interrogation.

"These are Pendeleu and Oggesfot," the Constable announced to the Sheriff, "two of the men you set to pose as carters in Sir Gerold's caravan. And of course this is the prisoner they captured."

The man in chains was hurled to his knees, where he slumped wheezing and coughing. His hands were bloody where his fingers had been pressed. Pendeleu, the younger of the spies, reached over and dragged the hood from the captive's head.

Little John couldn't help react as he saw the battered, beaten face of Will Stutely.

"You recognise him, then, Greenleaf?" the Sheriff spotted. "You have seen this man before?"

Little John was stricken. For a moment he considered turning on the men in the room and going for the Sheriff's neck before he was cut down. He felt sick as he saw his old comrade's torture wounds. He had no idea what to do next.

Will Stutely looked up and spat a bloody wad of sputum on him. "Reynold Greenleaf!" he snarled through swollen lips. "Little John will kill you!"

John realised that Stutely was beaten but not broken. The old bandit was saving his comrade's life.

"Aye, I've seen him," the giant replied, dragging his wits back. "He was with Robin Hood."

Shankshard recognised the old bandit too. "This is the fellow who came to the archery contest in disguise. The one we mistook for Robin Hood."

"And I beat your best, aye," snorted Stutely. His snarl revealed the gaps where his teeth had been extracted. "T'weren't hard."

"Where did you catch him?" Little John demanded of Pendeleu and Oggesfot. "How did you catch him?"

"Robin Hood's not the only one can do disguises," Pendeleu smirked at the big man. "He thought we were simple humble carters. He was so kind to us."

"He wouldn't hurt me," Oggesfot mocked. "I was a family man. He even paid me for my cart."

"And I joined him," Pendeleu went on. "I'm one of his merry men now. That's why he sent me off with Will Stutely here. That's how I got the old rogue."

"And why you'll die, you treacherous bastard," Will snarled through his pain. "Joining our fellowship, that's a sacred bond. There's a forest code, an outlaw code. Now Robin i' th' Hood will hunt you to the ends of the Earth."

"How will he even know?" sneered Pendeleu.

"He'll know," Stutely promised. He didn't look up at Little John.

"What have you got from this man so far?" the Sheriff enquired of his agents.

"Oaths. Blasphemy. A few teeth and his fingernails," answered Pendeleu. "But he'll talk. They always do."

"See he doesn't die prematurely," de Vendenal demanded. "No surcease from his pain until he's betrayed everything he knows about his master.

Only then will he hang, caged for the ravens."

Little John forced himself not to react. He could do nothing.

They dragged Will Stutely away. Reynold Greenleaf left the Sheriff's presence with a pouch of silver on his hip, walked past the sobbing red mess that was Turstin Guillaurme, and found a garderobe where he could be sick.

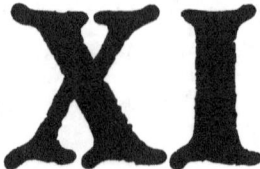

XI

Alan a Dale and Adam at the Lee rode exhausted horses into the outlaws' temporary camp in Barnsdale Forest only an hour before sunset. They'd crossed the Aire at Castleford, upriver of the outlaw's ferry ambush, and rendezvoused with Much and David at Featherstone. By now the young couriers were as tired as their mounts but they insisted on seeing Robin Hood before they rested.

"You can't," Friar Tuck told them. He handed over a wineskin and waited till they'd quenched their thirst. "Robin and Marion rode off this morning, right after Arthur brought in the black arrow."

"The black arrow?" Alan asked. It seemed to be something important and serious.

"Little John's in Pontefract Castle," Much blurted, "in disguise."

Tuck slapped him on the back of the head. "Still your fool mouth, boy! We can trust these two but they've far to go in dangerous places. What they don't know can't be racked from them." He turned back to the couriers. "But since our idiot miller's son has told you anyway, yes, John's secretly at Pontefract, where the Sheriff visits."

Adam's eyes were wide. Alan whistled softly.

"What John's up to doesn't matter now, but he was to send word by a black arrow shot by night from the castle walls. Only a tracker as good as Arthur a Bland would stand a hope of finding such a thing and retrieving the message."

"What message?" wondered Sir Adam.

Tuck grimaced. "Well that's the problem. John never learned his letters, so he had to memorise pictures he could draw, each one with a meaning. There was one–a snake–that he was to add to any message along with whatever else he sent to warn that he was caught, to tell us not to trust whatever else the arrow said. The message we got was *only* that picture, save a drawing of a man with a bow in his hand that wasn't any part of the code."

"That makes no sense at all," frowned David of Doncaster.

"Have they caught Little John?" Much fretted. "Has Robin gone to save him?"

"Getting a man out of Pontefract Castle is nigh impossible," Sir Adam worried. "I've been there. It's a huge place, as big as Nottingham, with a triple gate. Not only a military stronghold like the Sheriff's seat but an estate as well, so more people around. It'd take an army with siege engines months to reduce it."

"Well you know Rob," sighed Tuck. "He's not a lad to shy from a challenge."

"When will he be back?" Alan a Dale enquired. "We've brought word from Sir Richard at the Lee. It's going to get bad at Verysdale."

"I wish I knew when, lad. Take your ease tonight at least. Gilbert Whitehand's venison stew is very good. Rest yourselves and your horses and hope Robin's back from Pontefract by morning."

Another thought bothered Adam. "But my sister is with him."

Tuck nodded. "Aye. That's always trouble for someone."

The courier rode full pelt along the road from Doncaster to Pontefract, knowing that the end of his journey was in sight[26]. In the darkness ahead he could see the torches atop the castle's towers and the small flickering lights of the hovels that clustered beneath its walls.

He didn't see the rope stretched at chest height across the highway until it slammed into him and tumbled him off his horse to sprawl gasping in the dirt.

A hooded man leaned towards him pointing a bow and arrow. "Hello," the bandit said. "I'm Robin Hood. There's a reward for my capture. Do you want to try?"

The courier shook his head. He didn't have the breath to answer. His leg and wrist hurt; he suspected he'd broken them.

A woman emerged from the undergrowth with ropes to bind him. "You're a wise man," she advised. "Any other answer would have caused more of Robin's jolly witticisms. Just hold still while I pinion you. Mind that wrist, it looks nasty."

Marion bound the messenger with practiced efficiency. Robin dragged him to the roadside and used the rope that had straddled the path to tie

---

26   This would be the Roman Ridge, a diversion from Ermine Street, which branches west from the Great North Road. The Romans found the alternate inland route useful in winter months when the eastern marshes flooding occasionally made the usual route impassable.

him to a tree bole. "You're the Sheriff's man, yes? Excellent." The outlaw grinned. "Give me your clothes."

Dame Constanza wiped her bloody hands on the cloth Aliss passed her. "There now," she told the tanner's wife. "The worst's over, and you have a healthy baby boy."

The peasant woman, exhausted from thirty-one hours of labour, managed a thin weak smile.

"Now for the cord," Constanza announced. "Watch this carefully, Elaine. You tie it round here with catgut. Pull it tight. Then you use a sharp clean knife and you slice it just like this. "The old nurse severed the umbilical and demonstrated how to clean up the infant. The tanner's newborn son screamed in protest.

Elaine held the tiny child close to her. She'd never seen a baby so young or small. "Will he be alright? He's all bruised purple."

"Lord bless you, child, but that's every babe ever born into this wide world!" Constanza told her. "Now, give the lad to his mother. Lay him at her breast. He'll work out what to do fast enough."

The newborn was helped to his mother's nipple and began to suck.

"She's still bleeding," Constanza told Elaine and Aliss. "There's tearing down there that'll need to be stitched. Elaine, if you've been raised properly for your station you'll be neat at sewing?"

The former heiress of Loughborough nodded nervously. "I can sew," she admitted. "I've never sewn a person."

"It's a helpful skill for a woman to have," Constanza said. "Now, thread a needle while Aliss washes the mother down and I'll show you what to do. My eyesight's not what it was so it's better if you do the stitches."

Under the nurse's calm instruction Elaine had her first experience of midwifery medicine. Aliss held the candle. The tanner's son distracted his half-conscious mother.

"There now," Constanza declared at last, "As neat a piece of work as I ever did see. You've a talent for it, Elaine, and useful that might be if we've any more arrow-wounds to deal with later."

Elaine shuddered as she was reminded there was a world outside the cramped little pantry where the tanner's wife had increased the number of souls trapped in Verysdale by one. Sir Guy of Gisbourne had begun sending men to assault the gates, shielded by wooden covers, bearing battering rams. Three men of the castle had been injured repelling them so far. Ned Tyler had died from a lucky sling-shot.

"All of this won't matter at all when Black Guy breaks down our doors," Aliss worried.

Constanza slapped her on the hand. "Don't be talking fear and doom, girl! That's not your place. Have you forgotten that Master Adam's gone for help, and that our Marion's coming to save us with her Robin Hood?"

Aliss looked ashamed and shook her head, but she looked frightened too.

"I was trapped worse than this in Nottingham castle, but Robin Hood and my Alan saved me," Elaine pointed out. "This baby has had a hard time coming into life. Let's hope he has it better now he's here."

"Amen!" approved Constanza. "Now, we'll just keep watch over mother and bairn for a while to make sure they're settled. When the goodwife wakes she's to have warm broth to build up her strength again, and good fresh water no matter how much it's rationed. And Aliss, you'd best go tell the tanner that he's a father now. He can peep in to see his son but he's not to disturb him."

The young maid jumped to her feet and rushed off, glad of any errand that kept her busy, especially one bearing the first good news for days.

Elaine looked at the new babe and bit her bottom lip.

"What's troubling you now?" Dame Constanza asked her. The old nurse knew young ladies.

"Apart from everything?" Elaine answered. "The siege and Alan gone and what they're saying about my family being killed?" She paused for a moment summoning up the courage to speak her most personal secret. "Dame Constanza..." She touched her belly. "I'm late."

As Robin had hoped, there were none of the Sheriff's guards at the gate-house at Pontefract Castle. Old Hugh de Lacy was far too suspicious of his rapacious successor to allow de Vendenal's men to share the watch. The courier's garb and message pouch got Robin waved through despite the lateness of the hour. The precautions that might have tripped him up at Nottingham–a password or someone knowing the expected rider–were not in force here.

De Lacy's understeward was more than happy to return to his bed and leave the stable hands to unsaddle the courier's horse and see to the travel-ler's need.

"Nothing urgent in my scrip," Robin assured the sleepy official. "No need to wake his grace the Sheriff. It can wait till morning."

The stable boys weren't too happy about being woken in the middle of the night either, but they knew not to complain if they didn't want boxed ears. "Saddle me another ride, and a spare," Robin told them. "I might have to leave again in a hurry."

The grooms nodded. They perked up when the courier tossed them some pennies.

"What's happening in the castle, then?" Robin asked them confidentially. "What's the gossip?"

"Well, that posh squire that came in got flogged," one stable-hand an-swered with a happy smirk. "Blubbed like a girl when that savage brute the Sheriff keeps whipped him."

"What else?"

"They caught a bandit," another lad said thoughtfully. "One of Robin Hood's men."

Robin's heart lurched. "A big fellow?"

"No. Old and bony, from what I saw–which wasn't much. The Sheriff's spies dragged him off to the dungeon under the keep."

"Old and bony?" Robin tried to think then realised he was better think-ing somewhere else. "Ah well. Thanks for your help. Leave me a couple of good 'uns saddled for later and you can get back to your straw."

Marion kept watch on the road to the ford as best she could by the light of the waxing crescent moon. She hated waiting like this, not know-ing what Robin was facing, but she recognised that this was one occasion where he could do better without her. Her role was to keep vigil, tend the horses, and be ready to string ropes across the track to deter pursuit. She still wished she could do more.

As the clouds scudded over the sky the shadows of the forest shifted and changed. Marion remembered her first night in the woods and how strange and terrifying the tree-filled darkness had been. Her second night had been stranger still, lying wrapped with the outlaw rogue who'd kid-napped then saved her.

The dark silhouettes of the forest were more familiar to her now. The trees were comforting, not terrifying. She could tell just from shape and scent which flowers bloomed nearby. She knew that Robin, attuned to his Sherwood by years of experience, could discern even more.

Alone for the first time since that harrowing escape from Nottingham two weeks earlier, the young woman found pause to reflect on her changed life. No noble alliance now with some rich earl's son of her father's choosing. Even if she could go back to that destiny she wouldn't. That old life no linger fit. It would chafe like an outgrown tunic.

Marion wondered what it would be like to be the bride of Robin Hood. An outlaw's life was short and hard. May queens withered when the winter came. Was she willing to cast her life away to be with her forest king for a short season of freedom?

She worried about where Robin was now. Was Little John all right? Was this the night the outlaws' luck ran out?

The questions boiled through her brain like the clouds across the moon, but any answers were as dark as the forest depths.

The castle was asleep, except where the Baron of Pontefract's guards kept careful vigil and the Sheriff's retainers watched his tower. Robin did what any new visitor to the fortress would do and found his way to the great hall, where the main population of the castle was laid out to sleep on and under the trestles and benches.

A brazier by the hearth gave out a dim glow, enough for Robin to pick his way over the men, women, and dogs curled up across the floor. He made his way like a man seeking a good spot to lay his bedroll, checking the slumbering soldiers as he passed.

It was easy to find the biggest man in the hall. How well Robin remembered that raking snore.

The young outlaw sidled up to Little John and quietly pressed as hand over the big man's mouth. Steel fingers clamped over Robin's wrist as the giant came instantly awake.

Robin pressed his index finger to his lips to indicate silence, then gestured for Little John to follow him outside. The big man slipped from his trestle noiselessly, moving with a delicacy that belied his mass. The two of them escaped through the kitchens and found their way back into the courtyard.

"Rob, I'm glad to see you!" Little John said when it was safe to speak.

"We got your message. We couldn't understand it. What's wrong?"

Little John's ruddy face turned sober. "They've got Stutely. Those carters were the Sheriff's agents. Will's their prisoner. They're torturing him."

Robin clenched his fists. "I'm an idiot. The Sheriff underestimated me at Nottingham and I underestimated him at the wages caravan! Now Will's paying the price."

"I thought about trying to rescue him, but there's guards, lots of them. I'd take plenty of them down but I can't fight a whole castle."

"You did right to stay in cover and send me warning, John." Robin was pale with shock and fury. Stutely was one of his own, his inner circle. The young outlaw felt he'd let the old bandit down. "Right, you need to get back to the hall. Remember the big plan. We need Reynold Greenleaf at Verysdale. Many more lives than one depend on it."

"But Stutely…"

"I'll look to him," Robin promised. "He's mine. I won't desert him."

Little John nodded. He clasped his comrade's hand. "It's got bad, hasn't it Rob?"

"It's been bad all along, John. It's just that now we're trying to do something about it."

The two men ghosted off in different directions, John for his sleeping trestle and a good alibi, Robin for the dungeons of Pontefract Castle.

Will Scathlock had the watch. He leaned on the crenulations of the north tower, where he could see in all directions. The sickle moon gave just enough light to pick out any movement on the cleared turf banks that ringed the fortified manor.

He heard a motion behind him but took his hand from his hilt when he saw the maid Aliss clambering the ladder to the platform. She balanced a tureen of broth as she pulled herself through the hatch.

"What are you doing here at this time of night?" Scarlet enquired.

"The tanner's wife had her baby," Aliss replied. "Two nights and a day in labour. I needed a breath of air before I drop in my bed." She handed over her offering. "I brought you this."

The soldier accepted the crock and smelled the soup. "Thanks," he said tersely.

Aliss showed no signs of leaving. "My lady says that Captain de Wey-nold is healing nicely," she said at last. "The arrow didn't do anything too serious. He will be able to use his arm again."

Scarlet had dragged the wounded Captain off the wall when Gisbourne's archers had launched a volley to cover the men battering at the gate. That and Loren de Weynold's armour had saved his life.

Aliss tried again. "Elaine says that her Alan and Master Adam will have gone from York by now. They'll have talked to the Archbishop and they'll be passing through Sherwood on the way to London."

Scarlet sipped his broth. It was still hot.

Aliss persisted. "Constanza thinks that Black Guy won't really cripple every man of the fortress. She says that many captains make such threats in sieges, to weaken the resolve of those inside the walls. She says that even if Sir Guy wants to do it then other wiser men will reign him in for mercy's sake."

Scarlet sighed. "I'm on watch, girl. What do you want?"

Aliss stopped babbling and paused for a breath. "You're a soldier, aren't you?" she said at last. "You've been in lots of battles, probably. In foreign wars."

"Some."

"They call you Scarlet, because you kill men."

"Sometimes."

"And… and you've probably been in hundreds of sieges, all over the place. And you've known lots of pikemen and knights and archers and… and … girls." Aliss faltered and blushed, then turned away. "I'm not a slut, Scarlet, please don't think it, but they say we're all going to get violated and whored and I don't want to… I'm scared, and I've never known a man, and I don't…" She turned back to the soldier. "I want my first time to be… kind."

Scarlet caught her wrists as she reached for him. "I'm not who you're looking for," he told her.

She froze, then tried to pull away. He kept hold of her.

"Listen," he said, "all the kindness went from me a long time ago. All the love I can feel for a women died with a girl I knew before I was Scarlet. That's as much as you or anybody will ever hear about it." He relaxed his grip and stroked Aliss' hair. "Don't let fear decide your future. Don't throw your life away in fear it might get torn from you."

"I'm a fool," Aliss said, mortified at her behaviour.

"No. You're a lovely lass who's frightened and confused. I'm a brutal bas-tard who's got just enough decency left to see that. Like I said, I'm not the one you're looking for. But I will make you a promise."

Aliss looked up as he cupped her chin. "What?"

"If they breach the walls here then you come find me. I'll be looking for you. Come find me and I'll give you a quick, clean end, before ought worse happens to you. That's my promise."

It was a strange kind of comfort, but somehow it eased the maid's heart. "Thank you," she said.

She kissed the rough mercenary on the cheek and climbed down to her bed.

The rest of the castle was sleeping but Pendeleu and Oggesfot were still working on the captured outlaw. They'd heated tongs and were competing to see who could get the biggest scream out of the man chained before them.

"Not bad," Pendeleu told his fellow spy, "but I still think I can do better. Here's a little trick I learned from the chief torturer at the White Tower. Watch this closely…"

He broke off as the Sheriff's courier descended into the cell. "What's this?" the torturer asked.

Will Stutely looked up, his red eyes widening as he recognised the archer in the Sheriff's livery.

"This is vengeance," said Robin Hood, and transfixed Oggesfot with an arrow through the throat. The spy couldn't even cry out as he choked to death.

Pendeleu kept the red-hot poker in his left hand but drew a knife with his right. "Robin i' the' Hood!" he recognised. "You're a brave, foolish man to come here."

"And you're a dead man to swear to me then betray my comrade," the king of Sherwood said. Robin loosed a shaft that sliced right through Pendeleu's left palm, forcing him to drop his brand to the blood-slicked floor.

The spy called for aid. None came. Cries from a torture cell were habitually ignored, and the disgusted guards had all moved beyond range of the screams the spies had wrung from their helpless prisoner.

Pendeleu lunged forward and hurled his dagger. Robin ducked but the blade hit its target: Robin's bowstring was severed.

The spy came in with his bare hands, aiming for Robin's eyes. The young outlaw replied with a sharp jab to his enemy's kidneys and a hard knee to the face as his attacker doubled over; just as Stutely had taught him.

Pendeleu kicked out, sweeping Robin's feet from under him. The spy had somehow got another knife and he slashed down, trying to gut the fallen outlaw. Robin rolled back, catching Pendeleu's wrist in his own grasp and drawing his own hunting dagger. The spy's ruined left hand prevented him from catching the outlaw's wrist.

"Wait…!" gasped Pendeleu as Robin's dagger-point touched his chest. "I can tell you things!"

"Tell me you don't want to die."

"I don't. Please…!"

"That was all I wanted to hear," said Robin Hood, and drove his dagger home.

He dropped Pendeleu's limp corpse onto the bloody cobbles and climbed over to where Stutely hung. The old man's thin naked body was as red as the floor. "Will?" Robin called, trying to keep the horror out of his voice.

"Aye," replied the prisoner, forcing his gummed eyes open again. "What's left of him."

Robin cut the bonds suspending the old man from the archway and lowered him to the ground. Stutely's dislocated arms and legs dangled uselessly.

"Oh Will, I'm sorry," Robin said, looking down at the ruin of one of his oldest friends.

"Why, lad?" demanded the old bandit. "You didn't whack me on the head and drag me here."

"But I got us into a war with the Sheriff. I sent you off with the carter."

Stutely spat out a wad of blood from his toothless mouth. "I'm a bandit. Bandits get caught. I've had a good run. Now it's over." He managed a pained chuckle. "Except my chief's come to help me get away one last time."

"I have. I've got horses ready in the stable and Marion's prepared the road to deter anyone chasing us."

The old bandit shook his head. "I'm done, Rob. Knees are gone. I can't ride, won't even walk again. I hurt everywhere, worse than I ever thought I could. But you stopped them before they made me talk. I was running out of defiance. If they'd made me a traitor to my comrades in the forest then they'd really have destroyed me."

"I can carry you," Robin promised. "Little John's upstairs in disguise, and he can…"

"Robin, God bless you, there's only one way I can escape a bandit's end on the Sheriff's noose now, and you have to help me take it. Please." Stutely nodded to the middle of his chest. "Quick and clean, the way I taught you, lad."

"You want me to ease your passing," the young outlaw realised.

"The last getaway for an old rogue like me. I've had a good run, Rob, much longer than I deserved. And I can say I was a Sherwood outlaw with the best chief who ever led a bandit gang. I ran with Robin Hood." Will looked at Robin with tears in his eyes. "We robbed from the rich and gave to the poor and all sorts of bloody stupid stuff. We beat Gisbourne and the Sheriff of Nottingham, and all the people loved us. I've never been loved like that, Robin, not till then. Never felt proud of what I've done. So I want my chief to do me one last favour. Let's rob the Sheriff one last time, eh?"

Robin nodded. He changed knives. He wasn't going to dirty Stutely's flesh with Pendeleu's blood.

"I'll take your body to Sherwood," he promised the old bandit. "We won't let the Sheriff hang you over his gates. We'll bury you at the Major Oak, near the beck where the children play, where the sun sends dappled shadows when it comes up in the morning. You'll be one of us forever."

Stutely nodded, satisfied.

Robin leaned over him, held him close, and let him escape.

The grooms were asleep when Robin Hood returned to the stable with a heavy bundle of sacking slung over his shoulder. It was just as well; the outlaw's face was grim and deadly. He examined the two courier mounts left saddled for his use and slung Stutely's body on one of them. Then he looked down the stalls to where the Sheriff's expensive new Spanish hunting horse was stabled next to its rich tack and harness.

Then he knew how he and Will would be riding out of Pontefract.

Marion saw Robin galloping up the Doncaster road an hour before dawn. There was no pursuit yet. When he neared she saw he had a man-shaped bag strapped over one of the two horses tethered to his ride.

Robin and Marion exchanged no words when they met, only a tight handclasp as they sat on horseback. It was only when they were away from Pontefract and off the main roads that Marion dared to ask who was in the shroud.

Robin told her.

Then they holed up in cover while the Sheriff's men tore along the forest paths in vain chase, and Maid Marion held Robin while he wept.

XII

The bandits hunkered around a warm campfire and Alan a Dale sang the exploits of Robin Hood and Will Stutely. Friar Tuck passed around heavy tankards of good Barnsley ale and the company drank a toast to their fallen fellow.

Then Riccon Hazel struck up a lively tune on his penny flute and the company celebrated rather than mourned.

Robin kept Alan and Adam with him at the fireside to converse with Marion, Tuck, Gilbert Whitehand and Arthur a Bland.

"At York we hired heralds to my brother in Sussex, and to Lord Greystoke, my elder sister's husband, to warn of our coming," Sir Adam explained. "We dispatched letters to my oldest brother Mark and to King Richard Lionheart in the Holy Land, but of course they'll take a long time to arrive. Then we sought audience with Hugh de Puiset, the King's Justiciar in the North, but he's no longer in York. It seems he's in dispute with Geoffrey, the Archbishop."

Tuck supplied the gossip. "Geoffrey claims that as De Puiset's Bishop of Durham he should submit to York. De Puiset's grown too proud and powerful to do that. He says Geoffrey's not really Archbishop until the Pope consecrates him. Both de Puiset and Geoffrey have appealed to the Pope."

"Geoffrey was no keener to see us than de Puiset," Adam went on. "He wouldn't grant us audience at all."

"Would he not?" frowned Marion dangerously. "We'll see about that."

"He's not well disposed to outlaws since you hold his Canon Steven and five hundred pounds of his gold," Alan explained. The bandits of Sherwood had visited York before.

Robin stared into the fire. "So what are our options? Verysdale needs relief, and any rescue from the Fitzwarren family or allies will be too late to help. Sir Richard also sends for aid from we outlaws of Sherwood, asking that we chase off Gisbourne's marauders."

Arthur a Bland spoke up. "I've seen those woods round Verysdale. Some nice game there, especially big fat hares and plump woodcocks. But the forest's thinner than we're used to, harder to hide in, easier to ride through. We'd be exposing ourselves to counterattack by well trained soldiers or to hunting parties with dogs."

"It's the Sheriff's trap, of course," Marion said. "He knows I'll have to go whatever happens. He's hoping to catch Robin and the rest of you as well."

"We might be able to do it," Robin considered. "If we went in and out quickly by night. But I reckon that's what the Sheriff wants us to try."

"You have to do something," Alan a Dale urged. "Elaine's trapped there, and all Marion's kin and over a hundred people who've done nothing but live on the wrong estate. The walls of Verysdale are solid but not that high. Gisbourne's going to get past them in the end, and then things will get grisly."

Robin thought of Will Stutely after five days in the dungeon at Pontefract. "We'll do something. We've been doing something all along. Just not what the Sheriff expects us to do or wants us to do."

"Much said that Little John was with the Sheriff in disguise," Adam remembered.

"Much hasn't the wits he was born with and that wasn't many," Tuck objected.

"Yes, John's in there," Marion confirmed. "We'd better not tell you why yet in case you're caught. But Robin, I think the time's coming when we have to try your latest mad stupid plan."

The outlaw king nodded. "I think so too. And this one is madder and more stupid than anything we've tried before."

Alan blinked. "Madder than sneaking into the Sheriff's wedding and winning his archery contest?"

Marion had to confess that it was. "But we do need a fall back, in case something goes wrong. Robin, I'm going to take Tuck up to York and I *am* going to talk to Archbishop Geoffrey. I'm a lot harder to ignore than my polite brother."

Adam's jaw dropped. "Polite?"

"I'll take Alan with me too, if he'll come and Adam can spare him. Send Gilbert with my brother. I need a minstrel."

Alan and Adam conferred then agreed. Gilbert shrugged. "Been a while since I've seen London. Wonder if that Irish lass with the freckles still lives by the Cripplegate?"

"And you'll be careful, Matilda Fitzwarren?" Robin asked Marion.

"As careful as you, Robin in the Hood," his lady answered.

"And you'll be careful, Matilda Fitzwarren?" Robin asked.
"As careful as you, Robin in the Hood," his lady answered.

The attackers hid under new wicker thatched on a timber frame, enough to shield twenty men with a battering ram and still have room for a half dozen archers. They approached the wall with more confidence than before, knowing that the defenders had run out of oil the day before and had no way to burn out the men who were to hack at the gate.

"Here they come!" Scarlet called down from the battlements above the gatehouse to Sir Richard and de Weynold who stood ready in the yard in case the doors were breached. "Steady, lads. Steady!"

The assault party reached arrow range and the first shots came down at them from the wall. The master-bowman who commanded the archers shouted for his men to choose their shots. Arrows were also growing scarce inside the fortified house.

It was clear to Scarlet that Gisbourne cared nothing for his troops. Each day there had been at least one futile assault on Verysdale, mostly to harry the defenders and deplete their resources; possibly also for the black knight's amusement. Mostly the attackers had fallen at the walls.

Scarlet didn't like the mathematics of it though. Gisbourne didn't mind spending ten men to claim one of Sir Richard's, and he could afford to do it. The threatened royal force had not yet appeared but it seemed that every day the siege camp swelled with some new arrivals. Word was out about the destruction of Verysdale and the sell-sword vultures were gathering. Meanwhile three of the manor's defenders had fallen to missile fire and two more lay injured in the chapel. Kent the Steward had been knocked from the wall and would not walk again.

Gisbourne pressed them from all sides. He'd even ordered a foray up the sheer side of the eastern cliff, just to test Sir Richard's vigilance. As the number of fighting men available in Verysdale had dwindled, de Weynold had recruited serving girls and peasant women to keep watch too.

The outer gate had shattered three days ago and the metal portcullis was twisted and useless. The battering ram hit the inner gate with a shudder that set the whole gatehouse rocking. Only that last door kept out Gisbourne's rapacious horde.

"Right then," Scarlet declared, gesturing to the defenders of Verysdale to stand ready. "Next time they pull back for a run up."

The attackers under the canopy marched twelve paces backwards to take another charge at the gate. Will Scathlock dropped his arm in a 'now' gesture and the six strongest men in the castle heaved at levers that tilted one of the hall trestles over the crenulations and onto the defensive screen below.

It wasn't the wooden tabletop that caused the damage though; it was the half-ton cornice that had taken most of the night to prise down from the chapel roof and drag above the gatehouse. The heavy shaped stone crashed down on the assault party, shattering their sheltering canopy and crushing the men beneath. Those not pinned beneath their screen squirmed out battered and surprised.

The archers on the wall opened fire. A half dozen of the Sheriff's soldiers and a pair of mercenaries fell in ten seconds.

Sir Richard gestured for the sally port to be opened. "Havoc!" he called, "Dex aie! Charge!"[27] He rushed outside in his old crusader armour, wielding the broadsword he'd fought with in Acre, Damascus, and Tortosa forty years earlier. Captain de Weynold hurried to keep up with him.

The attackers were in disarray. The arrival of two fully armoured knights was enough to send them into panicked retreat. Another five of them fell, two to the knights' blades and the others to the wall archers. A ragged cheer rose from the defenders of Verysdale.

Scarlet kept his eye on Gisbourne's trenches and redoubts and was ready when he saw the twenty mounted men break out from cover and ride for Sir Richard and de Weynold before the gate. "Back inside!" he warned the knights. "Right now!"

Any hope of retrieving the heavy stone to use again was dashed by the charge of the attackers' cavalry. Sir Richard Fitzwarren was forced to retreat back behind the remaining battered door before the horsemen came too close. He wheezed as de Weynold helped him off with his helmet.

Scarlet watched the horsemen peel off and return to their lines. "Tomorrow, then," one of them called mockingly.

Scarlet leaned his forehead on the weathered stone battlement and closed his eyes. The siege was getting harder.

Sir Guy of Gisbourne had observed the sally from a newly-constructed timber watchtower. He turned away with mild disgust when his riders returned unbloodied.

Quimper Kinstain, Rulf Blakehelloc, and Black Dane rushed over to attend him when he descended. "Well?" he demanded.

---

27   Havoc is a medieval military word setting the rules of engagement to preclude accepting surrender or giving quarter; in other words: "no mercy". Dex Aie is old Norman for "God aid us" and was said to be the battle cry of William the Conqueror's forces at the Battle of Hastings. The Royal Guernsey Light Infantry were charging to this battle cry as late as World War I.

"They're weak, my lord," Blakehelloc declared. "You saw they used no oil today? They would have if they could. And there are few lights in their keep at night. They're short of supplies. And only the two knights coming out to fight? They're short of men also."

"That's all obvious, idiot. I have eyes, don't I? I mean what news of my reinforcements?"

Kinstain had been riding out for messages and had an update for his leader. "Nottingham has been making preparations, sir. He's arranged the hire of garrisons from Tickhill, Castleford, Wakefield, and Knaresborough, and raised his flag for mercenaries. Around five thousand men in the muster, called under Prince John's banner. Add in the Prince's own household knights and that's near to two thousand troops to beat the forests and box in Robin Hood and his cut-throats."

"When?"

"As I say, de Vendenal has been busy. He's negotiated passage for his forces from the Baron of Pontefract, from Huddersfield, from Tadcaster and Harrogate. De Puiset's in no position to object and Longchamp's too far off to care. The men are mustering now and should be here in good time for your Lammas-day feast."

"And Hood?"

Black Dane had every reason to know and hate Robin Hood. Dane had been right hand man to the brigand leader that Robin had killed to become bandit king. Robin had left Dane to be hung by the villagers he'd terrorised. The murderer had scarcely escaped with his life but now he'd found a new master to license his cruelties. "I've looked around the landscape," Black Dane reported. "There's some places an outlaw who thinks he's clever might try and creep up on your forces. I've marked them for your guard sergeants."

"I want him to creep up," Gisbourne said. "That's the point of this trap."

"And when he does he'll be seen," Black Dane promised. "You've cut down enough timber for the siege that there's only a few ways he could get to you. Every stranger to the camp is questioned to make sure it's not one of Hood's lackeys. When he comes you'll know about it. You'll have him."

Blakehelloc pointed to the stand of trees at the base of the hill. "You want them there, in those woods. To reach them the outlaws need to cross open ground down in the valley, fields we can close off after, trapping them. There'll be no way out. Then we just comb the surrounded forest, corner Hood and his bandits, then cut them down."

"Or burn them out," considered Gisbourne.

Black Dane had to admit that might work. The woods down to the river were green and plentiful, offering the outlaws good cover, but they would eventually be hunted or starved out if enough men guarded the perimeters. "I can find them for you, Sir Guy," the renegade promised. "You'll have Robin Hood laid bloody and begging at your feet."

"I'd better." Gisbourne had spent days penned naked in a pigsty as Robin Hood's prisoner before he'd seduced a stupid goose-girl and escaped. "Remember that I hang outlaws, Dane. The only reason you're not dangling like your comrades and their whores I caught in Barnsdale is because you can spot Robin Hood for me."

The renegade paled. "Sire, I've done good service too. I shot Sir Richard's captain…"

"He was back out there fighting today," sniffed Blakehelloc.

"How many men on the walls have you hit?" Black Dane demanded of Sir Guy's war commander.

"I'm not a coward. When I fight, I prefer to be eye to eye with the man I'm going to kill," Blakehelloc snarled. He pressed up to Dane. "Like this."

"That's enough," growled Gisbourne. "Kill each other in your own time, not mine. Now go and get the next attack on the gates organised. I want them every three hours from now on, day and night. No sleep for Sir Richard at the Lee and his brave heroes. Keep at it. Make them bleed. Make them cry. Then make them crack!"

Elaine still wasn't sure what she was going to call herself these days. She was no longer Elaine of Loughborough. Elaine Lambert had fled her father's house. She certainly wasn't Lady Elaine de Vendenal, praise Jesu!

She supposed she might be Elaine a Dale, except that she suspected there was no Dale, at least not one that her husband might have come from. Dale was also a surname given to bastards whose father wasn't known. A child born out of wedlock but acknowledged by his sire might be called Fitz-whoever-had-fathered-him; after enough generations there was no shame in that, as the Fitzwarrens proved. A child of unknown paternity might be a Wood, or a Dale, or a Greenleaf.

Maybe she should just be Elaine, and let the rest follow, she mused.

She finished the tally of military supplies, locked the cellar door, and went to find Scathlock. The grizzled soldier was up on the wall, shouting oaths down at the peasants who strained to lift yet another chunk of heavy masonry to position above the gate as a missile.

Elaine tried not to be frightened of the fierce soldier. Aliss said that he had hidden kindness but would not say why. But his fierce looks told of a savage temper barely contained. Elaine had never seen him without sword and armour.

"I have the inventory," she told him. "Do you want it now?"

"Tell me," Scathlock said, then remembered his manners. "Please."

"No more combustibles. Four hundred and twenty short arrows. A hundred and sixty-two long arrows. Six big bags of slingshot, old but good. Two sacks of caltrops. Three suits of horse armour, one of them with damaged straps. Seventy yards of bowstring."

"That's it?" Scarlet's face showed his concern.

"Everything else is given out. Everyone in the castle has a weapon of some sort. All the bows are used." Elaine thought hard. "Could we tear up the mattresses and bolsters to get feathers for more arrows, and beat the sling-shot to arrow tips?"

Scathlock shook his head. "Wrong sort of feathers, and soft lead's bad for arrows. Even if we had a proper fletcher we'd struggle. You said no oil at all?"

"Sorry. We're even out of spirits that will burn. And Sir Richard says no more cooking fires. Wood grows short, so we're to have our food raw from now."

"Lovely," sighed Scarlet. "Have you any good news at all?"

Elaine considered. "My true love is away bringing rescue from Robin i' the Hood and the Lady Matilda," she offered.

The soldier snorted.

"What?" demanded Elaine. "You don't think they will come?"

"Oh, I think they will," Scarlet confessed. "I spent over a week with those lunatics, trailing after them through village after village, giving out arms to the poor. I've seen what Robin and Marion do to each other."

"Then they'll save us."

Scathlock shook his head. "I know what woman can do to men. A woman like Marion, she can make it seem like night is day. She can make you forget all sense and reason and chase after impossible dreams. But eventually those kinds of women lead you to disaster and to death."

Elaine caught a bitterness in the mercenary's voice. "Is that how she made you feel?" she wondered.

"I'm here, aren't I? Penned up to die when I could have slipped over the wall in the dark and been far away. Here when I could slit Sir Richard's throat and end the siege today. But instead I'm stood on a crumbling gatehouse defending a lost cause for no other reason than... than..."

"Than what?"

"Than because it's *right!*" snapped the soldier. "When did that ever matter a damn in war?"

"I think Marion would be proud of you," Elaine told him.

She went off to begin her tally of the pantries.

Geoffrey Plantagenet was close to forty. He had close-shaved hair with a natural tonsure and he looked more like his father King Henry II than any of the old monarch's legitimate heirs. He had his father's temper too.

William de Vendenal, on the other hand, was calm and subtle. "I apologise for troubling you at this difficult time," he said smoothly.

The Archbishop of York glared at the Sheriff of Nottingham. "Where's my Canon? The one the bandits took."

"Where are all the things that belong to you?" de Vendenal replied. "Where are your taxes, withheld because Hugh de Puiset impedes your collectors from bringing in your due tithes? Where are your honours, withheld on technical grounds because of the disputations of jealous men? Where is your future, torn from you by good King Richard to prevent your rise while he ran off east to play crusader?"

Geoffrey blinked in surprise at the Sheriff's candour, and took a breath. "I had heard you were a cunning man, de Vendenal. They say you are John's creature."

"I owe my current office to Prince John, who arranged for my investiture as Sheriff. I am paying off my debt by instalments."

That won a humorous snort from Geoffrey. "I bet you are, de Vendenal. And he'll wring you for every penny he can get."

"What ruler would not? That is how the game is played. I farm my knights. They farm their peasants. The royalty farms me. Only the church is above such things, holy and perfect."

Geoffrey chuckled out loud at that one. "You've been listening to gossip, I think. What do you know?"

"I know that Richard's not happy with you. He set a new Dean and a new Abbot at Selby to watch you and appointed de Puiset's sententious nephew

Edric as your Treasurer at York. I know that Richard fined you £2000 and confiscated your estates until you accepted these keepers onto your staff and finally became a priest. I know the Pope rejected petitions from both you and your church enemies, just before you excommunicated them in what, since they were present at the time, must have been a very memorable service of public worship.[28] And then there were the Jews…"

"I had nothing to do with that," protested the Archbishop. "The people of York can burn Jews without any direction of mine. De Puiset should have stepped in if the King didn't want it." It was only four months since Clifford's Tower, the main fortress of York, had been burned down by the Jews hiding in there from the mob. Fire and the crowds between them had accounted for a hundred and fifty lives.[29]

"It doesn't matter, your grace," the Sheriff said. "What matters is that your enemies appear to be surrounding you, choking you of money, of men, of authority."

"And Prince John will treat me differently?" asked Geoffrey scornfully.

---

28   Geoffrey Plantagenet's appointment as Archbishop was controversial. Indeed, he was not finally consecrated in the role until two years after he was awarded the post. De Vendenal's summary here is a gross simplification of a tangled and lengthy political saga but perhaps illustrates the kind of church and state politics that Geoffrey played. Shortly after the events of the present narrative King Richard further required his half-brother to agree in writing not to return to England for three years; Geoffrey was arrested and imprisoned for breaking the promise. And this was only half way through his long and colourful life.

29   In 1198 the Jews had been 'encouraged' to loan-fund Richard's crusade. Believing they had bought the king's favour, Jewish dignitaries turned up to Richard's coronation but were stripped, flogged, and thrown out. Historians differ on whether Richard encouraged or simply didn't prevent the anti-Semitic London riots that followed. A few Jews escaped death, robbery, or forcible baptism by fleeing into the Tower of London. Persecution riots spread to other cities. Following the examples of the London Jews, 150 Jews took refuge in Clifford's Tower, York's principal stronghold. The siege went on for days, made more savage when a stone falling from the tower killed a monk who preached for the Jews' destruction. On 16th March 1190, unable to escape, many Jews committed suicide by burning the tower. Survivors were killed by the mob as they emerged.

The people who might have stopped this, including Archbishop Geoffrey and de Puiset, were all looking the wrong way at the time. Some scholars suggest that de Puiset deliberately chose not to intervene to hand the Archbishop of York another problem, or that the riots were fanned to show up de Puiset's inability to keep order in the North. In the end it was rival Justiciar Longchamp who marched in and restored order in York, to the annoyance of both Archbishop Geoffrey and Prince John, who each felt it made them look weak. The Sheriff of York was dismissed from his post; his former responsibilities may have passed to the new Sheriff of Nottingham.

"He was here less than a week ago, eating me out of house and home, making promises, offering gifts and veiled threats."

"Oh no. Lackland hates you as much as Richard does. He'll use you then crap on you and walk away laughing."

The Archbishop looked up sharply. "What?"

Now de Vendenal smiled. "I am a cunning man, as you say. I know, as you must, that nobody is really on anyone's side. There are only degrees of mutual interest. It so happens that today Prince John's interests and mine coincide, so there are good reasons for us to be allies. Likewise, my interests and yours overlap just now, so I have come to seek permission to bring armies through Yorkshire to destroy a little West Riding holding called Verysdale."

"I see. And why is that to my benefit?"

"Firstly, it will annoy Hugh de Puiset to have a large military force stamping over what he considers to be his territory. But because it is an army raised under John's flag in the King's name he won't be able to do anything about it. Secondly, the knight I will destroy is the same man whose gold was stolen from your own counting house. You have no reason to love old Sir Richard. The man has robbed you. And thirdly, the whole strategy is designed to lure and capture the outlaw Robin i' the Hood who flouts your authority and mine and who is trying to ransom your canon back to you." The Sheriff smiled slyly. "Is that sufficient benefit, my Lord Archbishop?"

The new reinforcements arrived at last and Sir Guy strode out to inspect them. This still wasn't the royal force he was awaiting but at last the six-score men who'd been delayed by Robin Hood's trick at the Aire crossing marched into camp. It increased the forces available to the black knight by almost a third.

Sir Guy's disposition darkened when he recognised Constable Shank-shard leading the columns. "What's that old idiot doing here?" he demanded of Quimper Kinstain. "The last thing I need is some cautious old prig telling me how to conduct a campaign."

"He's probably only here to make a report," Gisbourne's toady soothed him. "This siege might be happening under Prince John's banner but it's financed from the Sheriff's purse. You know de Vendenal. He'll want his reports."

Sir Guy suggested what William de Vendenal could do with his reports.

"Come on then. Let's make a show for the Constable. Blakehelloc, turn out the men. Hide the whores at the back. Kinstain, Dane, Evalgast, Slafot, with me."

Shankshard had dismounted by the time Sir Guy joined him. The Constable shielded his eyes with one hand to gaze across the entrenchments at the fortified house beyond. He was conferring with a giant of a man in studded leathers.

"Doesn't look too hard to take," Shankshard commented. "We should have sent for siege engines. We could have reduced the place in two days and saved a lot of expense."

"Depends what you want to do, Constable," Reynold Greenleaf replied. "Quick and quiet and a ballista or a bolt thrower's your best bet, or a catapult with burning pitch. But I thought your Sheriff wanted to take his time here and catch other fish."

Shankshard shot him a suspicious glance. "Where did you hear that?"

"I'm big, not stupid," the giant replied.

Gisbourne marched up, trailing Kinstain and Black Dane. "I wasn't expecting you," he said to Shankshard, not even trying to hide his feelings on the matter.

"That was rather the point," replied the Constable. "I've brought your men. This big fellow's the one to thank for your arms supplies, and I commend him to you. He's called…"

Black Dane stepped forward, mouth open. "I know him! He's…"

Reynold Greenleaf brought his quarterstaff up hard into the renegade's belly, bending Dane into a tight pained crouch. The giant leaned over, seized Black Dane by the neck, and snapped his spine with a single brutal twist.

Sir Guy's sword was in his hand as swiftly as Little John had taken down the man who could recognise him.

"I know him too," Greenleaf said, kicking Black Dane's corpse. "He runs with Robin in the Hood!"

Shankshard looked down at the dead man. He recovered from his shock. "This was Hood's man? You recognise him?"

"He was with Hood," Kinstain objected. "He deserted."

Greenleaf spat on the corpse. "Not long ago, then. He was there at Woodbarrow when Hood ambushed Dunstan. He was pally enough with Hood then, as I spied from the bushes when they were hunting me." He turned to Gisbourne. "I bet he came with some story about hating Robin Hood and wanting to help you catch him, right? And instead he'll have told the outlaws everything about your plans and they'll know all the traps you've set."

"Black Dane helped us to plan them all!" Quimper Kinstain blurted before a furious glare from Gisbourne could silence him.

Sir Guy looked down at the dead bandit. Black Dane sprawled on his chest but his head still looked up at his killer, twisted round far more than a living neck could manage. It fascinated Gisbourne. "You shouldn't have killed him. We could have put him to the question."

Reynold Greenleaf shrugged what could be an apology. "He knew he'd been spotted when he saw me. He was stood right next to you and he had a knife. I had to make a quick decision, so I went with my gut."

Gisbourne's own instinct was to maim first and ask questions later. He began to see possibilities for the huge fighter in front of him.

"I can see I got here not a moment too soon, Sir Guy," Shankshard noted. "I shall inspect the camp and the troops first, then review the disposition of your siege."

Sir Guy's venomous looks got more poisonous yet. "Show the Constable what he wants to see, Blakehelloc," he growled. He pointed at Reynold Greenleaf. "You—with me."

XIII

York was bustling in the dog-days of late July. The first harvests were in and the city was full of chandlers and farmers, of reeves and taxmen, of all the travellers whose business brought them to trade and treat in the second-largest settlement in England.

At the upper window of the inn on Stonegate[30], Ros stared out of with wide, excited eyes. The Saxon hamlet of Waltham where she'd been born and had lived most of her life would have fitted into one block of York's three-storey timbered houses. More people passed along the muddy street outside Ros' lodgings in half an hour than had dwelled in her childhood home.

It wasn't just the city. The milliner's horde had furnished Roslyn with an ensemble suitable for her role as companion maid to Lady Matilda of Leaford, the crusader's daughter. No ragged hem or threadbare seat shamed her. Ros' full skirt swished around her ankles when she moved, the first brand new clothing she'd ever worn.

For a moment Ros suffered a pang of guilt. This was serious business, the first time she'd had to leave her surviving child, Tad, to the care of others, and dangerous too. Matilda Fitzwarren took a great risk coming to York whilst in defiance of Prince John's summons, especially since John himself was resident in the royal castle's palace. Still, dressed so in such remarkable society Ros of Waltham, a girl who'd had to sell herself for bread crusts to keep her children alive after her man was hung for poaching, couldn't help but feel transported to some fairy wonderland.

Lady Matilda's return forced Ros out of her trance. Marion had easily transformed from forest queen to Norman heiress. She wore a rich loose gown with delicate Oriental borders, embroidered soft flat slippers, a corded off-the-shoulder cloak, with the ease and assurance of a lady born. A single silver band that spoke of tasteful reserve and hinted at wealth undisclosed fil-

---

30   The oldest public house in York is generally held to be the Olde Star Inne on Stonegate, which has been licensed at least back to 1644 and whose premises date back to well before that time. It is not unreasonable that lodgings for travellers were provided near the gates of the city even back in the twelfth century.

leted her copper-red hair. Ros had never seen a highborn damsel so beautiful or so noble.

Friar Tuck was dressed in clean robes for once. They were almost devoid of the wine stains and greasy finger-marks of his usual habit. Alan a Dale wore fine new livery suitable for a retainer of a highborn lady, and an outrageous feathered cap. David of Doncaster followed, carrying the carved wooden box that contained gifts to present when they called upon the Archbishop. Marion bore an armful of scrolls and parchments that she laid on the lodging room's polished table.

"Well done, everybody," Marion said when David had secured the door. "I think we've got all we need."

Ros hurried to help Marion unpin her cloak. "You got an appointment with the Archbishop?"

The lady smirked. "I gave his steward notice that I would call upon him tomorrow before Terce. I mentioned a gift for Lord Geoffrey." She pointed to the paperwork across the table. "And then Alan got me a roll of all the nobles and notables who are in York just now for Prince John's court."

"A right collection of rogues and opportunists they are too," judged Tuck. "Prince John's making his move all right, trying to undercut Lord Longchamp's popularity in London by making a big splash up here."

Marion glanced over the lists. She was disappointed that none of her father's friends seemed to be present. It would have been easier with some baron or knight of unimpeachable integrity to escort her to the Archbishop's court.

"What about the soldiers?" Ros worried. "When Prince John hears that you're in York won't he send men to get you?"

Town-bred David was worried about that too. He had a healthy fear of the watch.

"I'm counting on the general noise of Prince John's procession keeping him from noticing," Marion confessed. "By the time he works out I'm here I hope to be gone–or under the Archbishop's protection and the church's sanctuary."

Friar Tuck wasn't as confident. "I wouldn't count on Geoffrey's piety to protect you, my lady. Not if it conflicts with his ambition."

"But he'll be cautious," argued Alan. "The whole city's been on edge since last March's riots, when the Jews were slaughtered. The Archbishop must know it wouldn't take much to set the fighting off again." The minstrel paused and pondered that.

The conversation went on, with plans and contingencies and discussion of tactics, but Ros simply enjoyed the swish of her dress as she moved round the room and the feel of the clean fabric on her skin, as she lived her adventure in the greatest city of the North.

Reynold Greenleaf turned to Sir Guy for confirmation. "Five silver marks?"

"If you can do it, yes," confirmed the knight of Gisbourne. "In three weeks of siege they've ignored all provocation to come out to single combats. Otherwise I'd have gutted the old knight and his so-handsome captain long before this."

"But you didn't offer to wrestle without weapons or armour," the giant pointed out. "There's always some bully in their ranks who can't resist a grapple. I'll take him on, break his bones, and throw his crippled frame back at them to see what they do."

"If you can, it's five marks," promised Sir Guy. More like the big fool will get a dozen arrows in his guts, the black knight thought.

Greenleaf nodded. He laid his seven-foot stave down and strode alone over the ground between the siege earthworks and the fortified house. He bore a white scarf denoting parley.

"What do you want?" came a voice from the walls. "No nearer or we'll shoot."

"You're brave behind your battlements," Reynold shouted back. "But here I stand, without even weapons or armour. Is there any man inside that durst come out and wrestle me like this? Or are you all so scared by now that you're too busy sucking on your mothers' teats?"

There was no reply for a moment from the fortress. Then, at last, a voice shouted, "I'll take you on."

"Say your name," shouted Reynold.

"William Scathlock. They call me Scarlet."

A little smile crossed Greenleaf's lips. "I've heard of you. Come out and face me if you dare."

He stepped a little closer to the walls of Verysdale, so that he was equidistant between Gisbourne's trenches and Sir Richard's fortifications. Arrows from either side would be at long range, making the combatants a hard target and giving either man a chance of retreat to safety should the other side prove treacherous.

Scarlet was lowered over the side of the wall on a rope. The sally port was no longer usable. The final gate of Verysdale was so battered now that it had been reinforced with every moveable that could be stacked behind it.

The soldier held out his arms and turned around to show he wasn't wearing weapons or armour. He walked towards Greenleaf with a slow, confident tread.

Sir Guy's men began to shout their encouragement to their giant champion to break the challenger.

Scarlet reached Greenleaf and stopped six feet from him. "Hello, Little John," he said quietly. "What the hell are we doing?"

"We're going to grapple," the big man told him. "And while we're doing that I'll tell you Robin's plan."

Scarlet spat on his hands. "Right then. So I'm to go easy on you while you talk."

Little John laughed. "Just be glad I'm only going to pretend to snap your arms and legs. At the end I'll toss you back to your comrades and they can drag your poor broken frame back up to tend to your dying moments."

The soldier circled the giant. "We need to make it look good, then. I don't like throwing fights."

Little John closed the distance between them and caught Scarlet a heavy box on the ear. "You won't have to, lad. You're probably good, but I'm me."

Scarlet growled in reply and head-butted the giant in the belly.

Cries came from both camps now. Men and women crowded the wall at Verysdale. Money changed hands as the Sheriff's soldiers lay bets.

Greenleaf tossed Scarlet and flopped on him. "A few days from now Gisbourne's going to come and offer you terms."

Scarlet squirmed from under his opponent and got in a smack to the eye before rolling free. "Brickhead? He's sworn to see us all crippled or dead."

Greenleaf rolled to his feet and hooked Scarlet's knees from under him. He explained why the black knight would come and do such a thing.

"Really?" Will Scathlock gasped, winded but still struggling. "That's your plan?"

Greenleaf planted an elbow into the soldier's stomach. "Nope. That's Rob's plan. Sorry. And what comes after's worse." He explained that too.

Scarlet wrenched the giant's hand off his face, feinted a stab at his eyes, then kicked him in the belly. "Me? I can't do that. You're as insane as your leader."

Greenleaf caught him a vicious hammer-blow to the cheek, stunning the mercenary and sprawling him on the turf. Before Scarlet could recover, the big man had him in an unbreakable half-nelson. "If you have a better plan I'd love to know it right now. If not, that's what we've got."

Will Scathlock had no answer. He grunted in pain. His face was bloody.

"I'm going to pretend to break your arm now," Little John told him. "Scream so they won't wonder they didn't hear the snap."

A great cheer rose from the attacker's camp as Reynold Greenleaf shattered each of his adversary's limbs in turn, not once but twice. Sir Guy shouted loudest of all, delighted by the sport.

Scarlet tried to hold his limbs at awkward angles as Greenleaf lifted his limp body high in the air and carried it back towards the walls of Verysdale. When he was flung onto the turf he sprawled in a broken heap and didn't move.

The giant gave him a last kick. "Sorry. Remember."

"You owe me a pint," Scarlet hissed back at him through a bloody mouth.

Greenleaf strolled back to his camp and the celebrations of his comrades. De Weynold and four of Verysdale's defenders climbed down to gently lift their fallen soldier into a hammock and take him back inside.

"How did it go?" de Weynold asked Scarlet under his breath as the sling was prepared.

"I could have taken him," said Scarlet. "Oh, and there's a plan. The bad news is it's one of Robin Hood's."

"He wouldn't see me!" fumed Matilda of Leaford. "The Archbishop of York would not see *me!*"

"He wouldn't see your brother either, little flower," Tuck tried to calm the livid noblewoman. "He's in a very precarious position, our Geoffrey. Lackland's in the city breathing down his neck. He did offer to mediate between you and the Prince."

"There's nothing to mediate between Weaselly John and me," hissed Marion.

Alan a Dale thought through the ramifications of their call. "Geoffrey knows you're in York now, Marion. How long now before word gets to Prince John?"

"We might want to think about running for our lives," David of Doncaster suggested. "It's only a matter of time before one of the Archbishop's staff runs telling tales to Lackland's court. And in a walled city, if they close the gates we're caught."

"We need to do something quickly, for certain," Marion agreed. "Alan, show me those attendance rolls again. We need to find an ally, and fast."

Arthur a Bland slipped out of the undergrowth so quietly that even Robin didn't hear him. "I'm back," said the Lincolnshire poacher.

Much yelped and dropped the waterskin he was drinking from.

Robin took his surprise in good part. Nobody moved as secretly as Arthur. "What did you see?"

The poacher took a stick and sketched out a map in the dirt. "There's a pass runs north down to the Wharfe. The house is on a natural spur to the west. Woods all round, but few near enough to get men unseen. High ground to the south-east but Gisbourne's main camps are across the road through the valley and west of Verysdale."

Robin studied the diagram. "How many men?"

"Five hundred or thereabouts I'd say, and plenty with bows. About sixty mounted. They've got hounds as well. Almost as if they was waiting for us, Rob."

"Hounds," worried Much. "Hounds isn't good, Robin."

The young outlaw knew it. "Arthur, what can we feed those dogs to put them off the trail and keep 'em sleeping while we act?"

The old poacher considered the problem. "I talked this through with Gilbert Whitehand 'afore he went south. We can catch a few conies[31] like, and we lace 'em with the last of that poppy juice you got, or maybe just strong liquor. Then we toss 'em to the hounds. That'll see the dogs happy. I'll see what can be done."

"For the rest, how close do you think you can get our lads and still be able to retreat to safety?"

The poacher considered matters. "Well, if we set some deadfalls and other traps to slow down pursuit after, I reckon as we could get near enough to prick 'em with a few arrows. Nothing fancy. Then a fast away."

"Use fire arrows and aim for the tents," suggested Robin. "Right. Make sure everybody knows the landscape as well as you do, Arthur. Get ready to drug the hounds for me. And tell everybody to be set to go. Tell them this one's for Stutely."

Prince John stormed into the cellars of his royal palace in a foul mood for having been dragged away from his banquet. The noble young ladies he'd sat on his left and right promised to be far more pleasant and pliant company than the terrible creature confined in her basement cage.

"Well?" he demanded of his man Rothmere.

---

31   Rabbits.

The minion gestured to the thin bundle of rags in the cage. "It's true, your highness. She's dying."

The Tattooed Woman shifted as she heard Prince John's voice. One yellow eye opened and she managed a throaty chuckle.

"So what?" demanded John of England. "Why should the passing of one mad pagan witch interfere with my dinner?"

Rothmere didn't want to repeat the things the old woman had said to him, things he'd take with him to his grave. "She claims to have a last word for you, sire."

The Tattooed Woman's spidery fingers opened and closed convulsively.

John edged near to the bars. "What is it, then?" he demanded, making the sign of the cross to ward off the evil eye. "What do you want before you descend to hell?"

The Tattooed Woman cackled again. Her cracked lips bled as she whispered: "Revenge."

A shudder ran through the Prince. "What revenge? Die and be done with it, crone. You have no power to harm me."

"I have already done it," the hag breathed. "The arrow is shot. Let it hit where it will."

"Speak plainly or I'll kill you myself."

The old woman's eyes were turned upward now so only the bloodshot whites were visible. "You need not seek the hart. It will come to you. But the hunter follows behind it. Which will prevail, Crown or Hood?"

John grasped on the one word he followed. "Hood? Robin Hood? Matilda of Leaford and Robin in the Hood? Is that what you mean?"

"Revenge," said the old woman, and breathed her last. The room went cold.

Prince John found he had lost his appetite for supper and the ladies and retired early to his rooms.

The Earl of Huntingdon's household was packing up. Pages and maids rushed everywhere, making sure that their master's household possessions were properly stowed for tomorrow's journey. Chaos reigned.

Even so, the arrival of a highborn beauty decked in courtly finery, attended by her maid, a minstrel, a footman, and a simple brown friar, was enough to attract attention. A steward came over to enquire what they sought and received the gift that Matilda Fitzwarren presented for his master. He vanished into the interior of the Earl's townhouse to determine if an audience was possible.

"This place is very grand," whispered Ros as she waited nervously amidst the courtyard bustle. "This Huntingdon must be right powerful."

"He's the grandson of a Scottish king," Marion told her. "In fact he's got a claim on the throne of Scotland himself, if he chose to press it."

"He's got an awful lot of soldiers," worried David, looking around.

"He's preparing for a journey to Chester and he doesn't want trouble with outlaws," gossiped Alan. "He's to wed Matilda de Kevelioc, the Earl of Chester's daughter. She's thirty years his younger."

Tuck sniggered. "He's a lusty sort of chap–or he was in his youth. I well remember him when he hunted at Chesterfield. Wasn't only boars and stags he chased."

Marion was more interested in his recent history. "They say he's courted by Prince John and the Justiciars alike. He came for the Archbishop's blessing on his marriage and to receive the Prince's assent but he could just as well have done without them. They're more interested in him than he in them."

"Aye well," said Tuck slyly, "that's because they don't know quite what he'll do next. Will he take Chester's money and ride north to try for Scotland? Will he abide by his vow and sail to Richard at the crusades? Worst of all, will he cast his lot with de Puiset, or with Longchamp, or for Lackland, tipping the balance one way or the other right here? Nobody knows."[32]

"And that's why we're here," concluded Marion as the steward returned.

"My master will be pleased to receive you, my lady" the man fawned. "This way please."

Even packed up for transportation, the Earl's home made Sir Richard's Leaford estate look like a hovel. Marion ignored the comparison and glided across the hall to make a formal courtesy before David of Scotland.

Huntingdon looked down at the beautiful Saxon-haired noblewoman who'd unexpectedly brightened his day. "Please, rise," he told her. "I would know who is visiting me and why."

"And it please my lord, I am Marion Fitzwarren of Leaford, Verysdale, and Anston, daughter of the crusader knight Sir Richard at the Lee."

The Earl raised an eyebrow. "The same Sir Richard who fought beside

---

32   David of Scotland (c1144–1219) was grandson of Scottish monarch David I. Returning from crusade with Richard I to curb Prince John's ambitions, Huntingdon participated in the 1194 siege of Nottingham Castle and captured the Sheriff. Huntingdon was often identified as Robin Hood in Elizabethan dramas that overlooked his royal lineage. His crusader exploits with Richard the Lionheart were fictionalised in Sir Walter Scott's 1822 novel *The Talisman*. David's grandson was the famous Robert the Bruce.

the old king? The knight who held the pass?" Another association clicked into place. "The knight Prince John has declared recreant for withholding his daughter?"

"The same, my lord. But my father is not recreant, for I was given in betrothal at a contest of arms overseen by the Sheriff of Nottingham, and therefore am no longer Sir Richard's to dispose. It is my future husband who commands me and who defies the Prince. It is in his name and for his sake that I have come to you today."

The Earl of Huntingdon glanced at his stewards but none of them were able to offer any help. "Who then is this husband that would deny the will of a prince?"

Another curtsy. "My lord, I am also known by some as Maid Marion of the Greenwood. My betrothed is Robin in the Hood, the protector of Sherwood, leader of the free company of outlaws who defy tyranny and injustice, enemy of those without charity to the true word of God, and the king of my heart." She rose and looked straight into Huntingdon's face. "My love is Robin Hood–your son."

XIV

Sir Guy of Gisbourne had his camp stool set outside his tent so he could watch Verysdale burn.

Earlier that day he had ordered the usual sortie to break through the last gate into the battered mansion. For variety he'd sent two parties forward with rams and protective screens, wondering whether the defenders had enough masonry left to rain down in time. Then, as the men on the walls had strained to cope with a pair of breaching parties, the black knight had charged in his archers and had them send fire arrows over the walls at the wooden buildings beyond.

The tactic worked very well. The remaining thatch on the stables had caught and the blaze had spread to the main house itself. The defenders were torn between letting their fortress burn or defending the gates that kept out Gisbourne's bloodthirsty horde. They'd been so distracted that the attackers had even got three siege ladders up to the walls and put half a dozen men over the battlements.

Sir Guy's vanguard was cut down, but he knew they'd taken some of Sir Richard's men with them. The fires must have caused extensive damage too, consuming stores, destroying kitchens and workshops. Gisbourne could only guess how badly he'd hurt the defenders today, but he was well satisfied with the results.

Long after sunset he could see the red glows of hot timbers inside the fortified house's crumbling walls. The black knight imagined precious water supplies being used to quench fires rather than thirsts. Verysdale had its own well but it wasn't inexhaustible. He imagined that fussy old crusader quivering when each man of his died by fire or arrow. Sir Guy smiled at the mental image.

"Blakehelloc!" he called into the darkness.

His battle commander scurried over. "Sir?"

"I think tomorrow we'll try and get some boiling pitch over the walls. Speak to the engineers about it. Something that splatters, I think. I want disfigurements and minor fires, not deaths. Fitzwarren's the kind of fool who won't slaughter the injured to save resources."

"Yes, sir. I'll speak to them now."

"Also have them prepare some chains. That gate has been shored up with every piece of furniture in Verysdale behind it. Tomorrow I want the usual ram assault, but then I want chains attached to the door and horses to pull it away. With luck we can drag the gate to pieces and wrench it off before they realise what's happening."

"Yes sir." Blakehelloc thought of the condition of the remaining barrier. The plan might well work. "Sir, the Constable said that we weren't to take the castle until Robin Hood arrived."

"Well the Constable isn't here any more, is he? He's hiding with his men waiting to corner the outlaws. And I'm feeling bored. I want a woman, and the last available wenches in five miles are quivering inside that castle." The black knight considered for a moment. "That Lambert girl who was going to marry the Sheriff, she's in there, isn't she? She wasn't bad looking and she'd scream nicely. When the gate's down I'm going to..."

Gisbourne's plan for Elaine was interrupted by a strident horn blast. As he rose to see, three score of fire arrows arched up over his camp and seared down into the tents.

"Attack!" shouted the watchmen too late. "Ware arrows!"

A second flight arced in from the treeline. Sir Guy could see them clearly, blazing yellow streaks falling on men and equipment.

"To arms!" he bellowed, reaching for his helmet. "Blakehelloc, send Kinstain and two others with word to Shankshard to close his trap. Then form the men up on me and prepare to charge the woods."

Around the camp soldiers were hurrying out of blazing tents, grabbing water troughs to douse the fires. Others screamed for aid as they nursed shafts that had penetrated their limbs.

"Loose the dogs!" shouted Blakehelloc. Somewhere came a sound of savage barking in reply.

A third array of flame-arrows came in lower, aimed at the first of the soldiers to charge the woods. Gisbourne could see the outlaws now, lit by the torches they'd used to ignite their shafts.

"On me!" he shouted to his men. "Gisbourne! Gisbourne!"

The men at the wood's edge dropped their torches and vanished amongst the trees.

"Hold, sire!" called Blakehelloc. "It'll be an ambush. Remember Minsthorpe Woods?"

The black knight well recalled leading his men into the forest trap prepared by Robin Hood. He paused.

Reynold Greenleaf appeared at his side. "Let me take a couple of lads in there quietly," he offered. "We'll grab an outlaw and drag him back to ask him a few questions."

Sir Guy realised that he did need information about Hood's numbers and intentions. "Alright then. But be fast. I want answers."

"Evalgast! Slafot!" Greenleaf called the names of Gisbourne's most trusted—and brutal—men and headed off at right angles to the place where the bandits had vanished.

"Set a perimeter down by the treeline," Blakehelloc called to his sergeants. "Light torches along the edge so we can see if the bandits come back. Position archers. I don't want them getting this near again."

Gisbourne's battle-rage turned to bitter anger. "If you see them, kill them. I want blood. Blood!"

"And you'll get it now, sir," Blakehelloc promised him. "They don't know about Constable Shankshard's force. Once the Constable closes the forest they've nowhere to run."

Lady Mary waked Sir Richard from a deep exhausted sleep. It took him a moment to recall why he ached so badly, another to remember why he was sleeping in his armour.

"Loren is calling for you," the Lady of Verysdale told her husband. "He needs you on the wall."

"What time is it?" the old knight asked, wheezing out of his bed. The whole castle smelled of smoke, he noticed; smoke and defeat.

"Sometime around midnight," Lady Mary replied. "You have to go to the wall."

Sir Richard at the Lee staggered into the courtyard towards the makeshift ladder that had been fashioned to replace the burned out stairs onto the battlements. Captain de Weynold and Scarlet waited for him at the base of the north tower.

"What now?" the old knight asked, hardly daring to hear the reply.

Even as he asked, the third flight of fire arrows soared out of the woods and into the siege camp down the hill.

Will Scarlet's face broke into a rare smile. "I reckon Robin Hood might have turned up."

"I reckon Robin Hood might have turned up."

Of the three messengers who'd set out from Gisbourne's camp, Quimper Kinstain was the only one to arrive at Shankshard's file. The outlaws had proved adept at deploying archers along the likely routes where riders might be sent for aid. Only Kinstain's habitual custom of avoiding the lead had saved his life.

The Sheriff's Constable was already up and alert, having heard the horn blasts from the forest. "Is it him?" were his first words as Gisbourne's aide galloped into camp.

"If not then it's another band of outlaw archers," snarled Kinstain. "At least sixty of them judging by the flights they put up. I'd say Hood has brought his whole damn band."

"Excellent." Shankshard said, closing his fist as he intended to close his men around the little spur of forest. "Then we have him! Will Gisbourne seal the side of the woods nearest to the siege?"

"I imagine he'll already have done that by now."

The Constable nodded. "Right then. Gill o' th' Red Cap, take a hundred men and blockade the road. Nobody passes down it and nobody crosses it from the forest. Set guard-fires to spot movement by night. I'll take the river slope and then we'll have penned Hood on all three sides."

Gill saluted and called for his men. These were the Sheriff's regular guard, the soldiers who'd been disciplined and trained by Captain Aelstan in Nottingham Castle. They couldn't match the outlaws in woodland but on open ground at close quarters their numbers, armour, and discipline would make short work of Robin's irregular host.

Shankshard turned back to Kinstain. "Ride on to York. I'll provide an escort. Go straight to my Lord Sheriff and tell him the trap is sprung. If he can get the Prince's muster here in the next couple of days we can wipe out Robin Hood and his rebels to the last man and boy."

Kinstain nodded. "Prince John is also in York. I'll make sure that both of them know what's happening." It would do Quimper no harm to be the bearer of good tidings to the de-facto monarch of England.

"Everyone knows what to do," Shankshard called out to his troops. "Robin Hood's played the game his way. He'll find it's a lot harder now he has to play to our rules!"

Reynold Greenleaf led Evalgast and Slafot through the dark woods, silently and remorselessly. The two cutthroats had no idea where they were going. They were barely able to see the silhouette of the giant as he led them through the tangled undergrowth.

Then the big man turned round. "Right, lads. We're here," he said out loud.

"Here? Here where?" demanded Evalgast. "I don't see…"

"He weren't talking to you," said Much the Miller's Son, holding his knife to Evalgest's throat.

"He was talking to us," explained Arthur a Bland, similarly neutralising Slafot.

Robin Hood dropped out of the trees. "Hello, Little John," he said. "I was starting to wonder if you'd got a better offer."

"Well, the Sheriff's food was quite good, and I enjoyed the pay," admitted the big fellow, "but where could I get abuse like I do from you, Robin in the Hood?"

The two men embraced, hammering each other on the back.

"Wait. Greenleaf hates Little John," objected Evalgast. "He wants to kill him!"

"Well, maybe I want to die sometimes in a morning after I've drunk too much," admitted Little John. "As for the rest, I'm afraid that was just to get me a job where we could know what the Sheriff was up to."

Much called the other bandits. Riccon Hazel appeared to bind the prisoners' wrists.

"These are two of Gisbourne's nastiest bravos," Little John said. "They've tortured, raped, maimed and murdered for their master. And they've boasted about it after."

Robin turned his gaze upon Evalgast and Slafot. "Riccon, take them somewhere they'll be found by the soldiers tomorrow. Leave them hanging there, like Gisbourne left the women and children at the Barnsdale camp."

Much planted a fist into Evalgest's belly to stop him screaming for help. The thugs were led away.

Arthur remained behind. "This is your last chance to stop this foolishness before you walk into the lion's den," he warned the outlaws.

"We're already too near to get away," Robin judged. "I take it that Gisbourne's closed the borders of this woodland?"

"Shankshard's around somewhere with a hidden force," John of Hathersage explained. "I hope you weren't expecting to sneak the men out of here."

"Not without being seen, no. Arthur, make sure everybody's ready for the big escape."

"Right you are, Rob," agreed the old poacher. "Go and do your folly. If

God sends you down a stony path may he give you strong shoes, and may you be in heaven half an hour before the Devil hears you're dead!"

With the old outlaw's blessing ringing in their ears, Robin Hood and Little John ran through the forest.

Shankshard had hardly got his men into position along the Wharfe river basin when a shrill whistle from a sentry alerted him to movement in the forest. He turned his horse and led the mounted response force towards the signal at a gallop.

He was amazed to see a column of the Sheriff of Nottingham's own men emerging from the depths of the forest.

"What's this?" he demanded, recognising the huge man who strode beside a knight in arms on a quality stallion. "Greenleaf?"

"Sir," saluted the big man.

"Ah," said the knight on horseback. "This ees Constable Shankshard of whom I have 'eard tell?"

"Yes, Sir Marcel," agreed Greenleaf. "May I present his honour the Constable of Nottinghamshire? Your honour, this is Sir Marcel of Flanders."

"Sir Marcel?" frowned Shankshard.

"The same man that Robin 'ood captured and impersonated at the Sheriff's wedding, yes?" said Marcel. "It is the pleasure to meet you in reality this time, Constable."

The Constable glanced at the column of men who were moving in good order behind the French knight. "Excuse me, Sir Marcel, but I was unaware that you were in the area, or that any more of the Sheriff's forces had arrived."

Marcel tapped the nose of his helmet. "Need to know, Constable. I am sent directly from Prince John 'imself, and the Sheriff was keen that my coming with these men was not made known to the bandits."

"Sir Marcel insisted to Sir Guy that he be allowed to take a hunting force through the forest," said Reynold Greenleaf, trying to sound like a man who disapproved of such folly. "We did not encounter any outlaws." *Fortunately*, he didn't add.

The Constable caught the undertones of the giant's report. So here was one of King John's toadies, in authority he probably didn't deserve, with men he'd taken from the Sheriff's force, marching blindly into a situation he didn't understand. Marcel of Flanders had been lucky not to end up as

Robin Hood's prisoner again.

"We will find the bandits," Shankshard promised the knight. "We have a method. There is a plan."

Marcel nodded. "Good. You do your plan. I shall ride back around the forest and report to Sir Guy. These bandits are cowards. They will not fight a fair battle."

"But we have them trapped now. We only await the Sheriff's arrival with his main force and we can walk these woods from end to end with men shoulder to shoulder. Or we can take Sir Guy's council and burn the forest down. Either way we will capture or kill every outlaw in there."

"I am satisfied that you will," Marcel approved. "Carry on, Constable."

Reynold shot Shankshard a 'what-can-you-do?' glance as the Frenchmen led his column of soldiers away.

So Robin Hood marched his men out of the woods dressed in the uniforms they'd taken from the Sheriff's guard at the Aire crossing and left the Constable guarding an empty forest.

XV

Friar Tuck was no longer used to the regular routine of the clerical offices, but he heaved his bulk out of a warm cot and staggered his way to the chapel of ease to say Matins. Things were deadly serious and he felt he needed to explain matters to God in person.

He hadn't relished the idea. God always had sharp things to say to the recalcitrant monk.

It was the middle of the night. Few people were at the service. Tuck was surprised to see the Earl of Huntingdon there.

He was more surprised when David of Scotland recognised him. "I know you. Brother Thomas, it was. You've grown fat."

Tuck admitted it. He patted his paunch. "Yes, my lord. It's a very long time since I went hunting with your lordship in the West Riding."

"You were a merry fellow, I recall. I never thought you suited for a monk."

"I can eat, drink, and wench as well as a bishop, my lord."

The Earl snorted. He gestured for Tuck to sit down with him and waited while the other celebrants finished their devotions and filed out. "I couldn't sleep," he said at last.

"Nor I," admitted the friar. "I suspect we're both worrying about the same thing."

"Matilda of Leaford," said the Earl.

"Maid Marion," said Friar Tuck. "Do you know how brave she is to come to you as she did?"

"Bold, perhaps, and foolish. I could win much favour by bundling her up and sending her to John right now."

"But you haven't. Instead, you're here on your knees on a cold chapel floor."

Huntingdon sighed. "I'm not the young fool you once knew, Brother Thomas. That rogue's long gone. Now I understand the need to think things through."

"Marion knew what she risked when she declared herself in your court," Tuck said. "She's forcing your hand. Tomorrow whatever spies Lackland has in your retinue will send word that the lady's here. He'll demand her of you, and you must either bow and obey or else deny him."

"A choice between seeming a toady or a rebel," the Earl appreciated. "No wonder Geoffrey Plantagenet refused to see her. She sets her traps well, and baits them with herself."

"She's a girl in love, my lord. She'll risk all for her man."

The Earl quirked an eyebrow. "My alleged bastard? Peronell's child?"

"Aye, him. And you'll note we're not claiming he's yours for certain. I knew Peronell till her dying day–I was with her as she breathed her last–and she never said you were the only fellow who might have got her with Robin. But from what I recall it wasn't for want of trying."

Huntingdon snorted in old reminiscence. "Peronell of Loxley! Now there was a wild wench! No wonder her son's grown to a notorious wolfshead." He strained to dredge things from the back of his mind. "I think I remember a tow-haired infant hanging round the lists, pestering the knights and squires."

"That'd be him, my lord. Pestering's what he's good at. That and tricks and schemes." Tuck shook his head. "I tried to keep him honest, I swear, but you and God both know I'm hardly an example for a growing boy."

"So he seduced Lady Matilda?"

"As Christ is my witness in this holy chapel I'll testify that the girl's a virgin still, and if you saw her and the lad together you'd realise what a miracle that is. If he's not your son then he's the image of you when you were a youngster, my lord. And he's fierce as a lion when he's got the right of a quarrel."

"I can't fault that in a man," admitted the Earl. Nor in a son of mine, he didn't need to add.

"He picks fights when others would walk away, just because it's right to stand. He wins men's hearts because his heart's bigger than all outdoors. His people love him. They'd follow him down the jaws of hell."

Huntingdon looked at the fat friar. "And you with them," he judged.

"I'd want to see our Robin pick Lucifer's pocket and run away laughing!" Tuck chortled to himself for a moment, then grew sober. "Your son or not, he's a good man for all his outlaw ways. He's a good man facing powerful bad men. He's loved by a good woman, the best I've ever seen, and she's twined her fate with his despite the cost. They've fought for the things that seem right to them against overwhelming odds." The monk ventured one sly glance at the Earl. "Don't you want to see what would happen if it was a fair fight?"

In the darkness before dawn Blakehelloc rode out to check the sentries closing off the forest. He returned as another unit of the Sheriff's men arrived up the Harrogate road.

"What's this?" he demanded, watching the new column march in reasonable order towards the siege trenches. Then he saw the big man who strode beside their leader. "Why is Greenleaf with them?"

At the edges of the camp Reynold greeted men he knew and called out the watchword to pass the perimeter: "Hangman." The makeshift ditch gate was lifted aside for the reinforcements to enter.

"Hangman? Cheery," muttered Robin Hood as he followed Little John into his enemy's enclosure. His face darkened as he saw the rotted skeletons of the peasants Gisbourne had nailed up.

"Greenleaf!" called Blakehelloc, riding over. "What is the meaning of this?"

Robin took charge. "You will address me!" he demanded, affecting the French Norman tones of Marcel of Flanders. "I am from the Prince John. This man 'as guided me to your camp. I 'ave orders for your commander."

Blakehelloc paused. Robin had perfected that casual insolence that marked trueborn nobility. Blakehelloc knew better than to gainsay one of Lackland's heralds. "I'll take you to my lord of Gisbourne at once, sir."

Greenleaf fell into step with Sir Guy's commander and briefed him in sotto undertones. "That's Marcel of Flanders. He's one of Prince John's top men, a right bastard. Makes Black Guy look like a nun."

"What's he doing here? Where are Slafot and Evalgast?"

"Constable Shankshard said to leave them with him. I couldn't argue. He told me to escort this Frenchie back to camp. He sent Quimper on to York. Orders are orders."

Blakehelloc scowled. He didn't like the fussy pedantic Constable. Gisbourne's commander preferred a bloodier and chaotic kind of war. "Has Shankshard at least secured the woods while he was bossing everyone around?"

Greenleaf nodded. "But that's the least of our worries. I reckon this Marcel has some new orders for us. I don't know what."

Robin pulled his horse to a stop and handed it off to Much to hold. Like all Robin's men, the miller's son was dressed in the captured livery of Nottingham. The outlaw had brought sixty outlaws into the centre of Gisbourne's siege camp; they were surrounded by six hundred of the Sheriff's soldiers.

"You will go away," 'Marcel' commanded Blakehelloc. "My words are for Sir Guy de Gisbourne alone. But you do not go," he told Greenleaf as the big man turned away. "You are strong. You may be needed to carry my things. Come with me."

Blakehelloc glowered as Robin marched off towards Gisbourne's tent trailing Little John behind him. Much gave the commander a sunny smile.

David of Doncaster's qualms about the big city mostly vanished after his third pint of ale. By the sixth he was content. By the ninth he hadn't a care in the world.

The big youth trailed, later staggered, after Alan a Dale as the minstrel progressed through the taverns of York. It was always the same: first a song about Good King Richard on crusade. Then a bawdy story about a bishop and a nun. Then the first song about Robin Hood, followed by tales of the outlaw: Robin and the Black Knight, Robin and the Sheriff of Nottingham, Robin and the Golden Arrow, Robin and the Old Crusader, and always at the end, Robin and Marion.

By that time the minstrel had his crowd. They sang for the outlaw, cheered his daring, booed the wicked Sheriff, hissed at Weaselly John Lackland. When Alan finished (before anyone could call the watch) he would raise his cup and toast. "God bless Robin of Loxley and the Maid Marion!" And the tavern would explode with cheers.

Then David would follow Alan on to another public house for another drink.

Alan a Dale was chuckling. He loved a good audience, and York was ready for his stories. "The Sheriff of Nottingham didn't think a mere bard could do him any harm," he laughed to David of Doncaster. "I need no sword or mace when I have words and music. And he thought me a fool!"

Despite the lateness of the hour William Longchamp still worked in his solar. The Chief Justiciar of England had not risen to his present state–King Richard's most trusted officer, Chancellor of the nation, keeper of the Tower of London, Bishop of Ely, papal legate, lawmaker, perhaps the richest man in England–by indolence and apathy. Longchamp enjoyed the vast processions and elaborate festivities his office required, but he paid for it with diligent attention to the detail of his offices.

He completed the work in front of him, a long set of decrees and instructions to the marcher lords regarding the campaign against Welsh rebel Rhys ap Gruffyd, and called for the lad who'd been waiting all day to see him to be brought forward.

Longchamp's sister Melisend showed Sir Adam Fitzwarren in. She took a proprietary care of the handsome young rider who'd risked all to save his father and his people. Indeed, she'd sat and heard Adam's tale of folly, imprisonment, rescue, and wild hope all day; the young knight had no idea that he had already pleaded his case to the most sympathetic hearer he could hope for. It was Melisend who had ensured that Sir Adam was on her brother's agenda.[33]

Adam at the Lee came in, bowed, and fell to one knee. Gilbert Whitehand had polished his armour and groomed him till he looked every inch a paladin on quest. "My Lord Justiciar, I come to you for justice!"

His tale spilled out again, just as Melisend had told it, of a greedy Sheriff raised by an ambitious Prince, of the House of Lambert imprisoned to death and the House of Fitzwarren hounded towards destruction; and of Robin Hood.

"The North again," sighed Longchamp. It was mere weeks since he had deposed his rival Justiciar Hugh de Puiset, mere months since he had quelled the riots in York. Now the fool Prince John and the too-clever de Vendenal looked set to tear all apart again.

Melisend hovered, watching what her brother might do.

The Chief Justiciar of England took a breath and reached for parchment and seal.

Will Scarlet stared over the wall into the darkness.

"What can you see?" asked Loren de Weynold nervously.

"Nothing," answered the gruff mercenary. "Didn't expect to."

"But Hood is moving? That was the message."

"If he moves then nobody will see," replied Scarlet. "Not until he wants them to."

The defenders of Verysdale continued their vigil.

---

33   History notes that Longchamp's older sister Richildis wed the castellan of Dover Castle. The fate of his younger sister Melisend is unrecorded.

Ros returned to the bed she was sharing with Marion. The elaborate four-poster with mattress and down pillows and heavy tapestry curtains was a marvel to the peasant woman, but even that couldn't distract her from her concern. "There's two men guarding the door," she reported. "There's no way out."

Marion continued to brush out her hair. "Why would we want to leave, Ros?"

"Because that Earl might mean to sell you to Prince John Lackland, that's why. I know how these lords go on. You can't trust them."

Marion worked on a knot. "Either way we win," she said.

"Win? How do we win if the Prince ravishes you and murders us in our beds?"

"Then the Barons who Adam rallies will have cause for war. And Robin will kill Prince John. And if Huntingdon doesn't turn us over then that will cause a stir as well. John will be outraged and there'll be a huge quarrel, loud and messy. I'd prefer that latter eventuality, of course."

Ros wasn't comfortable in the world of high politics. "We should have stayed in the forest with Robin. Nothing can stop Robin in the forest. Out here he can't win."

Marion smoothed Ros' cheek gently. "Don't worry so," she said. "Fretting won't change anything for good or ill. We've made the play, now we have to see what comes. But I'll tell you a secret, shall I?"

Ros nodded, uncertain but curious.

Marion leaned in. "When a hero goes on a quest he must enter the forest and go off the path. But when Robin Hood has to quest, well, he's already the forest lord, so he needs a different kind of forest and a different path to stray from. Not an actual forest but some other kind of dangerous tangle. Somewhere alien to him, somewhere far from where he's comfortable and safe."

"Like... York?" Ros guessed.

"The Prince's world," Marion said. "But here's the secret. You're right. Robin can't be stopped in Sherwood. But there's something even he doesn't realise yet."

"What's that?"

Marion smiled. "Robin in the Hood makes every place he goes into Sherwood Forest!"

The fire arrows had not touched Gisbourne's tent. Now he'd had it covered in wet furs to further protect it. Reynold Greenleaf nodded to the guard outside the pavilion but marched straight past him as if he had the right. Robin just strode behind, looking important.

Gisbourne wasn't asleep. He sat on his camp bed scraping a whetstone along his sword, waiting for morning and the bloodshed he planned. He looked up as the giant entered his tent, followed by a hooded stranger.

"What?" Sir Guy asked bluntly.

The time for deception was over. Greenleaf pointed to the man he'd entered with. "I found Robin Hood."

Before Gisbourne could react to his sudden recognition of the outlaw, Robin punched him in the face. The knight toppled backwards off his pallet. Robin kicked his sword away then jumped on him.

Gisbourne landed a heavy blow on Robin's cheek. If he'd still had his gauntlet on he'd have broken the outlaw's skull.

Robin replied with an accurate and devastating knee between the black knight's legs. Gisbourne would have cried out but for a hammer-punch to the throat that squeezed all the breath out of him.

His last memory was of the outlaw leaning over him and drawing back his fist.

Robin toppled off the downed knight shaking his injured knuckles. "Ow! What happened to us both grabbing him?"

"Didn't seem fair," Little John replied. "Besides, his guard heard something."

Robin noted for the first time that the big man was holding the tent-watchman's head in a lock under his left armpit. The man's face was crimson.

Robin sucked the back of his hand. "When we called Gisbourne 'Brickhead' who knew we were speaking the literal truth?"

John made sure the guard was down then dropped him to the floor. "What now?" he wondered.

Robin opened Gisbourne's heavy clothes trunk and emptied the contents on the floor. "Get Gisbourne's armour off him, hogtie and gag him, and dump him in here with your friend the door guard. In fact tie them so they're cuddling. Make sure neither of them's going to wake up any time soon."

"You're not going to kill Gisbourne?"

"Maybe later when I know we won't need him. I've not forgotten Min of Babworth. Right now I need his armour and helmet more than I need

Brickhead, but that might change if things go wrong."

A watchman rang his bell and called the hour of Prime. The camp began to stir.

In Sir Guy's tent Little John strapped Gisbourne's armour onto Robin in the Hood.

Prince John did not rise for breakfast. He was served in a huge quilted feather bed in the sun-lit chambers of York's royal fortress. The castellan had wisely given him large comfortable rooms whose windows looked away from the jagged Jew-burned tooth of Clifford's Tower.

The Prince had just finished a compote of custard and glazed honey with raisins and was picking his teeth when the Sheriff of Nottingham was shown in. John dismissed the doxies who were warming his bed and threw aside the remains of his meal.

"De Vendenal. What's going on?" he demanded.

"Several interesting things," the Sheriff answered. "The muster is complete and our troops now march to Verysdale. They'll be in place the day after tomorrow to give Sir Richard at the Lee a most memorable Lammastide. Quimper Kinstain rode in a short time ago with news that Hood and his men are surrounded, confined in a stand of woods near the manor. And I am reliably informed that Matilda of Leaford is in York seeking allies to aid her father."

John sat up. "In York? Where?"

"She called yesterday to see the Archbishop. He had the sense to be unavailable but not enough to detain her."

"Damn that bastard!"

De Vendenal went on smoothly. "However, my sources indicate that she may then have called upon his grace the Earl of Huntingdon and received his hospitality."

Prince John was perplexed. "Huntingdon? What's he got to do with any of this? I thought he was trotting off to Chester to marry some plump nubile brood-mare and her fortune?"

"Who can predict what David of Scotland will do, sire? I imagine the intention–his or Matilda's–is to have you command for the wench to be sent to you."

"He'd better send her," growled the Prince. "I'll hang him and his whole household else!"

De Vendenal knew how unwise that would be even for the Prince of England. "Or," he suggested, "you could play a subtler game, which will be all the more satisfying. If your highness would care to hear a suggestion…?"

Blakehelloc didn't get to see Sir Guy up close that morning. The knight sent word to him via Greenleaf to personally supervise the south edge of the ring of men surrounding the woods. He was to pay special attention to where Gisbourne's troops handed their watch over to Shankshard's men to make sure there was no gap in the cordon.

By the time the commander returned from his inspection–and the summary flogging of a man found drunk at his watch–Sir Guy had already mounted his attack on Verysdale.

Blakehelloc couldn't believe it. "What is he *doing?*" he asked the captain of archers incredulously. "Is he mad?"

Gisbourne had ridden out with the column of men that had arrived in the night, charging straight at the broken gatehouse with no cover or precaution. Even a reduced number of defenders would wreak havoc with arrows before the soldiers reached the walls. If half the Sheriff's men returned intact from the assault it would be a miracle.

"Said he had his orders," the archer captain replied phlegmatically. It wasn't him facing a lethal flight of missiles.

"Marcel of Flanders," concluded Blakehelloc. "And where is Prince John's bum-boy this morning?"

"Asleep in Sir Guy's pavilion. He's not to be disturbed, the poor lamb. He's had a long journey."

Gisbourne's commander shook his head in disbelief. "What is Prince John thinking to order a direct attack? Is Gisbourne out of favour now, so he's sent to his death?"

Even as he spoke the attacking column neared the walls of Verysdale; but the expected massacre never happened. A few arrows came from the wall but they all fell wide. Blakehelloc knew from past observation that there were seven good archers and perhaps twenty indifferent ones to man the walls–or there had been. Even now there were at least five good shots.

"Where are they?" he breathed.

Gisbourne reached the gatehouse unscathed. No masonry tumbled down to join the graveyard of stones that had ended so many other thrusts.

The knight reached the battered remnants of the gate. Reynold Greenleaf and some other sturdy fighters made swift work of dismantling what was left of the inner door.

"He's got in!" Blakehelloc gasped. "God's wounds, he's just taken the castle!"

"Looks like," the archer captain agreed, less sanguine now. If the new arrivals were there at the kill then they would get the spoils of conquest. The archers and footsoldiers who'd ringed the manor for a month now would see little booty for their efforts. Unfortunately Black Guy had been specific in his orders about staying put and not following into the fallen fortress.

Blakehelloc swore. "That man has the devil's luck!"

"He'll be the only man in Verysdale to have any kind of luck today," predicted the archer.

Marion attended the Earl of Huntingdon with some trepidation to hear her fate. Tuck, Alan, Ros, and David followed at her heels as she entered the hall.

"I had intended to ride to Chester today," David of Scotland told her when she'd made her courtesy. "It seems that good Prince John has other ideas."

Marion swallowed. "What does he command?" she asked. *What will you do?* She wanted to know.

The Earl held out a scroll with the royal seal affixed to the bottom. "The Prince is planning a banquet tomorrow night. There will be clowns and jugglers and fire-eaters and diverse wonders. There will be sixteen courses. And there will be justice."

"Justice?" Marion echoed.

"Evidently so. Prince John will hear the case against Sir Richard at the Lee and his recalcitrant daughter Matilda. I am summoned to state my views, as are any who bear testimony in the matter." Huntingdon pointed to the neat clerical script on the summons. "You are invited to be present as my guest."

Tuck crossed himself.

"May I speak at this hearing?" Marion asked.

"Is there any way to stop you?" wondered the Earl.

The man in Gisbourne's armour rode under the crumbling gateway arch and doffed his full-face helm. Its distinctive horsehair plume trailed in the dirt as he dismounted.

The defenders of the castle broke into cheers as they saw Robin Hood amongst them. De Weynold and Scarlet quickly quieted them.

Sir Richard limped forward and embraced the young outlaw. He'd never expected to be so glad to see his daughter's kidnapper.

"Hello, folks," Robin greeted the defenders of Verysdale. "Nice job holding off Brickhead."

Will Scarlet shook his head. "Robin Hood! Who'd have thought that your crack-brained scheme would work?"

"Well, you'd be pretty dumb to go along with it if you thought it wouldn't," Little John pointed out. "I never doubted Rob could pull this off for an instant. No, honestly. Why would I?"

The big man's innocent face brought a peal of laughter from the crowd. It was the first merriment in the oppressed confines of the fortified house for many days.

Robin clapped his hands. "Right, well, fun as it is, we don't have time to mess about here. We've got places to go and people to annoy."

Sir Richard looked up. "Where's Matilda?" he demanded.

"York. I'm going there to join her now. Meanwhile Brickhead and Reynold Greenleaf have other things to do. The Prince's orders from Marcel of Flanders, you know?"

Much scratched his head. "We're going to let Sir Guy free? And John is going with him?"

Little John grabbed Much's head in a lock and scrubbed his hair.

"Scarlet, I need you to be Gisbourne now," Robin told the soldier. "I need someone who can give orders to soldiers and know what he's doing." He tossed the helmet to Scathlock.

"Me being Gisbourne?" Scarlet still didn't know the full extent of Robin's plans.

"I'll be with you to relay your orders to the rest," Little John promised. "Keep your helm down and growl a lot and we can pull this off."

Sir Richard moved forward. "What do you intend?"

Robin swept his hand round to the disguised outlaws of Sherwood. "This might seem like a rescue but there's ten times more Sheriff's soldiers outside, and many more of John's muster a day or two behind them. Even if we'd brought stores and stacks of arrows to reinforce Verysdale they'd take us eventually. So we have to get rid of those armies permanently."

Lady Mary saw the sense in that. "Is that why Matilda is in York?"

"Alan went with Adam to appeal for intervention from the barons," Elaine ventured. "Is he–are they well?"

"Adam headed south with Gilbert Whitehand and a few of my lads to carry out his mission. Alan's with Marion," Robin reported. "She's recruiting the Archbishop of York to our cause. Geoffrey Plantagenet has the power to stop the Sheriff's venture. Probably. At least he can provide a distraction for the big finish I've got planned."

"Another of these so-called Robin Hood plans," de Weynold surmised.

"The best," grinned the young outlaw, "My favourite." He clapped his hands again. "Now, who's for some lunch? I reckon we could send over to the siege camp for a few choice provisions?"

XVI

Constable Shankshard and his best men rode into the courtyard of Verysdale manor to consult with Sir Guy of Gisbourne. There were less flayed corpses around than the Constable had expected. Then again, there were more men holding drawn-back longbows than he'd been prepared for.

"What is this?" he demanded, looking at the walls where serious-looking archers covered his retinue from all sides.

Robin Hood dropped down from the wain where he'd been perching. "This is a dinner invitation," he said. He took another bite of the apple from the commandeered siege camp stores and tossed it to Much. "Hello, Constable. We meet again."

Shankshard had never met an undisguised Robin Hood but he knew at once whom he was facing. "Wolfshead!" he snapped.

He instinctively reached for his blade. An arrow whizzed past his head.

"For an observant man you don't seem very good at sums," Robin told him. "You have fifteen officers on horseback, dressed for dinner. I have sixty woodsmen with English longbows pointing iron-tipped arrows at the vulnerable points in your mail. It would be a really stupid time to try and draw a weapon or sound a horn."

The Constable could do the maths. He raised his hands. "How?" he asked.

"Sheer brilliance, really," Robin said with his usual modesty. "I'll leave you to figure out the detail while you're locked in the cellars with your men. I need you out of the way so Gisbourne can steal your company to add to his own for some manoeuvres we have in mind."

For the first time Shankshard realised that the black knight was present in the courtyard, being helped to mount his huge black stallion by the equally huge Reynold Greenleaf. "They'll hang you for this, traitor," he warned Gisbourne.

"Well, I really deserve it," replied the man in Sir Guy's armour. He saluted the Constable insolently as he rode with Greenleaf towards the siege camp.

Arthur a Bland and Riccon Hazel supervised the capture of Shankshard's

172

men. Gisbourne's personal baggage contained plenty of chains. The soldiers were stripped of weapons and armour, hooded with old grain sacks, shackled, and led off to the cellars. Robin disarmed the Constable, tied his hands in front of him, then led him into the main hall.

The big house betrayed the signs of a long siege. Charred timbers showed the effect of fire arrow barrage. The trestles and benches were rough new-cut timber requisitioned today from the besiegers' stores. But the women of the castle bustled with renewed purpose, scurrying to make good what they could and return their home to its former efficiency.

Elaine handed a newborn babe back to the tanner's wife and brought goblets of wine over to Robin and the Constable.

"You're welcome for dinner," Robin told Shankshard. "Of course, there'll be a fee. But we can discuss ransom while you're locked under Verysdale. Tonight you're our guest and we'll dine and talk."

"I won't tell you anything," the Constable warned.

"There's nothing else I want to know," Robin assured him. "You think clearing the villages for miles around silences the common people? Chase them into the hedgerows and you've just given me a hundred spies. Burn their homes and you send them to my camps. Murder them and their kin will support me forever."

Shankshard caught his breath as he realised just how dangerous this young outlaw was. Robin *understood*.

The wolfshead went on. "For example, I know that the Sheriff's bringing levies from a whole bunch of garrisons over to quarter those woods I'm supposed to be trapped in. I know he intends to destroy Verysdale and everyone here in the most ignoble and cowardly way. I know it's all a larger plan to catch Marion for Weaselly John and to get rid of me. I know the odds are stacked against us and the Sheriff thinks he's got an unbeatable hand."

"What are you going to do?"

Hood tapped his finger on the side of his nose to show it was a secret. "For now all you need to know is this. As far as those thugs out there are concerned, these Sheriff's lads here are going to hold Verysdale under Lackland's orders. Marcel of Flanders will take Sir Richard captive back to the Prince in York. Gisbourne will take all the soldiers he can muster and ride out on another mission." He paused reflectively. "I think an army's the biggest thing I've ever stolen."

"The Sheriff will hunt you till doomsday," Shankshard threatened.

"He won't need to," Robin promised. "I'm working to even the odds, and then I'm going to do some hunting of my own."

"Hunting? Hunting what?"

"A greedy High Sheriff. A rapacious Prince." Robin smiled a secret smile to himself. "A beautiful white hart."

The watchman clutched his helmet in his hands and sweated. He usually reported to his watch commander, a man who swore and belched and drank, a man he could understand. He was not brought into the palace of the Archbishop of York to stand before the prelate himself; until today.

"Tell his grace what you reported," a knight in a Templar tabard commanded the unfortunate watchman.

"An' it p-please you, your eminence," the man faltered, "There's talk in the street. Folks muttering, men gathering. There's been songs in the taverns, see, and rumours spreading like fire."

"Tell him what," commanded the knight.

"They say Maid Marion's in York, but you turned her away. Maid Marion what loves Robin Hood. Robin Hood the outlaw of Sherwood."

"I know who Robin Hood is!" snapped Geoffrey Plantagenet. "What else?"

"There's an ugly mood. In the crowds, I mean. They're waiting."

"Waiting for what?"

"For Robin Hood, my lord." The watchman swallowed. "They're waiting for Robin Hood to come for Maid Marion."

Blakehelloc scrambled off the ground, clutching the cheek that Sir Guy's studded gauntlet had laid open. His face would need stitching, but he knew his survival now depended on keeping the black knight calm. "I'm sorry!" the commander stammered, tasting the blood in his mouth. "Of course it's not my place to question your orders. I'll muster the men."

"They're not my orders," Gisbourne said, his voice muffled and distorted by his full-face helm. "They're the Prince's orders. Next time you balk I'll have you crucified."

Blakehelloc knew it was no idle threat. He'd seen Sir Guy's notions of discipline before.

Gisbourne turned back to the map table where Reynold Greenleaf and a couple of Shankshard's sergeants had joined the war council. "Right. Are we clear what we're doing? We march out today and we take the Harrogate Road and the lane to Swindon. We burn Pannal, Follifoot, and all the farms outside Harrogate's walls. We ride in to the sheep fair and plunder what we can. Then we sweep east, pillaging as we go, all through Claro, harrying Knaresborough then off down the Nidd valley."

Blakehelloc held his tongue. He's already objected that those lands belonged to the church. Archbishop Geoffrey and Hugh de Puiset would both be outraged.

"When we're near Wetherby there's lot of rich fat manors for us to take," Sir Guy went on. "They belong to Prince John's enemies so we're allowed to do what we please." He glared at Blakehelloc and the men around the table. "Any objections?"

Nobody was stupid enough to comment.

"Then let's get on the road. Tell the men this is their reward for their service." Inside Gisbourne's armour Scarlet grimaced. "This is when they get what's coming to them."

Marion twirled to flare out the skirts of the rich brocaded dress that the Earl had provided. The embroidered panels were Damascus silk and the bodice was scattered with seed pearls. She turned from the looking-glass towards Ros of Waltham. "Well?"

Ros closed her jaw. "He'll be impressed," she promised.

A day had passed. Tonight was the feast where Huntingdon was required to speak on the matter of Richard at the Lee.

"Prince John? I care nothing for impressing him. It is everyone else at the banquet I must sway."

Ros shook her head. "No, Marion. *He'll* be impressed. When he comes for you."

The lady blushed. "Oh, him. Yes. When he comes for me, despite Prince John's court and the Sheriff's army and all common sense."

Ros nodded. "That is the plan, isn't it?"

Marion spun again, and giggled. Robin made certain death seem like a glorious adventure. "It's the plan. One last stand."

Ros tweaked Marion's silver-filleted hair. "And then maybe a lie down at last, eh?" she suggested with a wink.

The Sheriff of Nottingham came before Prince John expecting to plot more about the Fitzwarren hearing at tonight's banquet. De Vendenal was certain that the ploy would flush out Lady Matilda. At the same time the Prince's levies would be destroying the outlaws of Sherwood, crushing Verysdale, and capturing Sir Richard and what remained of his family for the Prince's dubious mercies. Quite a result, calling for quite a reward.

The Sheriff was surprised to find John's council chamber so full of dignitaries. He recognised the arms of de Puiset and FitzPeter, de Glanvil and Marshall, but there were others too. Nor were these envoys clothed for diplomatic meetings or cosy revels. They were armed for war.

"Your highness?" de Vendenal asked, making a bow. He didn't like the glares he was getting.

"De Vendenal," said Prince John dangerously. "Tell us again how your troops are deployed."

The Sheriff turned to his war captain for a report. "My lords," reported Aelstan, snapping to attention. "We have over seven hundred men at Verysdale, surrounding Sir Richard's manor and a wood where the Sherwood rebels are trapped. More than two thousand hired swords are marching to join them and will be there tomorrow."

The room remained hostile. The Sheriff frowned. "Why do you ask, highness?"

The Prince's voice trembled in his fury. "Because these *several* envoys tell us differently. They tell us that your men are riding east along the Nidd Valley, plundering and burning as they go - through Earl de Puiset's lands and the estates of all these lords represented here."

De Vendenal winced. He was sharp; he knew how close to civil war such an act would push the country. For once he had no explanation and no plan. "Sire, my Constable is with that force. It is led by your own Guy of Gisbourne…"

"We have no part in this treachery!" hissed the Prince, slamming his hand down, playing to his audience of angry emissaries. "None! These are not acts of our doing!" He glared at the Sheriff. "That means they must be yours."

"Not so, your highness. There must be another explanation. I'll ride out now, right now, and set this to rights."

"You'll go nowhere, de Vendenal, and especially not to the head of your rebel marauders to plunder and pillage more. Stay here, under close watch. We have already sent Marcel of Flanders to take command of the hired columns and use them to crush your army of reavers."

The Sheriff stood alone. Aelstan stood baffled and shocked. Even Morgan of Shrewsbury had backed away. Too late William de Vendenal knew what had happened.

"Robin Hood!"

Sir Richard Fitzwarren rode into York with a handful of retainers. They passed through Micklegate Bar[34], crossed the river, and made straight for the cathedral precincts. There, like his son and daughter before him, Sir Richard was denied access to the Archbishop.

Unlike his children, Sir Richard Fitzwarren would not take no for an answer.

"Won't see me?" he thundered in the forecourt of the Archbishop's Hall. "The Archbishop of York will not see me?"

"Sir, he is a very busy…"

The old knight slapped the steward's hand away. "Hear me, Geoffrey Plantagenet!" he thundered outside the prelate's windows. "I am Sir Richard at the Lee, knighted by Henry II, who stood with him in the fields of war. I am a crusader who took oath to God and fought in the Holy Land, with the Pope's blessing upon me. I am God's warrior, and by God's grace and the majesty of Christ Jesu, God's priest had better stand forth and meet me! Come out of your palace and be a man of God, or by our Saviour on his cross I'll ride this horse in to find you as surely as I rode as Christ's knight against the Saracen!"

Elaine and Constanza exchanged glances. "It's best not to get him worked up like this," the old nurse advised. "He's old now, but great in deeds of glory. They could lock him away out of sight when nobody was watching, but here, in the Cathedral forecourt, with half the nobility of England in the city…?"

"And he knows it," Elaine guessed.

"Bless you, child, no," sighed Constanza indulgently. "This is just him." She looked at the fuming knight. "If any man *is* God's warrior on this Earth then it's that one. This Archbishop had best be sharp and answer. His Master's watching!"

Servants rushed about, seeking orders. Guards watched helplessly as the old knight raged up and down on a barded warhorse, shouting at the palace.

---

34   This ancient and royal entrance to the city is still extant. The oldest parts of the structure date to the twelfth century although the portcullis and higher levels were added in the 1300s.

"Seven times these limbs were hewed for Christ's sake! Five hours I stood at the Lee, holding back the heathen horde from plundering a piece of the True Cross! Dear friend, our dead king called me! True defender of the faith, Pope Hadrianus[35] named me! Will God's chaplain now turn away from an old knight who appeals God's justice?"

Much looked up at the skies to see if thunderbolts would fly down from heaven right then and there. A crowd began to form.

"As Christ entered the Temple and cast out the iniquitous moneychangers[36] so a knight of God will root out the usurer and the apostate amongst the congregation of the faithful!" bellowed Sir Richard. "As Jesu condemned the Pharisees who pretended to holiness, as Moses smote down the Midianites, as Elijah shamed the prophets of Baal and put them to the sword…"[37]

At that point a harried looking priest hastened from the palace. "His grace will see you now."

Arthur a Bland wasn't comfortable inside stone walls, or speaking with gentry. The Lincolnshire poacher had only ever known poverty, and sleeping in ditches, and running. Even Riccon Hazel knew more about castle life than he did.

Now the bandit found himself having to report to Lady Mary Fitzwarren and to deploy Robin's men to restore and defend fortified Verysdale. Crippled Kent the Steward lay helpless on a mattress in the chapel. Loren de Weynold's festering wounds had split again; the lady in waiting Aliss attended at his bedside with a gentle care.

---

35   This is the Latinate form of Adrian IV (c1100-1159), the first and only English Pope, who served from 1154 to 1159.

36   Jesus' dismay and fury at finding the Great Temple of Jerusalem filled with illegal commerce is described in *Matthew* 21:12–17, 21:23–27, *Mark* 11:15–19, 11:27–33, *Luke* 19:45–48, 20:1–8, and *John* 2:13–16. Christ's just and holy wrath was a favourite theme of medieval sermons.

37   Jesus' public debates with the self-proclaimed religious expert Pharisees fill the Gospels. Some examples may be found at *Luke* 10:25ff, *Matthew* 22:34ff, and *Mark* 10.2. The much earlier conflict of Moses and the Midianites is told in the *Book of Numbers*, chapter 31. Elijah's encounter with the bloodthirsty priests of Baal is described in the *First Book of Kings*, chapter 18.

That left Arthur with a fortress in his charge. He tried to speak as little as possible and tug his forelock a lot.

He was reporting on the supply situation and how the outlaws had re-stocked Verysdale's larders through some judicious foraging, when the outcry came from below. Lady Mary hurried with him to the cellars where Shankshard and his men were loose.

"At 'em, lads!" Arthur called, happy to have something within his field of expertise. "Knock 'em down 'afore they can get weapons!"

"Really?" called back Riccon Hazel. "Why didn't we think o' that?" The Flintshire cobbler head-butted Gill o' th' Red Cap, ending the champion archer's bid for a heroic escape.

Arthur's happiest reminiscence in after days was how he knocked out the Constable of Nottinghamshire.

It took ten frantic minutes to recapture the prisoners and discover what had happened. They found the two villagers tasked with guarding the cellars stabbed dead, the hidden silver with which they'd been bribed still clutched in their hands. The solitary cell of the man who'd paid them with coin and death before freeing the other captives was still empty.

Lady Mary crossed herself. Arthur swore.

Sir Guy of Gisbourne was on the loose.

Blakehelloc was slightly drunk, but not as drunk as most of the men that followed him. The Sheriff's soldiers had degenerated into an undisci-plined mob, six hundred armed thugs with licence to loot. There was little order now and no chance of reining them in. Blakehelloc didn't care.

"You promised booty," he slurred at the man in Gisbourne's armour, "and there was booty! You promised pillage. We burned... whatever the name of that place was. And that other place. They all ran. Ran away!"

That was because Little John had ridden ahead with warning. As Reyn-old Greenleaf he had the authority to come and go as he pleased. It was taking all his and Scarlet's ingenuity to limit the harm the marauders were doing on their drunken rampage.

"There's more to come," Scarlet promised from beneath Gisbourne's helm. "Much more. Tomorrow you'll take the men on ahead, making to-wards York. More troops will meet you. Keep heading east."

Blakehelloc nodded. Right now, with the taste of blood in his mouth

Lady Mary crossed herself. Arthur swore.
Sir Guy of Gisbourne was on the loose.

and stolen sack in his belly, it all sounded good.

There was a call from the perimeter of the disorganised field camp they were starting to throw up around the remains of Hunsingore. The few men with enough sense left to mount a guard had spotted a rider approaching.

It was Quimper Kinstain. Gisbourne's aide rode past the dissolute army and reigned in beside the man in his master's black armour. "Sir Guy! What are you doing? You've burned the fields and villages of the Bishops of Durham and York both! You've embarrassed and endangered Prince John himself!"

"There's a good reason," Reynold Greenleaf told him. "Come off your horse and hear it."

Kinstain stayed where he was. "The Sheriff's confined, maybe under arrest. The columns that were coming to reinforce you are now commanded to destroy you!"

Gisbourne seemed unconcerned. "Where are they?"

"Not far behind me, closing from Wetherby and Boroughbridge. De Puiset has sent a third force out from Knaresborough. They'll be on you by nightfall."

"What?" gasped Blakehelloc, sobering a little.

Scarlet and Little John exchanged glances. "Sounds good," admitted Little John.

"Yep. Our work here is done," judged Will Scarlet. "No-one's going to muster any force against Verysdale now. No treaties to cross territories. No loaning the Sheriff troops. No trusting Prince John." He looked at the seething soldiery of the way-camp. "I didn't think Robin Hood could really destroy whole armies but he has."

Kinstain began to apprehend that something was very amiss. "Robin Hood? What's he got to do with…"?

Little John grappled Kinstain's horse and wrestled it to the ground. Scarlet caught Gisbourne's aide as he fell and kicked him in the head.

Blakehelloc gasped. "Sir Guy…?"

Scarlet turned on the commander. "He's mine, John. You deal with Kinstain." The soldier rounded on the man whose siege had tormented him for so many days.

"I'll take this one with pleasure," agreed Little John, standing over Quimper Kinstain. "We told him before what'd happen if he didn't mend his wicked ways."

At last Kinstain recognised the giant towering over him. "R-robin Hood's man!"

"To my last day," agreed Little John as he wrung his enemy's neck.

That distracted Blakehelloc just enough. Scarlet slid his sword into the commander's belly and twisted it round. "This isn't enough for all those people you nailed up," he spat into the dying man's face, "but I hope to God they're all waiting for you to drag you down to hell!"

The soldiers nearby had witnessed the carnage. Now they paused in their revels and reached for their blades.

"They wanted us to stop, lads!" shouted Reynold Greenleaf. "But will we?"

"No!" a drunken sergeant shouted back, His cry was taken up by the others around him. "Never! No! The lads! Cut 'em all!"

"More ale!" ordered Scarlet. "Drag these carrion away and give 'em to the dogs. More drink for my brave fighting boys!"

A ragged cheer rose from the disorganised mob.

"Time to go before those other armies get here," Little John judged.

Will Scarlet nodded. "I'd rather be somewhere else when the hanging starts."

XVII

arion entered the royal hall on the arm of the Earl of Huntingdon, and all eyes were upon them. They walked with stately gravity towards the places reserved for them at high table, followed by Friar Tuck, David of Doncaster, Ros of Waltham and a train of attendants. They ignored the stares of the court and took their places.

"I do like to make an entrance," admitted the Earl.

"We have their attention," admitted Marion.

The lady looked around the high hall. The vast chamber was decked with candles, lighting it as bright as day, painting the colourful tapestries and royal banners with a warm glow. The benches of the lower tables, laid out in a U-shape to leave a space for performers and animal spectacles, were already full. Many great lords filled the top table, unexpected additions to a feast that had now gained a much greater significance.

This was no longer the celebration of power and luxury that John had intended to rival William Longchamp's famous festivities. With the assaults on clerical lands and the suspicions of the barons aroused, this was a tense and dangerous meeting of men on the brink of war. Neither Prince John nor any of the outraged lords held enough power to be certain of victory. Armies were already in the field; less than twenty miles away blood would be shed tonight.

Marion recognised the emissaries of de Puiset, of de Glanvil, of Geoffrey Plantagenet himself, all waiting to see what would unfold. Like every lord in the hall they had worked out that she was Sir Richard's daughter. All were watching her.

She allowed herself a little smile. Whatever happened now, nobody could ignore her father's case any more.

The Sheriff of Nottingham sat at the end of the trestle, unspeaking, pale. He looked worried.

The hall filled up, packed to the walls. Lesser knights and their squires were forced to content themselves with hastily raised additional benches at the edges of the room.

Prince John's planned schedule had changed. The jongulers and beast-baiting were deferred, as was the sumptuous planned banquet. Nobody was ready to eat or be entertained just yet.

When everyone was seated Prince John made his entrance. The guests rose at the royal fanfare. He gestured for them to take their seats again.

"My lords spiritual and temporal," Lackland declared, "you are most welcome. But before we devote ourselves to fellowship and camaraderie there are matters that must be addressed." He frowned across the room at the disturbance as the Archbishop of York and his retinue made a late appearance. Trust Geoffrey Plantagenet to try and upstage him.

Prince John went on. "It has been brought to our attention that there is some concern over the matter of Richard at the Lee, a knight who has been appealed of treason by the Sheriff of Nottingham, and about the events which have proceeded from this accusation. We have therefore summoned those who can speak to these allegations and to what has since occurred. We intend to hear now the testimony of those who have obeyed our summons." He shot a smirk over at Marion. "We note that the daughter of Sir Richard Fitzwarren had finally submitted, but of the knight himself there is no word."

Marion was on her feet in a moment. "My father is under siege by the Sheriff's soldiers! They have ravaged the land for miles around. How can a noble knight be here to defend himself when he is ringed by marauders who threaten to murder every defender in Verysdale?"

"Silence your guest, Huntingdon!" Prince John ordered. "There will be time to interview her later. We intend to question her thoroughly." His face twisted into a brief leer. "All night most likely. For now we need only note that Fitzwarren is not present to offer any defence for his treason."

There was movement in the Archbishop's party. The clerics parted to reveal an old knight in crusader whites. "I am here," announced Sir Richard at the Lee. "Who accuses me?"

Elaine entered the tavern uncertainly. The inn was packed to bursting and this was unfamiliar territory for the former heiress of Loughborough. Her fears vanished like mist when she heard the minstrel's voice.

"Even now," said Alan a Dale to his rapt audience, "even now in the palaces of the Norman overlords, the powerful and the rich are gathered to hear the old crusader plead for justice. Prince John and the Sheriff of Nottingham seek to do him down. They hate him and all who stand for right over privilege. Even now they meet to decide his fate."

There was an angry murmur amongst the listeners.

Much shouldered a way through so Elaine could make her way to the front. She edged around until she was as near to her husband as possible and settled at his feet.

Alan didn't see her. He was in full flow. "Even now Maid Marion stands before lustful Prince John, but she does not fear. He has guards and soldiers, assassins and torturers—but she has Robin Hood!" The audience stirred. "The Hooded Man is come to York, and he has come for her. For her and the evil Sheriff and for venal John Lackland. Yes, friends. You do not stand alone against these cruel lords any more. Robin Hood had come as your champion!"

The name started as a murmur somewhere in the crowd, then spread from throat to throat. "Robin Hood! Robin Hood! Robin i th' Hood! Robin and Marion!"

Alan had drawn them taught as sure an archer with a bow. He had aimed them with lethal precision. Now he fired. "Robin Hood at the Archbishop's palace! He needs us now. He needs us there!"

And the riot began.

Alan managed to stay behind as the tavern cleared and angry men went to spread the news. He heaved a sigh of relief that he'd managed to make it work.

Soft feminine hands reached around him from behind and caught him in a tender embrace.

The minstrel stiffened. "I'm sorry my dove, but I'm a wedded man," he apologised to the unseen woman.

"And glad I am to hear it," said Elaine in his ear, "for there's nowhere else I'd be but in your arms."

Much turned away, grinning, as Alan a Dale held tight to his reward.

Sir Richard was not a public speaker but he told his tale with a blunt forthright honesty that compelled the listener. He spoke of Prince John's visit to Leaford; of John's attempt to seduce his daughter; of his son's futile absurd duel with one of John's toadies that ended with the envoy's death and Adam's confinement in Nottingham Castle; of the Sheriff's depredations; of Canon Stephen's usurious bargain and the breaking of it; of the murder of the old knight's retainers by men released from the Sheriff's dungeon; of the black bargain he'd been forced to make to offer Matilda up as prize at the Sheriff's games; of the downfall of the house of Lambert; of the rape of Verysdale by Guy of Gisbourne. And he spoke of Robin Hood.

Prince John would have silenced him but the bishops and barons present over-ruled him. It was too late to cover this up.

At some point in Sir Richard's testimony Marion joined her father on the floor. Her own comments were brief and to the point, assigning blame with devastating accuracy to Gisbourne, to de Vendenal, to Prince John himself. When Fitzwarren had completed his statement it was Marion who summed up:

"Sir Guy is a knight, sworn to uphold the code of chivalry. Instead he has dishonoured himself, his lord, and his class. William de Vendenal took the office of High Sheriff, keeper of the King's peace and justice. Instead he has torn his shires apart with bloody tyranny and has tortured and destroyed great and humble alike for profit and power. Prince John is of royal blood, of the line of Henry, of the line of William of Normandy, brother of Richard whom God has set as king over England. He has severed all fraternal loyalty, all feudal fealty, all grace and morality to indulge his lusts and prejudices. None of these men have served God, king, or people. None of them."

She turned to the barons and bishops. "My lords, there is only one man in this tale who has kept faith with his oaths, save my father who stands before you. One man who has done right, who served justice when the law failed, who defended the weak against the tyrant, who comforted the destitute and brought down the wicked. Gisbourne, de Vendenal, Prince John himself are proved wanting. The man more worthy than all of them, the hero of this day, is Robin in the Hood!"

Her words provoked turmoil. Cheers and shouts of praise were mingled with outraged cried and angry denials.

"She is a formidable lady, I deem," the Earl of Huntingdon said to Friar Tuck.

"Terrifying," admitted the monk. "But now it's Lackland's move."

Prince John demanded order. Rothmere called for silence.

Lackland rose from his throne and addressed the room. "We have listened to accusations and insults. We have allowed the poison of our accusers to spew out for all to witness. But we have heard no evidence to refute the charges of our Sheriff of Nottingham." He glanced to the end of the table. "De Vendenal? Have you anything to say?"

The Sheriff rose, his sober garb marking him out from the peacock finery of those around him. He looked dangerous. "I have, highness," he replied. "You rightly say there is insufficient evidence to make a judgement. I maintain Sir Richard's treachery. He maintains his innocence and that of his kin." His lips contorted into a cruel smile. "There is only one recourse. Let God settle it. Let Him settle it by wager of battle."

Marion saw her father stiffen up. She recognised what the Sheriff had done. De Vendenal knew that an old traditionalist like Fitzwarren would not deny trial by combat. "Hold!" she objected to Prince John. "My father is a great man but he is past his fighting years. He has endured a long and unjust siege that has taken what strength he has left. If there is to be a test of arms to determine the right of this case then he must have a champion."

Prince John looked across at the Sheriff. "Do you have a man to fight for you?" he asked.

The Sheriff nodded. "I'll put up Morgan of Shrewsbury to stand for me. But who would champion Sir Richard at the Lee?"

It was a loaded question. Whichever man spoke faced a formidable opponent who lacked the scruples of a knightly champion, but worse he would declare himself an enemy of Prince John; and all had just heard first hand what became of men who earned Lackland's ire.

"Nobody?" asked the Prince with satisfaction. He ranged his gaze around the room. Even Huntingdon was silent.

Marion took her father's hand. "There'll be a champion," she promised him with perfect confidence.

"Oh, I know, Matilda," replied the old knight. "I brought him."

The Archbishop of York was surprised when one of Sir Richard's retainers moved out to stand beside the old knight. "I'll fight for him and the lady," said the man. He cast his cloak aside to reveal hunting leathers of Lincoln green.

He made an extravagant sweeping bow to the whole court. "Hello, my lords and ladies. They call me Robin Hood!"

Little John and Scarlet passed into York disguised as carters, but the city guards had no interest in them. The watch was occupied with the civil unrest that had already split half a dozen heads and started a dozen fires.

"What's amiss?" Will Scathlock asked a harried officer.

"Haven't you heard?" the man shouted back as he rushed his men towards the fighting on Fossgate. "Robin Hood's in the city!"

"Robin Hood?" repeated Little John with eyebrows high. "My goodness!"

John and Scarlet abandoned their stolen wagon and hurried to the inn on Stonegate.

They met the mob halfway there. The crowd raced down the street with torches, shouting.

Alan a Dale, Much, and Elaine followed after. Much hailed Little John over. "Everybody's fighting for Robin!" the miller's son gasped excitedly. "They're fighting the watch and everything."

Scarlet shook his head. "That man could set fire to water."

Little John looked at the mob. "Good job, Alan a Dale! You've got us another army. Now we've got to use it."

He raised his voice in the bellow he'd once used to call sheep in distant Hathersage. "To the royal palace! To the palace, boys! To the palace for Robin Hood!"

Marion returned to the Earl of Huntingdon and drew her father with her. She was surprised to find her nurse Constanza waiting beside Ros, Tuck, and David. Constanza said nothing but corrected the neck-hem of her lady's dress.

"Fitzwarren," said the Earl, clasping the old knight's wrist.

"Huntingdon," replied Sir Richard; they said no more.

Prince John had a dilemma. The grinning outlaw that had thwarted him stood brazenly before the court, daring Lackland to arrest him; but Robin stood for Sir Richard's right, and if the Prince prevented the combat he was as good as admitting before the barons that his cause was false.

Worse still, the Prince knew from Robin's grin that the outlaw understood just what he was doing.

"De Vendenal," Prince John said through gritted teeth. "Have your man kill this wolfshead and be done with it."

"Morgan," commanded the Sheriff, gesturing his brutal enforcer forward.

Stewards rushed out with quarterstaffs. Traditionally commoner trials by combat were fought on foot with staves.[38]

---

38   Wager of battle was introduced into English common law after the Norman Conquest. It was usually used when there was no conclusive evidence for judgement by jury. This trial at arms assumed that God would give victory to the just party. It was usually fought in a judicial list 60 feet square, to the death or surrender by the admission "Craven!" (literally "I am vanquished!"). Lowborn combatants used quarterstaffs. Knights often fought fully armed and armoured.

Robin twirled the six-foot pole with practised ease; he came second to Little John every time with this weapon–but nobody beat Little John with quarterstaff. "It'll be a new experience for you, battling a man who can fight back," Robin said to Morgan.

Constanza, who'd been flogged by the bodyguard, spat a harsh "Ha!"

"Talk all you want, Hood," Morgan replied, circling. "Now you die." It wasn't sparkling banter but the brutal beast had other skills.

William de Vendenal watched as the combatants circled each other. The banquet guests were all caught up in the unexpected drama that had diverted the course of the evening, the contest of life and death that played out between the trestles. The Sheriff of Nottingham thought furiously. He was a man who liked plans.

He knew that the clash of his bodyguard and an outlaw was only one level of the fight. He began to plot out his strategy for the rest.

The horses were blown. At the outer limits of Stamford, Gilbert White-hand had to admit as much.

"My lord, we need to find new mounts else rest these animals we have," he called to Adam Fitzwarren. "Killing them won't speed our journey."

The new knight slowed his horse to a mere trot. It was hard to coax her to more. They'd sped up the Great North Road through Stevenage, St Neots, and Peterborough. The milestones warned that there were still 109 miles between them and York.

"We'll seek new rides at the town ahead," Adam declared. "We must keep going." His hands moved to the scrip slung over his shoulder, the vital pouch that contained the Chief Justiciar's ruling. It could change everything; but only if word arrived in time.

"We'll see what we can get," agreed Gilbert. He'd traded horses before, and stolen them too. "But even with fresh steeds we won't be there before morning, perhaps midday."[39]

The Tractatus of Glanville, c1187, describes wager of battle as the most common form of trying nobles.

39   A 210 mile journey from London to York in a single night was considered remarkable enough to form part of the folklore about 18th century highwayman Dick Turpin, who was credited with riding his horse Black Bess between the cities overnight to establish an alibi, although the noble mare died at journey's end. Daniel Defoe first conflated the actual escape ride of gentleman rogue John "Swift-Nick" Nevison with deeds of Turpin, spawning a legend.

Adam knew it was true. Until then, his father, his sister, and everybody who stood with them were on their own.

The combatants closed without any warning. Robin's staff caught Morgan's and twisted it aside. His counterthrust at Morgan's gut was blocked and he had to back away in turn as the thug went for him. It was clear the men were closely matched.

Prince John leaned forward in his seat, eager for blood.

Robin exchanged knock for knock with the big bodyguard. Morgan was the stronger, but not as strong as John of Hathersage and not so fast either. Robin took a glancing blow to one leg but exchanged a crack that set Morgan's nose streaming with blood. Morgan closed, forcing the outlaw to give ground.

Robin saw his strategy. Morgan was trying to force him up against the trestles, to limit his movement and make it impossible to avoid the heavy tip of that whirling stave. One good hit would knock him down. A follow-up would cave his skull.

The outlaw allowed himself to be backed up to the table. He ignored the shouts of the diners, the catcalls and cheers of an audience caught up in this combat of blood and honour. He waited his moment then used his staff as a vaulting pole and leaped atop the trestle.

Morgan hadn't expected that. His blow went wide. Robin kicked a platter of beets into the thug's face then danced away.

Morgan lumbered after him, blaspheming, furious.

Robin ducked down, grabbed a chalice of wine, sipped it, then hurled the rest over Morgan. People laughed.

Robin danced along the table, now dodging, now attacking, catching every blow that Morgan struck and returning with a trivial smack to keep the bodyguard angry. He paused to blow a kiss at Marion.

"Don't show off," the maiden told him. "Finish it."

Robin ducked a wild swing from Morgan, saluted the lady obediently, and rolled off the trestle. Morgan thundered after him, closing for the kill.

Robin came up and vaulted again, this time catching the hanging chandelier wheel. He swung up with easy grace, scattering lit candles down on Morgan below, and squatted there while Morgan tried to knock him down with heavy arcs of his stave.

Hot wax splattered over the livid scar the Sheriff had left Morgan, adding to the disfigurements. He howled his fury and prodded upwards to displace the mocking outlaw.

Robin somersaulted off the chandelier, landed gracefully in a roll, and came to his feet by the top table. He grabbed the silver trencher in front of the Sheriff and hurled it like a discus. The platter caught Morgan in the teeth.

Robin followed it, hammering his stave into the bodyguard's midriff, then following with a swing that brought its full weight across Morgan's jaw. Everyone in the room heard the bone shatter.

Morgan went down and did not rise again.

Robin stood over him and kicked his adversary's staff away. "Sir Richard and the Lady Matilda are innocent," he proclaimed.

The Sheriff rose to his feet but could not find anything to say. The Prince was white with fury.

"Seize him!" Lackland spluttered at last. "Seize that common outlaw!"

But the Earl of Huntingdon rose too. "Hold!" he called. "That is no common outlaw. That is my son."

Even Robin's mouth dropped at that.

The sudden silence was broken by the hall doors being flung open. A red-faced man in black fighting garb stalked into the hall, sword in hand. "Robin in the Hood!" shouted Sir Guy of Gisbourne. "Now you die!"

XVIII

he garrisons from Tickhill, Castleford, Wakefield, and Knaresborough, united under the command of Marcel of Flanders, fell upon the recreant Nottingham soldiers by night. Ill disciplined, drunken, and outnumbered, lacking leadership or understanding, the Sheriff's men broke and fled in all directions.

The Prince's man and the bishops' and lords' representatives who rode with him hunted the marauders down without mercy.

Marion's hand closed on Tuck's arm in a tight reflex grip. "Gisbourne!" she hissed. "How did he…?"

"The devil's knight," replied the monk. "He won't be stopped till he's buried at a crossroads with a stake in his black heart."

Sir Guy stalked into the room bearing his naked sword. He glared at the victorious Robin Hood beside fallen Morgan of Shrewsbury. He yelled Robin's name once more.

Prince John overcame his indecision and called again for guards. There were not enough armoured men between the Prince and the madmen.

The Sheriff of Nottingham rose. "Your highness, if I may? It seems to me that we have something of a unique opportunity here. Recent report has claimed your envoy Gisbourne turned rogue and reaver. Many lords spiritual and temporal are here tonight because of depredations to their lawful holdings."

There were mutters of assent from envoys of de Puiset and others.

De Vendenal went on. "It occurs to me though that Sir Guy may not have been leading that rogue army. Sir Guy may have been a victim of Robin in the Hood."

Richard at the Lee interrupted. "Gisbourne is a bastard black-heart without honour or conscience, unfitted to be a knight, unfit to breathe on God's clean earth!"

Sir Guy said nothing, keeping his eye on Robin stalking slowly towards him.

"We have just witnessed a trial by combat to determine the guilt of Sir Richard at the Lee and his family," the Sheriff went on. "God has proved their innocence on the charges of treason and murder, true. That case must now be closed, and the Fitzwarrens may walk free. Except there is also a charge to be made against this Robin of Loxley, outlaw, raider, rebel; and against all those who associate with him, such as the Lady Matilda and her father."

Another murmur ran around the hall. Prince John, Plantagenet, Huntingdon, Fitzwarren and the more astute observers realised at once what the Sheriff had done. The accusations against Sir Richard and Adam had been disproved, but new and even more damning charges stained them with Robin Hood's crimes.

Robin's agile mind tried to follow what was happening, but he was distracted by the murderous black knight closing on him.

Then Marion was with him again, stood at his back, facing Prince John. "Your highness, my lords," she called, "you have heard an accusation against this good man, Robin Hood. You have been told of the wickedness of black Guy of Gisbourne. One is right and one is wrong." She pointed at the Sheriff. "This man is frightened for his post, for his power, for his wealth. He schemes to hold onto it at any cost and wants Robin Hood silenced." She turned her accusing finger at Prince John. "This man wants me as his toy, to despoil and destroy. Robin Hood has withheld me from him as is a betrothed's right–and indeed his duty. So now it comes to this: a combat of arms between Gisbourne and Robin."

The Sheriff's lip peeled back in a snarl. He'd wanted to engineer a death match between Hood and Sir Guy. He hadn't wanted Marion to set the terms.

"God sees all," proclaimed Lady Matilda of Leaford and Verysdale. "Let there be a judgement by steel of who has the right. If Gisbourne kills Robin Hood then the black knight is proved blameless. I am widowed before I am wed and nothing can keep me from this Prince's lust and malice. My father and many others are guilty by association. The champion of the people is fallen and all is lost. But…"

The Sheriff made to rise and interrupt but this was Marion's time. The Saxon-haired beauty had captured the court. Even Gisbourne was halted.

She spun around, gathering their attention, locking their gazes. "But," she declared, "if Robin Hood triumphs then he is absolved, and all of us with him. He wins his freedom and our innocence to leave this place in peace." Finally she looked at Robin. "And he wins me."

Robin couldn't hold back a grin. "My lady, am I… in a Maid Marion plan?"

Marion laughed back. "I believe that you are. Don't die."

Huntingdon spoke up. "My son has a right to defend himself from these charges by main force of arms. Let him fight." Others round the room nodded.

"There is no other resolution," agreed the Archbishop of York, enjoying Prince John's discomfit. He made the sign of the cross. "God give strength to the hand of the righteous."

Sir Richard at the Lee rose. "I believe the young man has only a quarterstaff against a knight full armed. But here I have a sword I won in Antioch, of Saracen steel. No other but I has lifted it in battle since." He unbuckled the blade and held it out. "Robin Hood, this is yours, with my blessing."

Marion blinked back tears. She took the sword from her father and girded it onto her love.

Sir Guy of Gisbourne's black rage was not abated, but now it was focussed. He understood what the Sheriff had given him. If he only killed Hood he was saved, able to win back his position, his future, all. He had only to slaughter the man he hated most in all the world.

Robin kissed Marion. "For luck," he said. "And because, y'know, it's really nice."

Marion ungrappled his wandering hand. "First kill the black knight and save the day," she chided him. "*Someone* captures your white hart tonight, Sherwood. Make sure it's you."

Robin drew the crusader's sword and turned to face Sir Guy of Gisbourne. "For justice, Marion, and the people," said freedom's outlaw.

Gisbourne charged.

The rioters had reached the walls of the royal fortress. Worried guards held them back and hoped the watch would bring reinforcements.

"Robin Hood!" shouted Little John. "Robin Hood! Robin Hood!"

The mob took up the cry again and amplified it, shouting for the outlaw as they surrounded the Prince's palace.

"Well, that should get a response," admitted Scarlet as the crowd hurled stones. "Shame all the garrison's out chasing marauder armies, isn't it? Makes breaking up stuff like this a lot harder."

Little John laughed out loud. "Ah, we do stuff like this all the time. Why aren't you with us, Will?"

Scarlet found he had no good answer. In the end he joined with John's laughter and clasped his hand.

"Keep up the shouts," Alan a Dale urged the throng. "Robin Hood! Maid Marion! Sherwood forever!"

Elaine drew him back a little. "Try not to get killed," she requested her husband. She leaned in close to embrace him and whispered, "Our child will need a father."

Alan a Dale found himself lost for words.

The mob closed in around the royal fortress, screaming for Robin Hood.

But suddenly there were soldiers; not the struggling watch but steel-clad guards drawn from the personal retinues of the lords within the palace. They moved out to bracket the crowd, spears ready.

"Lay down your torches and weapons!" shouted Captain Aelstan. "Surrender in the Sheriff's name!"

The mob paused, shocked, uncertain. Then Little John hurled his staff like a dart. It flew through the air and caught Aelstan full in the mouth. "That for the Sheriff!" cried Robin Hood's lieutenant.

Scarlet and David surged forward to tackle the guards moving to support their captain.

"The Sheriff or Robin Hood!" Alan yelled. "Whose side are you on?"

The mob found its spirit again. They surged forward, overwhelming the soldiery by sheer numbers. Aelstan shrieked as he was seized up by vengeful hands and dragged away.

The crowd surged forward, angry, jubilant, defiant, to hammer on the gate of the royal fortress. They called for Robin Hood!

The Sheriff had done his calculations. True, Matilda Fitzwarren had blunted the finesse of his trap, but Hood and Gisbourne still crossed swords. Sir Guy had been raised as a knight, trained in the list and on the combat ground since the age of six. Robin's weapon was the bow, a peasant tool. Gisbourne was supreme with the blade. One fatal stab would restore the Sheriff's fortunes as much as Guy's.

The black knight came in fast and furious, allowing his rage to fuel his attacks. It became obvious to the seasoned veterans present at the banquet that the young outlaw was outmatched. Robin struggled to catch Gisbourne's strokes on the notched Antioch steel. Every blow forced Hood backwards.

Robin knew it too. Gisbourne was more practiced at the sword and was clad in leather and mail. Robin's hunting garb offered little protection against a heavy blade. One good blow would end him. He fell back again and played for time.

Robin could not win by matching Sir Guy. This was Gisbourne's kind of battle and his advantages were unassailable. Robin was an outlaw of Sherwood; his weapons were stealth, guile and boldness. As Gisbourne forced him harder and harder he realised he should never have left the forest.

And then he knew what Marion had known, what she had seen in him with a lover's insight, what had made her name him the people's champion. She'd even called him it just moments before!

Robin wasn't out of Sherwood. He was Sherwood.

Robin in the Hood laughed at Sir Guy of Gisbourne.

"What?" frothed the black knight. "This isn't funny! I'll kill you!"

Robin was pressed up against a trestle. Fruit rolled across the floor as his off-hand seized up a three-branched candelabrum and stabbed it at Gisbourne's face. The hot beeswax splashed over Sir Guy's skin. "You?" mocked the forest trickster. "I already told you if I ever saw you again then you were dead."

Gisbourne struck the candlestick from Hood's hand with a sharp blow. Robin was already rolling aside, dancing aside. He made no attempt now to match Sir Guy with steel on steel. He dodged, he ducked; and always he laughed.

"Don't play with him, Gisbourne!" snapped the Sheriff. "Cut him down!"

"Oh please," scoffed Robin, skidding aside so the knight lurched off-balance and smacking him hard on the rump as he passed. "Brickhead's a powerful bully when he's raping a peasant girl or crucifying villagers but he's a foresworn dishonoured loser else."

Gisbourne's blade swung at Robin's face. The tow-headed youngster pulled his head back just in time. The sword-tip passed half an inch from his eyes. Sir Guy was dangerous.

"And he's going to hell." Robin went on. "He swore in the Virgin's name not to harm Min of Babworth. There's a place awaiting him in the eternal fire."

Sir Guy lunged once more. This time his thrust sliced into Robin's arm, drawing blood. Marion bit back a cry.

"For all his pretensions he's just a jumped up lackey, dancing on Prince John's chain," Robin scorned. "A pet. A performing bear, maybe. A mad pet that needs to be put down."

"Shut up!" roared Gisbourne. He could fight. He could kill. He was ill-suited for the war of banter that Hood was waging on him. "Shut up and die!"

"Or what, you'll kill me?" the outlaw scoffed. "You're already trying that. And sweating quite a lot. Maybe it's your exertion from trying to catch me, but it might be guilt or fear."

He'd got too close. Gisbourne lashed out with his mailed left fist and caught Robin on the cheek, sending the youngster spinning backwards to tumble on the floor.

Robin fell but rolled, avoiding Sir Guy's death-strike by a hair. He tried to find a quip but the room was spinning and his breath was short.

"Not so clever now?" Gisbourne crowed, missing with his next slash but managing a reverse pommel into Hood's back. Robin dropped again. His sword skittered away across the rushes.

Sir Guy closed in. Hood didn't back away as the knight had expected, but rather rolled forward under Gisbourne's legs. Sir Guy swung round after him. Robin's fingers tightened upon the cloak he'd discarded earlier. He flung it into Gisbourne's face and used the distraction to regain his sword.

Gisbourne unwrapped himself from the garment and closed again. The black knight's fury seemed unending. His entire world was focussed on the destruction of Robin Hood. He came in slowly now, implacably, allowing his enemy no chance to dance away, relying on stamina and persistence to batter down Hood's defence. The fight was coming to its bloody conclusion.

"It's you that dies, Robin in the Hood," breathed Sir Guy of Gisbourne. "I'll enjoy taking a turn with your woman when the Prince has finished making her scream."

Robin fell backwards onto the rush flooring. He'd manoeuvred the battle just right. His hand closed over the fruit he'd spilled ten minutes earlier, just where he needed it. A ripe plum filled his fist. He hurled it with an archer's accuracy.

The rich fruit splattered in Gisbourne's eye, half-blinding him with its ripe juice. A hard red apple smacked him on the nose.

Robin sprang up and kicked him in the belly, bending him over. The outlaw's reversed sword went pommel-first into the black knight's teeth, shattering them.

Gisbourne swung back, wildly. Robin didn't oppose the strike but instead let it past, catching Gisbourne's blade on the back edge, knocking it further out.

Then he brought that ancient Antioch steel back on a straight-line arc with the black knight's neck.

The arterial spray spilled over the top table, drenching the lords there with Gisbourne's life-blood. Sanguine-drenched William de Vendenal watched Sir Guy stagger and fall on the great hall floor. The black knight's head arced over the trestle and rolled to Prince John's feet.

Friar Tuck was the first to break silence. "Praise God!" he called in a loud voice. "Robin Hood's innocence is proved!"

The young outlaw ignored white-faced John Lackland, the suddenly-shouting nobles, the furious blood-drenched Sheriff, Sir Richard's praises, Huntingdon's claims of the court, the thousand other consequences of his duel. He paid no heed to the harried Rothmere hurrying in with news of the York mob at the gates calling for Robin Hood. It didn't matter.

Robin kissed Marion and the world stopped.

Robin kissed Marion and the world stopped.

XIX

The following day, Sir Richard at the Lee and his son Adam joined Robin and Marion at the Earl of Huntingdon's board for a mid-day meal.

"The Prince has seen the warrant," the old crusader said. "Weaselly John might not like what Longchamp has to say but he's not yet in a position to deny it. Robin's pardon is confirmed. The King's peace protects us."

"For now," Adam added. "Who knows what will happen next? My brother and sister's husband have rallied at last, but I think I'd better head back to London and ensure the Lord Chancellor's favour stays upon us."

"And see Melisend Longchamp?" suggested Alan a Dale slyly. He wrapped an arm around his beloved Elaine and smiled indulgently. "I'll write you a song for her."

"You and your people can winter at Verysdale," Sir Richard promised Robin Hood. "I imagine winter is a hard time in Sherwood."

"I have a lot of people," Robin warned. "They won't all fit in your manor."

"He means all of Sherwood," Marion translated for her father. "All of England. Knowing him, maybe all the world."

"Someone said I had to be the people's champion," the young outlaw protested. "I remember it distinctly. It nearly got me killed."

"We're safe for now while the mob disperses," Little John judged. "When Marion ordered the banquet be sent out to the crowd it blunted their anger, and the bishops and barons are all taking care to be kinder to their villeins for a time."

"We robbed the rich and gave it to the poor," the lady of Sherwood replied. "It's what we do."

The Earl of Huntingdon clapped his hands together. "Well then, I can finally be off to my wedding in Chester. I assume I can travel safe from fear of bandits?" He looked at Robin. "Later we must talk about your future. An acknowledged bastard of David of Scotland can go far, you know."

"Robin Fitz Huntingdon is quite a good match for a younger daughter," Constanza admitted to Marion. "It allies the house of Fitzwarren to the Huntingdons and it ties in Fitzwalter, the Bigods, de Mandeville, de Percy…"[40]

"I am available to conduct the sacrament of marriage," promised Tuck, his voice muffled by the hock of ham he'd stuffed into it. He reached for the wine jug again. "Shortly."

"They're saying there'll be new alliances now," Will Scathlock reported. "The streets are filled with rumours. De Puiset's on the up again with support from that Archbishop of York, ready to go against Adam's Longchamp. And Prince John's still spitting venom and blood from his shaming yesterday."

"Will you go a-soldiering again, then?" Much asked the mercenary.

Scarlet shook his head. "I need a rest. I thought I'd try the forest life for a while." He was surprised how easy a smile came back to him again after so long.

"Well, you can't be any worse than them as has already taken it up," Ros declared, poking Little John in the ribs–and winking at him. The big man's hand came down and pinched her rump.

Robin laughed and took Marion's hand. "There's just one last thing to do, then," he said. "I have a plan."

Rothmere waited outside Prince John's private bedchamber for his master to retire. "Sire," he reported, "there is an unexpected development."

It had been a bad day for the would-be ruler of England. His loss of face had forced him to compromises. They were laughing at him in the streets, and the tales would run to Nottingham and Lincoln and London, maybe all the way to Richard on crusade. Disciplining William de Vendenal hadn't begun to quench the Prince's fury. "What now?" he snapped.

"An interesting development," Rothmere said significantly. "Lady Matilda of Leaford has come to sue for grace."

"Matilda Fitzwarren? Here?"

Rothmere nodded his head to the bedchamber door. "She and her nurse await within."

A nasty smile twisted across Lackland's face. "Well then. She finally understands."

He dismissed Rothmere and the stales he'd intended to bed, stationed his guards at the door, and went into his chamber.

---

40   These are many of the principal signatory barons who forced King John to accept the *Magna Carta* in 1215, curtailing royal power and establishing forever the rule of just law in England.

Marion waited for him beside his bed, her flaming red hair unbound and glorious. "My lord Prince," she said.

Prince John was so distracted by her beauty that he almost missed the other details of the room: a discarded nurse's wimple on the floor, his personal strongbox forced and empty, and a new red bloodstain on his bed-sheets.

He noticed the knife at his throat well enough though.

"My lord Prince," said Robin Hood into his ear. "It's time we talked."

Prince John did not dare move, even when Marion removed his dagger and rings. "You came to my bed unbidden to steal from me," she told him. "Now it's my turn."

"You set your hounds after me," Robin told Lackland. "You thought yourself untouchable." His blade dug deeper at the Prince's neck. "Learn now that you're not."

The Prince whimpered. He tried to squirm away.

"Behave yourself, your highness," Marion warned Lackland, "or I will charge Robin Hood to destroy you. Understand?"

"Yes," said Lackland in a strangled whisper.

"So stop chasing me," Marion commanded. She leaned in and breathed in the Prince's other ear. "You're too late. I'm already caught." She giggled. "The proof's over there on your bedlinens."

"Well, you were a bit tardy at dinner and we got restless waiting," Robin explained to the outraged ruler. "But now Marion is *mine*."

The Prince stared at the Saxon-haired beauty. She nodded. "Three times his," she confirmed with a smirk.

John stared at the laughing couple in disbelief.

Suddenly Robin Hood grabbed John by the collar and slammed him to the floor. He straddled the Prince and held him down helpless. And he stopped laughing.

"Marion's mine," he swore. "Sherwood is mine." He leaned in close and stared at John's wide watery eyes. "I *am* Sherwood."

And Prince John stared into the dark woods, the eternal forest that seethed and plotted and laughed and kept its mysteries, at the secrets the peasants had never forgotten, at the primal urge of every man to live free, at the rage and the glory of a people that would not bow forever... and at the man who wore those things like a hood and aimed them like an arrow.

The primal fear of the forest came upon John. It would never truly leave him.

"I am Sherwood," Robin repeated. "I am England. *Remember*."

The trees of Sherwood were turning brown when Robin and Marion returned to the greensward. The dappled light through the leaves of the Major Oak danced like fairies on the forest floor. In the distance the children laughed as they climbed over Little John. Ros of Waltham paused to watch the game as she brought water from the brook. Alan a Dale sang and Friar Tuck quaffed. Gilbert Whitehand stewed a haunch of venison brought down by Arthur a Bland. Scarlet drilled the new recruits while Much and David watched and shouted veteran encouragement. Two loaded carts stood ready for the next journey to the villages with provisions to the poor.

Robin helped his love down from her horse, though she didn't need it; it gave them an excuse to embrace. He held her in his arms and grinned that smile of pure mischief.

"Not another scheme?" Marion protested, matching him grin for grin.

"Why not? The Sheriff still seems to think those taxes are for him."

"But you think differently."

"I'm the king of Sherwood. The arrow of justice. Freedom's outlaw. My queen says so."

Robin kissed Marion.

The world started.

And They All Lived Happily Ever After?

An afterword by I.A. Watson

I've enjoyed writing the exploits of Robin Hood far more than I ever expected when it was suggested to me as a topic. In penning the stories in *King of Sherwood*, *Arrow of Justice*, and *Freedom's Outlaw* I've come to appreciate much more the archetypal relevance of the outlaw who upholds justice when the law fails.

With the ending of our third narrative I've completed the story I'd originally intended to tell in a single volume and left Robin and his merry men in the condition most readers will naturally picture them, together in Sherwood fighting the Sheriff and caring for the people. However, it is an integral part of our character from our youngest days when a tale is told to ask, "But what happened then?"

Sequels are nothing new. Entertainers who lived by telling stories were quick to "cash in" on successful tales. *The Odyssey* followed *The Iliad*. The wealth of Robin Hood stories that has survived to the modern day hints at the greater range of oral material which must once have supported the livelihood of many a roving troubadour.

Perhaps the main difference between the legendary characters of old and modern story icons like James Bond, Superman, Doctor Who, and Indiana Jones is that the modern heroes, owned in the real world by copyright-holders who need to derive an ongoing income from them, never truly die. The much-touted 1992 "Death of Superman" storyline lasted a year before the Man of Steel's inevitable revival.

Many ancient heroes' passing is the capstone of their legend. Achilles' heel, Hercules' poisoned shirt, King Arthur's final battle at the field of Camlaan and his sailing over the waters to the Isle of Avalon, each offer a sense of completeness and resolution that satisfies some deep need in us to know "the full story"–right to the end.

So what became of Robin Hood? What became of Marion, and Little John, and all the merry men who followed him? Did the Sheriff get his come-uppance in the end? Was the struggle against oppression, the hardship and the sacrifice and all that shining courage *worth it*?

For those who insist on knowing how fictional characters probably ended up there are some historical and literary clues to offer an answer.

In 1192, eighteen months after the story in this volume, Richard the Lionheart and Saladin agreed to a three-year truce, with provision for Christian pilgrims to safely pass to holy sites in Jerusalem. Richard turned his attention homeward, where Prince John had displaced and exiled both of the king's Justiciars and was ruling England. However, Richard was shipwrecked near Aquileia and had to travel across Europe by land. Just before Christmas he was captured by his enemy Leopold V, Duke of Austria, then given into the hands of Henry VI, the Holy Roman Emperor. Leopold and Henry were excommunicated for imprisoning a crusader, but still Henry insisted on a ransom of £65,000–thrice the national income of England!

This is a fertile time for Robin Hood mythographers. While Richard's mother Eleanor of Aquitaine struggled to raise the sum, Prince John had every reason to prevent the ransom's payment. In fact John joined the King of France in offering Henry money if he kept hold of Richard. The huge ransom was met through confiscating a quarter of the church's treasure and through yet more scutage and carucage (taxes instead of military service and on lands farmed). One might imagine that Robin and his band had much to do curbing the usurper John and mitigating the hardships that the tax-squeezed peasants had to endure.

Richard was released in February 1194. King Philip of France wrote to John: "Look to yourself; the devil is loose."

Robin Hood readers will recall old legends of Richard's return to England; of how he came alone and disguised into Sherwood, faced the outlaws, and secured his freedom by wrestling down Little John or duelling Robin himself, before revealing his identity and commanding the merry men to bow. In this tale Richard pardons Robin and his men and commissions them to join him in reclaiming the country from Prince John.

Historically, Lionheart and his allies chased John's forces across England. The Earl of Huntingdon captured Nottingham Castle with Richard, the only time that fortress was ever taken by force. Huntingdon also caught the Sheriff, and at this point William de Vendenal disappears from history. William de Ferrers, 4th Earl of Derby, becomes Nottingham's Sheriff thereafter. Might we infer that Robin FitzHuntingdon played a principal role in de Vendenal's downfall?

There followed a period of relative peace in England. Lackland fled to France but was eventually reconciled to his brother, who proclaimed him "a child who has had evil counsellors", stripped him of all land and power (except Ireland) and kept him out of England.

During Richard's captivity, France had conquered his kingdom of Normandy. Lionheart sailed to liberate it. He spent the remainder of his life fighting in Europe. On 25th March 1199, sieging the tiny castle of Chales-Chabrol in Limoge despite it being Lent, Richard was hit in the shoulder by a crossbow bolt. The surgeon bungled its removal, the wound festered, and Richard died in his mother's arms on 6th April. Richard had named his brother as his successor.

John's accession proved a difficult time for Richard's supporters. Fortunately Lackland was distracted by a series of embarrassing European conflicts which gradually stripped him of his continental lands. By March 1204 he had lost all of them save Aquitaine. In England he was unpopular, deemed arbitrary, venal, cowardly, and weak. The crowds called him "Soft-Sword". John's opponents began to organise against him. Whether John moved against Robin and Marion or not, doubtless Robin Hood would abandon whatever comfortable life he might then have achieved, call together his old allies, and take up England's cause once more.

The historical King John I probably did more for England than his famous beloved brother. He strengthened the courts, improved administration, and developed mechanisms of government. But high taxes, military incompetence, and John's policy of *ira et malavolentia*–malice and ill-will–against those who thwarted him–were the spurs that united the Barons in opposition. After revolt and warfare John was forced to Runnymede, near Windsor Castle, on 15 June 1215, to seal the *Magna Carta* that guaranteed English rights forever.

Many of those who forced and signed as witness to the Great Charter are those mentioned in *Freedom's Outlaw* as united by Robin and Marion. Romantics are free to speculate on how that unstoppable pair might have impacted upon the document that enshrined fairness in English law.

The literature of Robin Hood itself provides our hero's end. Several stories describe Robin's death by being excessively bled (for medicinal reasons) by a monk or nun. The most complete account is Childe ballad 120, *Robin Hood's Death*, set at Kirklees Priory, with his cousin the abbess deliberately letting too much blood from his veins. This version also implicates the wicked Sir Roger of Doncaster, whom Hood kills before dying.

To fit *Freedom's Champion*'s continuity, this cousin would likely be some offspring of Earl David of Scotland's or some child of Marion's elder sister, Anne, who is "married to Lord Greystoke" in our narrative. Her motive for her crime must remain nebulous. Robin instructed Little John to take no revenge on her.

Things get legendary then. Robin still resides in the greenwood at the time he goes to Kirklees. Little John and Will Scarlet still serve him. On the way he encounters a lamenting lady who predicts his end–perhaps Sherwood would not allow its hero to pass without one last meeting with Robin's lost Queen of May?

Robin fires a last arrow before dying, asking to be buried where it lands. The shaft flies high into the forest, landing somewhere in the depths of our imaginations.

We remember.

IAW
November 2011

Those who really want more Robin Hood are directed to http://www.chillwater.org.uk/writing/robinhome.htm wherein I.A Watson presents a wealth or additional material including maps, character profiles, historical notes, and some additional Robin Hood stories, along with links to other works he has written.

BIRTH OF A LEGEND

In 1190, two years after wresting the crown from his father, Henry II, Richard the Lionhearted departed France for the Holy Lands and the Third Crusade. He left behind regents, Hugh, Bishop of Durham and his chancellor, William de Longchamp. But his younger brother, Prince John, lusted after the crown and saw Richard's absence as a golden opportunity to seize control. John began a program of heavy taxation that threatened to destroy the social-economic stability of England.

While the royals conspired against each other, it was the people of the land who suffered. Working under inhumane laws, they became no more than indentured slaves to the landed gentry. Amidst this age of turmoil and pain, there arose a man with the courage to challenge the aristocracy and fight for the weak and helpless. He was an outlaw named Robin of Loxley and how he became the champion of the people is a timeworn legend that has entertained readers young and old.

Now I.A. Watson brings his own vivid imagination to the saga, setting it against the backdrop of history but maintaining the iconic elements that have endeared the tale of Robin Hood to readers throughout the ages. With beautiful covers by fan-favorite artist Mike Manley and interior illustrations by Rob Davis, this is a fresh and rousing retelling of an old legend, imbuing it with a modern sensibility readers will applaud.

Airship 27 Productions is extremely proud to present –

Robin Hood
King of Sherwood

&

Robin Hood
Arrow of Justice

PULP FICTION FOR A NEW GENERATION

WWW.AIRSHIP27HANGAR.COM